# #MNGirl

## MIDWEST BOYS SERIES BOOK ONE

# #MNGirl

## MIDWEST BOYS SERIES BOOK ONE

## A.M. BROOKS

**#MNGirl**
By A.M. Brooks
Copyright © 2020 A.M. Brooks

Cover: Amanda - Pixel Mischief Design
Formatting: Elaine York - Allusion Graphics
www.allusiongraphics.com
Editing and Proofing: Rebecca - Fairest of All Book Reviews
Proof Reading: Athena and Darlene - Sisters Get Lit.erary

# #Acknowledgements

*** This book is the first in a brand new series that I am so excited to share with readers. I left a part of my heart in this book. That being said, I have a lot of people who I owe a huge shout out too. ***

*My Husband-* Thank you for letting me live my crazy dream. I know you miss me when I'm in the cave and on busy weeks when my manuscript is due for editing, and yet you don't complain... much (Haha). Thank you for continuing to be a great dad to our babies while I'm working and building my business. We're lucky to have you! XOXO

*My Family-* Thank you for continuing to be supportive and cheering me on. You guys are my #1 fans and your encouragement means the most to me. I'm sorry for the random texts and calls that sometimes happen. I promise the reasons are within the pages. I love you!

*Kiki and the girl boss squad, Colleen, Nicole, and Kristina, at The Next Step PR* -Thank you for your hard work, dedication, and guidance. Thank you for working on my emails, sharing all my info and release materials, and creating eye catching flatlays and designs for my book. I appreciate everyone's push for #MNGirl to be seen and promoted. I'm so thankful to be part of this team!

*Darlene and Athena- Sisters Get Lit.erary-*Thank you for taking on the challenge of being my PA's. Our calls and calendar are my favorite! Having you both on my team has made it easier for me to step back and just be able to write. Thank also, for beta reading and proofing this manuscript. I can't thank you enough for all that you ladies do!

*Rebecca- Fairest of All Book Reviews* - I can't thank you enough for editing and helping me craft the perfect version of this story to share with my readers. I appreciate your time and making me feel my book was your top priority.

*Amanda Simpson- Pixel Mischief Design-* Thank you for patiently working with me on this cover. You took my idea and created and something unbelievably perfect. Thank you for honestly answering all my emails and offering advice when I need it. I'm excited to work on this series with you!

*My Readers-* Thank you for your purchase. It is because of you that I can continue to write and live my dream. I love you all! I'm happy to share the first book in this brand new series. I hope you enjoy the beginning of Ciaran and Saylor's story. Welcome to the Midwest Boys Series!

XOXO Ashton

# #Playlist

Pity Party- Melanie Martinez
Die For Me- Post Malone (Feat. Future and Halsey)
King of Everything- Wiz Khalifa
Antisocial- Ed Sheeran and Travis Scott
Breathe- Mako
Friday Night Lights theme song- W.G. Snuffy Walden
Holding Out for a Hero- Elise Lieberth
Codeine Crazy- Future
No Guidance- Christ Brown and Drake
All the Good Girls Go to Hell- Billie Eilish
Lie- NF
Ruin My Life- Zara Larsson
Money in the Grave- Drake and Rick Ross
Time- NF
Roxanne- Arizona Zervas
Heartless- The Weeknd
Everything I Wanted- Billie Eilish
7 Rings- Ariana Grande
What Happens in a Small Town- Brantley Gilbert and Lindsay
Ell
I'm So Tired- Lauv and Troye Sivan
Kick It In The Sticks- Brantley Gilbert
Highest in the Room- Travis Scott
Mirrors on the Ceiling- Mike Stud
Breaks Down- Brantley Gilbert
Falling- Trevor Daniel
Wow. – Post Malone
Man of Steel- Brantley Gilbert
Give Me Back My Hometown- Eric Church
Youg Dumb & Broke- Khalid

Girls Need Love- Summer Walker and Drake
Nights Like This- Kehlani and Ty Dolla $ign
Servin- A Boogie Wit da Hoodie and 6ix9ine
Take It Outside- Brantley Gilbert
Somethin' Bout A Truck- Kip Moore
God's Country- Blake Shelton
Back in Black- AC/DC
Ride- Chase Rice
Surrender- Natalie Taylor
Cryin Game- Bad Wolves
Heartless- Diplo and Morgan Wallen

# #One

*Saylor*

**"I** don't think anyone is coming," my best friend, Oaklynn, whispers next to me, while gripping my hand tightly between hers. My eyes scan the room one more time, taking in the pastel pink, lilac purple and teal balloons, the gold confetti over the tables, and the three-tiered strawberry cake with pink whipped frosting that sits uncut. An angry flush covers my cheeks, and I swallow the painful lump in my throat.

"Let's wait a little longer," I tell her, hating the way my voice wavers with indecision.

"Say," she starts to argue, then slams her perfectly pink glossed lips closed, when she sees the sheen of tears in my eyes. It's my seventeenth birthday, and we've been planning this party for the past eleven months. Oaklynn had pulled extra volunteer hours at her mom's charity, so her mom would call and make the reservation for us. I had stashed away the majority of my allowance each week, foregoing movies, nights out with friends, and the perfect pair of Versace Medusa high heels in order to pay the cost to rent the top floor party room at one of New York's upscale restaurants. I was not leaving before midnight, even if no one else showed up.

"Nash said he was on his way," I remind her gently, while running my free hand over the plum, crushed-velvet skirt of my dress. Of course, that was over two hours ago when my on-again, off-again boyfriend had texted me. Turning my phone over in my hand, I check the screen again. No messages and no missed calls. It suddenly felt like all the blood was rushing to my head, and it hurt to breathe, which only makes me grip Oaklynn's hand tighter. I'm fully aware of the questioning and lingering gazes of the minimal staff that were assigned to this party tonight. They've stayed diligently in the background, but I can hear the murmurs.

"The staff need to leave," Oaklynn says, leaning closer to me. "The manager needs to cut them from their shift if no one is coming."

A lone tear falls down my perfectly contoured cheek, and I wipe it away furiously. My chest heaves because I know what I need to do. "Okay," I tell her, signaling that we will leave. I don't want to hold people up or keep them away from their families. I'm not a brat, and despite the designer label I wear on the outside, I would rather die than be the cliché rich girl from the Upper East Side. But, as I make this decision, I swear I hear my heart crack in my chest for yet another time this week.

"It's going to be okay," she tells me, pulling my frozen body into hers, hugging me tightly. I want to believe her, but the horror of the past few days crashes into me all over again.

"I can't believe he didn't come." The words fall from my lips, as I swallow down another surge of anger.

"Nash is an asshole, Saylor. His mommy probably told him he couldn't come after all the publicity." She waves her hands around. "You can do so much better than him, girl." I nod, knowing she's right. Nash Aimsworth is an enigma at Trinity Prepatory, our elite private school, in Manhattan. He's lusted after by girls, while guys are dying to be in his group of buddies. Nash plays sports, and he is in the top of his class academically. Ivy League schools have been showing an interest in him since his sophomore year. He's the classic boy every society mom wants their daughters to date. He'll grow up to own one of the most lucrative companies in the world, and he carries all this on his plate with a crooked smile and a hidden, cunning gleam in his eye. He's a senior while I'm a junior, and every girl in school has told me how lucky I was to have caught his eye on my first day.

That was last year, and, since then, nothing with Nash has been quite the fairytale that the female population likes to think it is.

We often go back and forth on if we're a couple or not. We went to parties on the weekends and often spent time at his parent's club. I didn't need a grand gesture, but if we're together, I'd like to know we aren't seeing other people. Nash is gorgeous. I know it, and he knows it. His thick dark hair is always styled perfectly, and his deep brown gaze glitters with mischief. He may have been trying to get my attention the first time I saw him, but he also had two of the most popular girls in the senior class draped all over his body, feeling up his sculpted arms, which were thanks to his years of playing football. Of course, he was also the all-star quarterback of the school, and his influential family had just donated the money for a brand-new stadium. Everything I had seen and knew about him screamed egotistical manwhore. I should have known better, but I had been intrigued by the confidence he has. He carries himself in a way that doesn't allow others to look down on him. For a girl who was changing schools and didn't have many friends, I was lacking that confidence in myself. I thought I could be the one to change his playboy ways and I stupidly ignored the red flags that had been waving in my face.

For the first few months at my new school, I had been known as "new money." I learned quickly that it was *not* a friendly endearment from my peers. I didn't grow up wealthy and privileged. I had not been in class with them since they were wearing golden diapers at their elite preschool. My family was new to having money. This made me an outsider -- someone who was in the running to achieve a scholarship or place on a team that they had already spent years working toward. I was a target because I was someone who didn't understand the hierarchy that ruled from inside the academy; the fact that the older the money, the higher up the food chain a person sat.

Oaklynn had done her best to shield me, to warn me and protect me, but she could only be in one place at a time. Monopoly money was shoved in my locker on a daily basis. Within my first week there, my regular underwear had been exchanged for a sparkling G-string during gym class, and I was constantly asked if it was my mom or I who had been prostituted to help further my dad's career. One kid, who excelled in technology classes, went out of his way to produce my face in a porn flick. He swore up and down that that was how I earned my tuition. Yeah, kids are cruel. The kids at Trinity Prep, though, took things to a whole new level.

It wasn't until I caved and started going on dates with Nash that the outright bullying stopped. Once in a while, I would still hear *bitch* or *whore* muttered under people's breaths in passing. I guess as much as they loved Nash, they also feared him. I clung to him and the little bit of protection dating him offered. In the beginning, he was different. I thought I knew who he was from all the time we spent together outside of school. In the end, though, I found out he wasn't the world's greatest boyfriend, and I wasn't proud of myself for the way I used his name to survive last year in high school.

At the beginning of this year, everything was manageable. No more pranks occurred. The name calling stopped, and I was making friends. So, I guess I was lucky Nash liked me. My past and the fact that my family hadn't always been wealthy had never been an issue for Nash. His mother, maybe, and maybe that was why he kept dating me. My lips pucker at the sour thought. At this point, I know for sure he isn't coming. He probably is at home or with his friends, instead of being here for me on a night like this. A night when my whole world was crumbling around me, and I needed the two people who I thought were on my side despite my family issues, to be here.

"Are there any news crews out there?" I ask timidly. The last thing my family needs is another headline this week.

Oaklynn peers over the balcony and shakes her head. "Not yet, the room was under my mom's name, so they probably don't know the party was for you."

"I'm sorry," I tell her, my voice cracking from the weight of this colossal disaster.

"It's not your fault, babe," she soothes me, shaking her head. "I can't believe all these douche canoes didn't show up. Who cares what your dad did? They're still your friends!" Were they though?

When I move my head in agreement, the pressure in the front of my skull builds and thrums painfully. I thought they *were* my friends, too. I should have known tonight would be a disaster, especially when people started distancing themselves from me since the news broke at the beginning of the week. I chose to ignore it, just as I chose to ignore my dad's shady phone calls at odd hours of the night, the way we suddenly had money to move to Manhattan and attend the most prestigious schools, the way he started going on business trips and would be gone for days at a time. The biggest sign should have been the wear and tear I noticed in my mom, but I closed my eyes to it all. I knew she rarely slept. Even though she was lavished by my father in designer label clothes, shoes and make-up, the smile on her face was tense. She stopped making our evening meals and let *staff*, because we had staff now, too, do it. She suddenly had headaches when my younger sister, Mila, would ask her for help in math. All this should have been the biggest clue that our world was about to be flipped, but I kept on going as if things were normal.

On Monday, a local New York news station broke the story that my father, Calvin Torre, had been laundering money through the company he started five years ago, as well as a litany of other fraudulent practices. Before noon, every major channel, including CNN, was covering the story. My dad had bankrupted thousands of people who had invested with him and broke business deals with the parents of the kids from the school. And now, our family was being investigated by some of New York's finest criminal investigators. It was also discovered his company was involved with oversea accounts, making his crimes international. His face was plastered over every television screen in the country. Needless to say, prison time was hanging over his head. And what made everything worse was the fact that people questioned how my mom, my sister, and I had no clue what was happening. Our family was torn apart in front of the nation. Paparazzi waited outside our home to tail my mom as she dropped us off at school. We were accused and found guilty, without having the opportunity to defend ourselves.

By Tuesday, we were made aware that my father had depleted a different offshore account in the Virgin Islands, purchasing a one way ticket to Cuba. He was gone, and the coward that he is left my mom and me to face the world by ourselves, to be shamed and ridiculed for his sins. When my mom's monthly payment for Mila's Christian middle school bounced, they were unsympathetic and gave my mom one week to pay or Mila could no longer be enrolled.

On Wednesday, my school locker was checked, making sure I wasn't stashing any evidence or information on my father. I stood by, fuming, while the principal wore a smug smile. Almost like she enjoyed humiliating me more with this process. The school was now fully aware what was happening with my family because of my father, and that's when my peers, people I had started calling friends, couldn't meet my eyes. The whispers started. The glares commenced. The shunning at lunch tables and lab stations had my stomach dropping. I was used to being looked down on by them. I was able to get past their prejudice that I wasn't good enough because I hadn't been born into a blue-blooded family. But now my family and I were seen as criminals, and the hate that flared in their eyes and the evil twists in their lips are what made the week completely suffocating.

Thursday, I started receiving notifications that the friends I had invited could no longer make it to my party. But I refused to cancel. I refused to let the fuck up that my dad was responsible for have any impact on the person I was. Even if it was only my best friend and boyfriend who showed up, I had a point to prove. I wanted to show everyone that this wasn't going to break me.

Today, my mom kept me and my sister home from school because there had been numerous threats to our family and my father. She tried to hide most of them without us seeing. But even if she destroyed the letters in the mail, it didn't stop the YouTube videos. People holding grudges, people who lost everything because of my dad made videos with graphic details about how they wanted to kill him. Another detailed everything about myself and Mila and the best way to kidnap us before school. My face paled after it was over. As if that wasn't bad enough, the police were currently working on trying to figure out who threw the brick through our living room window with another death threat attached to it. My mom couldn't work; her anxiety and lack of sleep over canceling clients made her more on edge. For the first time since we first moved into this home, her face broke with real emotion: fear. As I was getting ready for my party, we fought the whole time I curled the long strands of my dark auburn hair and rimmed my deep brown eyes in black liner. She didn't want me to go, and I kept reminding her this wasn't my problem. It was between her and my dad.

It is now Saturday at 12:01am. I am officially seventeen, and nothing is as I had hoped it would be. I send a quick text to Nash, letting him know that, once again, we are done. And, I mean it this time. My time is too precious to be wasted on a boy who cares more about appearances than the actual truth of a person. With our hands locked together, Oaklynn and I find the elevator and cruise to the bottom. I crumple into the waiting vehicle she had ordered for us. The small back space is crowded with the handful of balloons she grabbed on the way out.

"I'm so sorry, Saylor," she says again. I can hear the emotion in her voice, and it takes all my strength not to cave into the storm inside me.

"I'm so mad at him, Oak," I whisper through my clenched teeth. Seriously, I would be lost without my best friend. Despite her cold looking exterior, Oaklynn is the warmest and most loyal person I know. We've been friends since first grade, before she moved to Manhattan. When my dad came home and surprised us with his promotion and plans to move us to Manhattan as well, Oaklynn's parents helped mine get settled. We were so happy to be back together.

"Your dad's a prick," she huffs next to me. "You're amazing, Say. What he did has nothing to do with you and the person you are. This whole thing is ridiculous."

"Thanks for being here," I tell her. "Tell your mom I'm sorry we wasted the reservation and the space."

"She won't care." Oaklynn smiles. "She just wanted you to have a good birthday, no matter what."

"Your mom is awesome," I tell her, before shifting my gaze out the window.

"Kelly is, too, Babe. She will bounce back, once she figures out how to move forward. Don't discount her yet," she answers. A small sliver of guilt creeps in, and I know she's right. My mom is a victim just like me. I just wish she'd snap out of her funk and figure out what needs to be done. Mila and I are losing our spots at school, and now I know my dad is behind on our house payments as well.

By the time the black town car pulls up to my home, the small pounding in my head is now a full-blown headache. I scan the front yard, checking for unwanted paparazzi waiting to snap my picture, before opening the car door.

"Don't forget these." Oaklynn hands me the bouquet of balloons. It makes me want to laugh and cry at the same time, but instead, I give her a small smile and take them from her.

"Happy Birthday, Saylor." She gets out and hugs me, holding on extra tight, because she knows I need it. I'm not ready to end the night; I don't want to go back to my reality. And, I *really* don't want to face my mom and Mila. I don't want them to know my night was a disaster. Mom had begged me to cancel, somehow knowing this was probably going to be the result. That my heart would be crushed.

I run up the front stoop and wave over my shoulder as Oaklynn's car pulls away from my curb. The light is on in the front entry, and it's safe to assume my mom is still awake. I slip off my favorite pair of gold, butterfly winged heels, my sixteenth birthday gift from my parents, and tiptoe toward the stairs.

"Saylor?" My mom's voice calls from the kitchen. I freeze, one hand on the banister, and step lightly. The instant groan from the ancient wooden floors gives me away. Within three heartbeats, my mom's figure emerges. Kelly Torre looks haggard. For the first time in days, I take the time to actually see her. Blue smudges, evidence from lack of sleep, under her eyes contrast with her pale complexion. The freckles across the bridge of her nose are more prominent. She's in her pajamas, her honey brown hair piled on top of her head, and a loose bathrobe hangs off her shoulders. She pulls the extra material tighter to her body. She's lost weight. We haven't had a meal together all week, and, looking at her now, I'm guessing she hasn't eaten that whole time.

"How was the party, Sweetheart?" she asks, yawning at the same time. I have to fight the urge to hurl an insult or a jab. I want to shake her and ask her how she thinks it was now that I'm a social pariah. Instead, my shoulders shrug, and I choke back my emotions.

"I have a headache," I tell her, while pinching the bridge of my nose between my fingers.

"Oh." She quickly scurries back into the kitchen. I hear bottles rattle and then she returns with two reddish orange pills. "Take these. You'll feel better." I hold out my hand, and she dumps them into my waiting palm.

"Thanks," I mutter, and start ascending the stairs.

"Happy Birthday, Saylor," she calls to me softly. My eyes slam shut because, as much as I want to crumble into a crying mess in her arms, I know there is nothing she can do about the pain twisting my insides. She isn't the one who is responsible. But she's here and he's not. I don't get the luxury to unload all my anger on the parent who deserves it. Instead of thanking her, I climb the rest of the stairs to my room.

With my back safely pressed against the closed door of my room, I finally release the balloons from my grip. I watch as the pastel colors float to the ceiling and spread out. Frustrated, I take the little pain relievers form my palm and swallow them down quickly, before washing my face in my bathroom. My body is bone tired. The week long anxiety wave I've been riding has now crashed. I'm drowning in unknowns. I shut off the lights and welcome the darkness. The pain in my temples throbs a little less, as I slide the material of my party dress down my body and leave it pooled on the floor of my closet. I snatch my favorite sleep shorts and tank from their drawer and dress quickly, barely making it to my bed before my legs give out. My eyes close, and my breathing shallows. Sleep is my friend, and tonight, I welcome it wholeheartedly.

# #Two

It isn't the screaming or crying that shakes me awake. It isn't the front door being ripped from its hinges or the shattering of the glass coffee table that she is thrown into. What pulls me from the deep recesses of my dream world is the feeling that I'm suffocating. A pressure across my face yanks me from my sleep, my body jumping in response and my eyes flying open.

"Shhhh!" Mila begs me. It's her little hand that's covering my mouth. Tears slip down her cheeks and snot runs from her nose. Her tiny frame is shaking inside the flannel nightgown she loves to wear this time of year.

"They're in the house. They're hurting Mom," her young voice cracks. I can tell a sob is waiting to escape. I'm fully awake now, my body moving in sync with my heartbeats. Blood rushes to my ears while I tiptoe across the floor and carefully move my hand to nudge the door open farther. Mila's hand snakes out, grabbing my arm painfully, as tears fall faster and faster down her face. "No!" She mouths in silence, but damn, the words echo loudly in my brain.

"It's okay," I whisper, my hand peeling her fingernails from my skin. I push the door open farther, but not far enough for the hinges to groan. Biting my lip, I turn my head and look out. Only the hallway light illuminates the area. I can't see anything. I slip my leg out the door followed by the rest of my body. Carefully, I step on the boards where I know the wood floor won't creak.

When I reach the banister, that's when I hear it. The sound of a backhanded slap. I flinch and glance back at my room. My mom cries out and all that does is earn her another smack.

"Where is he?" a dangerous and lethal voice asks.

"I swear," she groans out, "he left. I have no idea where he is. The detectives said he had a private offshore account and may have headed to Cuba."

Slap! Slap!

"Do not lie!" the voice gets louder, and my mom screams in response.

"I'm not! I promise. He left us!"

"Pull her up," he commands. "Where the fuck is your husband?"

Instead of words, only noises can be heard, like she's trying to keep her pain inside. "Who else is here? Do you want us to start looking around the house then?"

"Nobody!" she answers quickly, her words sounding garbled. "It's my daughter's birthday. They're at a sleepover," she lies.

"Daughter, huh?" the voice replies. The way it curls around the word *daughter* sends chills over my skin and vomit rushing to the back of my throat. This could be very bad.

"Hit her," the voice commands. I cringe when the loud smack triggers another howl of pain from my mom. My heart races to interfere, to call for help, but I retreat backwards, careful to step in all the right places again, and close my bedroom door softly.

"Come here." I wave to my sister's shaking frame. She collapses into me, instantly soaking my night shirt with her warm, wet tears. Moving us slowly toward the side of my bed, I reach for my phone and quickly hit the call button.

My phone illuminates, but No Service stares back at me.

"The fuck?" I question, turning it off and right back on.

"I think they're doing it," Mila whispers into my chest. "Mine didn't work either."

I'm about to protest, when boots thudding against the wooden stairs pull my attention.

"Down!" Not thinking, I push Mila to the carpet, wrestling her under the bed, before slamming into her. The first set of booted feet is joined by another. They yell rapid fire directions to each other in another language, and it doesn't take a professional translator to understand their meaning. They're looking for whoever may be home. In the confined space, I slam my hand over Mila's mouth and keep her head tucked into my shoulder. Closer to the ground now, my ears pick up on more noises coming from downstairs. The inhumane cries and sound of flesh being pummeled and torn is unmistakable. My insides curl and threaten to rebel. My eyelids slam shut, and I squeeze Mila into me harder, hoping my shoulder can act as a barrier to cover her ears. No child should have to hear her mom in pain, let alone a thirteen-year-old.

Every instinct I possess is kept on edge while waiting for it all to be over. I replay in my brain every noise and every word I'm forced to listen to so that I can remember. The booted feet stop outside my door. Mila goes still beside me, both of us scared to even breathe. Her tiny nails dig further into my arm, making me wince, and I know I'll have little crescent shapes in the skin after this is over. When I feel the vibration of his steps move away from the door, my body sags in relief. Minutes feel like hours as they drag by; my muscles ache and the arm cradling my baby sister's head is numb. I'm not sure how much time has passed when the house is finally silent. The screams and grunts are done. My ears strain to listen for any movement from downstairs. Sweat covers my body as I slowly peel away from Mila.

"I heard a door close," she whispers, her voice still shaky.

"Wait just a few minutes," I whisper back, while flexing my arm and trying to restore blood flow. Sliding to my stomach, I peer out from underneath where the blanket drapes over the edge. Silence hums loudly in my ears. I slam my eyes closed to stop tears from leaking out. My chest squeezes in pain. I don't want to leave this small protective bubble, and yet, I know I have to get downstairs to my mom. She's going to need help. I need to call the police, but my body is in shock, and I'm frozen in place.

"Saylor," Mila whispers, through more tears, next to me.

"It's okay, Mi," I reassure her, trying to smile, but I fail. My lips won't curve or stop shaking. Slowly, I use my arms to crawl on my stomach out from under the bed. Tingling pain radiates from my fingers to my shoulder. I bite my lip to keep from making any noise. Mila starts to scoot out behind me, and I stop her.

"Door," I mouth, and she halts. Adrenaline spikes through my system while I creep my way toward my door. I hold my breath and concentrate on my surroundings. Twisting the knob, I let the door push open, before sliding my head out into the hall, just like before. The lights are now completely out, and my eyes need to adjust to the pitch black.

Reaching back into my room, I grab the softball bat from behind my door, before motioning for Mila to follow me. Keeping my eyes trained on the hallway, I don't move until I feel her body pressed behind mine.

"Stay by me," I whisper, and she nods. We slide along the wall, avoiding the wooden planks that groan, until we get to the staircase. My stomach tightens, and my breathing grows shallow. It's completely dark downstairs, except for the single sliver of light coming from the direction of the kitchen. Goosebumps rise on my arms and legs. Step by step, we ease our way down. My sweaty hands grip the titanium handle of the bat, twisting with the need to hit something. Once my feet hit the landing, I can hear it. The shallow breathing and muffled cries call to me, pulling me toward her.

"Wait," I tell Mila, pulling her off to the side. "Take this and don't look." She takes the bat from me wordlessly, silent sobs racking her body again. She doesn't make a sound as she crouches to the ground. Following the light from the kitchen, I tiptoe across the cold tile.

"Mom?" Her name escapes my lips, and it takes all I have not to fall apart when I see her.

"Saylor," she whispers my name from where she lays on the ground, covered in blood, broken and bruised. Her body is cradled between the cupboards and the island where she sits half propped up.

"Mom." I fall next to her. Taking my hand in hers, I notice she visibly winces in pain. "What do I do?"

"My phone." She tries to lift her hand; my eyes follow the line of sight until they land on her purse. Getting up slowly, so I don't jostle her, I grab her purse strap and yank it to the floor, cursing in my mind the whole time about its size, while my hand dives in frantically looking for the small block. My fingers slide across it, before I snatch the phone from her purse and the home screen lights up. I grab her hand and hold her thumb to the button for it to unlock.

"Saylor!" Mila's voice frantically screams my name, breaking my concentration. My head snaps up, right as a huge, bulked up body slams into me. My head bounces off the linoleum floor, causing streaks of light in my vision. The phone slides from my grip and across the floor, while my hands push and shove at the beefy ones trying to control mine. My body thrashes against his to get free. My eyes connect with his soulless, bloodshot ones. His huge paw wraps around my neck. I instantly panic at the loss of breath. My eyes widen, and I fight back harder, using my nails to scratch and dig into his skin.

He's temporarily shoved, when my mom throws herself over me. "You dumb bitch!" The man's voice hollers, spit flying from his mouth, his hand raised back to throw a punch. I flinch, waiting for the impact, waiting for the pain. My eyes widen in shock when Mila's arms swing the bat, and I watch in slow motion, until the bat connects with the back of the man's head. He freezes, a confused look crossing his features, before his body slumps forward then crumples to the side.

"Gun!" my mom shouts, and I scramble to the man's side, tugging the weapon out from his waist band, and slide it to her hand.

"Is he dead? Did I kill him?" Mila shrieks, falling on her knees next to me. Wrapping one hand around her, I use the other to reach for the man's pulse. My fingers find nothing. "He's alive," I lie, over and over, until she stops convulsing next to me.

"What the fuck!" Another man's voice yells from the doorway. Three gun shots ring out right next to my ear. My hands slide to cover them, but it's too late. Warm liquid splashes against my tank and across my neck. My head buzzes, and my hearing fades. Mila's screams sound as if I'm swimming under water. I watch, in horror, as the other man's body slides down the wall. I scoot back across the floor, my feet slipping in blood, until my fingers reach the cell phone again.

"I'm calling the police." I frantically pull up her screen and grab her finger, again, to unlock again.

"No." Her voice is hoarse, her breathing sounds labored in her chest. "Matt, call Matt."

"Who?" I want to shout because she makes no sense. We should be calling law enforcement. She needs to go to the hospital, and there is for sure, one, possibly two, dead bodies in our kitchen. "No."

"Matt." She stretches to reach for the phone, but stops, cradling her middle. "Call Matt, Saylor. Not the police. They can't help us now."

"Saylor," Mila's voice whispers softly next to me. Her eyes haven't left the body of the man she hit with the bat. I watch her shed a layer of innocence. She's pale and probably about to lose her mind.

"Fine." The word falls from my lips with more venom than I planned. Adrenaline is the only thing keeping me focused at this point. I slide through her contacts to the M's and double and triple check. "There is no one named Matt in your phone," I tell her frustrated.

"Rogue," she mumbles. Her eyes are heavy; she's losing consciousness. Panic races up my spine. I don't want her to die.

"Saylor, do something," Mila cries next to me. She shifts, bringing our mom onto her lap and holding her head.

Tears prick the corners of my eyes as I slide back through her contacts.

"Rogue," she tries to say again next to me.

"I stop on the R's and, sure enough, ROGUE is saved in all capital letters. Without thinking, I hit the call button. It rings twice, before a man's voice answers on the other side.

"Hello? Kell?" His voice is gruff and sleepy. I forgot it's in the early morning hours.

"Is this Matt?" I ask quietly, swallowing to keep my voice steady.

"Who's this?" he asks, sounding more awake. I hear a shuffle in the background, and I wonder if he's sitting up now.

"My name's Saylor, my mom told me to call you," I start to tell him.

"Kelly? Is your mom, Kelly?" He asks.

"Yes." I nod, even though he can't see me through the phone. "She needs your help. It's bad," I tell him, as the tears I'd been holding back start sliding down my face in warm, wet currents.

"What happened Saylor?" he questions. There's more shuffling in the background, and the sound of a zipper echoes in my ear. I tell him about the men who broke in and about me hiding under the bed with my sister and then finding our mom. I tell him everything that led up to this phone call.

"I'm at least four hours out before I can get there. Check her pulse," he instructs. I move closer to my mom and keep my fingers pressed against her neck.

"It's there. Not as strong, but there," I tell this faceless man.

"Okay, here's what I need you to do. Is there a closet, bathroom or bedroom on where you're at with a lock?"

"Yes, there's a bathroom," I answer automatically.

"I need you and your sister to lay your mom down. Find a sheet or table cloth or towel to lay her on then pull her into that room. Do not move her head or neck or sit her up. Get her on the floor in there then lock the door. Can you do that?" he asks, firing off the directions at me. My eyes scan the kitchen and fall on the table cloth.

"I can," I tell him, sounding more confident than I feel.

"Do not open the door for anyone except me," he instructs. A car door slams, and I hear keys in an ignition fire up. My eyes slam shut against more tears, tears of relief.

"Yes," I whisper.

"Okay," he replies. "I'm going to hang up now. I will be there as soon as I can. Send me a pin of your location and which floor and room you're in and turn this cell phone off the minute you send that text."

"Okay," I reply, my fingers flying over the screen. The call ends, and I watch as the texts I sent go through, before turning the power off.

"Here." Mila stands next to me, holding the table cloth in her hands. We work quickly to lay it out flat and slide my mom onto it to move her. I take the top corners while Mila takes her feet, and we move her over the floor, then across the hallway, until we reach the smaller bathroom. I ignore the squish and slide of the blood between my toes while we work, sidestepping the broken glass, and focus on keeping my eyes only on my mom and not the gore and splatter on the walls around me.

"Get in the tub," I instruct Mila and watch while she hunkers down. I move my mom's body, so she's laying horizontally from the door, before grabbing a wet towel and heading back into the hallway. Quickly, I wipe up the bloody trail we made, giving off our location. Ditching the towel by the back door, I run back to the bathroom and close the door, sliding the lock in place before my legs give out. I barely make it into the tub with Mila, before the shaking starts. My skin vibrates with energy, and it takes all I have not to dry heave.

"Breathe." Mila's small hand runs in circles over my back. Lifting my head, our eyes connect, and we share a sigh of relief. Help is coming. I have no idea who this person is or what he can do, but for the first time all night, I don't feel like the world is ending. Gripping my sister's hand, I pull her against me and stroke her tangled blonde locks. Soon, her breathing evens out, and I can't tell if she's just calm or asleep. My other arm slides over the lip on the tub and finds my mom's pulse again. It's still there, and I send a silent prayer of thanks.

The house remains quiet, only the tick of the clock in the living room echoes in the silence. I count the chimes for each hour that passes. My eyes never leave the door knob, fearing it will turn, and another murderous, hateful face will charge at us. My legs cramp, and I have to pee, but I don't move. I can't move. I let the anger replace the denial inside my mind. Those men were here because of my dad. My mom is hanging between life and death because of them, and my dad's off cruising around with millions of dollars. He left us. Mila and I could be like our mother right now. We all could have been murdered, and no one would know until a news crew picked up the story, once we failed to show up for work and school continuously. My skin prickles with the rage crawling underneath it. I want to hurt him. The man, who I trusted most, who was supposed to love his children unconditionally, left us to rot because of his messed-up choices.

"What time is it?" Mila's small voice whispers. I glance down and meet her crystal green eyes with my brown ones.

"I think sometime after four. He should be here soon." I run my hand over her golden crown again, hoping it soothes her.

"Have you ever heard of Matt?" she asks, and my hand stills.

"No," I answer honestly. "I'm just hoping Mom knew what she was talking about. He sounded legit, though," I attempt to reassure her. Even though we're four years apart in age, I love my baby sister and would do anything for her. The minute my parents told me I was getting a sister, I'd never once felt resentful or jealous. I happily would share any of my clothes or make up with her because Mila is the sweetest child with the kindest heart. It kills me knowing she saw everything here tonight. I couldn't shield her from the darkness. I couldn't protect her and that failure weighs on me. "It's going to be okay," I tell her again, and I feel her body relax a little more against me.

"I know," she whispers. "I have you." Those three words pierce my heart, and I vow, from now on, nothing will ever happen to her again.

I want to tell her how great she is and that I love her, but the words choke in my throat, the minute I hear a key scrape in the front door lock. Time stops moving for me, and my adrenaline spikes. I pull Mila closer to me and slide farther down into the tub, ignoring the pain that licks up my calves.

"Saylor," she calls my name, and I can hear her fear. I place my hand over her mouth to hold her together and shake my head. *Please be Matt. Please be Matt.* My brain serenades over and over.

The footfalls crunch over the broken glass from the coffee table. The steps are not as loud, as the booted feet from before, as they move into the kitchen. A voice mumbles as the person walks past the door to the bathroom. The stairs creek before padded footsteps are heard over our heads. My eyes close, and I picture what they're seeing as they move from Mila's room to my parents' room then finally to mine. There's a soft thud from outside the door, and I jump slightly, barely able to contain the small scream that's lodged inside my throat.

A tap to the door is soon followed by, "Saylor, it's Matt. Open up." I hesitate. My mind swirls over tonight's events. Matt never said how I'd know it was him. It could be the third guy from earlier, finally coming back to find his friends. Mila pushes against me. I read the questioning and panic in her eyes.

"Saylor, my name is Matt Jakobe. Your mom calls me Rogue because in high school, out of our group of friends, I was always the one going off on my own and pulling pranks. She had to bail me out many times," he fires off, and I can hear the small trace of a smile in his voice.

Pulling myself from the tub, I flick the lock and open the door part way. The man I assume is Matt stands in dark jeans and a faded black winter jacket. It's name brand, and it actually looks warm. His gaze is intense as his eyes trace over me then move over my shoulder to where Mila sits in the tub holding her knees, before sliding to my mom's form on the floor. "Kell," he mutters her name, and the devastation that flickers in his eyes is genuine. Opening the door farther for him, I slide past and lean against the jam. He kneels down and starts looking for her pulse.

"Hand me that bag." He nods to the dark gym bag that is propped against the wall. I slide it to him. "I need you to go get a bag and throw some clothes in there for you and your sister. Grab anything that's important but not that can be used to find you. No phone and no computers or smart watches." He fires off more directions, while pulling a liquid bag and needle out of his gym bag. I watch in fascination as he inserts the needle into my mom's arm and tapes it off, before taping the bag to her arm.

"Go Saylor," Matt's voice is sharp and brings my gaze to his, "I got this. You need to get the bag, so we can get out of here. Upstairs is clear, I already checked." I don't know why I trust him. Something about his muscled frame and kind eyes eat through the distrust I felt earlier.

Not having to be told a third time, I turn and flee for the stairs. My heart hammers in my chest, while I quickly throw on a pair of jeans from my drawer and an oversized hoodie that I had taken from Nash this past summer. Using the hair band next to my bed, I throw my hair in a messy ponytail and empty my school bag. At this point, my calculus homework seems pointless anyways. I stuff the bag with anything in my reach and make sure to grab the essentials like my toothbrush and underwear. After one last sweep of my room, I dash into Mila's and do the same, then head into my mom's. I have no idea what she would deem as important right now, so I just grab her yoga pants and exercise shirts from her closet and her toiletries, before running back downstairs. I just want to get out of this house. Our time is limited; I can feel it.

"Done," I breathlessly tell Matt. He's got my mom's neck supported with a brace, and he's leaning her up against the door, checking her heart and lungs.

"Mila," he nods to my sister, "throw on some pants and a jacket." Mila follows his instructions, while I search for some shoes for us. Everything in me screams for comfort and practicality as I rifle through to the back of our entryway closet for something decent.

"Ready?" Matt asks, suddenly standing next to me. Mila is dressed, and I hand her the bubblegum pink Converse I know she loves to wear. Matt is cradling my mom in his arms, his jacket fitted around her.

"Yeah," I nod and shrug at him. I'm as ready as I'll ever be, and I still have no idea what we're doing. All I know is that he's taking us out of this death trap.

"I'm going to go first and put your mom in. I will wave you over when I'm done. Do not move from this spot until I tell you," he instructs, before sliding past us and down the front steps with my mom against his chest. My heart jolts painfully, thinking he's going to leave us. My arm drapes across Mila protectively, while my eyes eat up Matt's every movement, as he opens the door of a deep red SUV. Once my mom's secured, he closes the door. He keeps his back to us and glances at his watch. My heart beats painfully against my rib cage; I step forward, only to be yanked back by Mila.

"Wait," she says and points to the camera across the street.

"Go," Matt calls to us suddenly, waving us over. He has the back door open and ready. I push Mila ahead of me and hand her off to Matt, who lifts her in. He grabs my arm and lifts me in as well, before closing the door and rounding to the other side. He has his truck fired up and is pulling away from the curb, before I even have my seatbelt completely fastened.

His eyes dart to the rearview and side mirrors constantly, as he drives us south and out of the city.

"Where are we going?" I ask timidly, my lips cracking from being so dry.

"Motel first," Matt replies, his eyes meeting mine briefly in the rearview mirror. "Your mom needs some medical attention, but I don't trust bringing her to a hospital right now. I need to get her awake, so she can make some decisions."

"What kind of decisions?" I question, hearing secrecy in his voice.

"Don't worry about it, kid," he answers, his eyes boring into mine, "you've both dealt with enough tonight. Let's get your mom in a good place, then she can fill you in." He must see the guard that shutters my eyes because he sighs. "You can't go back, Saylor. It's not safe there. I can get you guys to safety, then, from there, your mom needs to be the one who decides what happens. We're about two hours away from our first pit stop. Try and sleep if you can."

I don't know why, but his words cause tears to sting my eyes. My nose prickles, and a bubble of pain is determined to get out. Nodding my head, I push down the emotions and rest my forehead against the cold window. I force my body to relax and breathe evenly. "What did you get yourself into, Kell," I think I hear Matt say, his voice low. I balance between consciousness and darkness. I should check on Mila again. I should check my mom's pulse again, but no, Matt is there. Matt is here, and my dad is not. I've left behind my best friend, my ex, my entire life. Before submitting to the dark recess of sleep, my last thought is that I'm pretty sure this is the worst birthday ever.

# #Three

*Saylor*

"**S**aylor," a deep voice, one I don't recognize, calls to me. I know it, but I don't. "We have to get inside, kiddo," the man says again. He sounds friendly while also a little like a drill sergeant.

"Say," Mila calls out to me. The sound is an echo in my nightmares. My eyes fly open, then shut again from the blinding sunrays, as my body jumps up in the seat.

"Are you okay?" I ask, reaching across the console toward her.

"I'm fine, but we're here," she answers. I look her over and notice her hair is now braided, and she looks somewhat rested as well.

"Where are we?" I ask, facing front, my eyes landing on Matt. The events from last night come crashing down on me.

"At a motel," Matt answers, watching me warily in the mirror again. "We have to get inside."

"Okay," I answer, reaching for the door handle. I notice then that the interior is different; the vehicle itself if completely different. "What happened to the SUV?"

"We ditched it already," Mila reports. "This is actually our third vehicle."

My eyebrows lift at her news. "I don't remember any of this." I remember hitting my head on the floor. Do I have a brain injury or a concussion?

"That will happen sometimes with trauma. Your body was so overworked, it shut down. I carried you at each transfer," Matt answers my lingering questions. Heat rises in my cheeks, and I feel terrible he had to carry my mom and me.

"I'm sorry," I start to tell him, but he waves me off.

"It's not a big deal. Let's get inside, though, so we can sleep before we have to move again." Matt pops his door open and moves to the passenger side to help my mom. In the daylight, it's easy to see the blood caked on her legs and hands.

My eyes dart around to make sure no one is watching. Panic threatens to coil up my spine again, before Matt reassures me. "This is a safe place. The owner works for me. No one will say anything." I follow him to the door at the corner room and notice the doors are not numbered. "Find the green card," he says, handing Mila a worn brown wallet. Her fingers move deftly through the various colored cards, before pulling out an all green card with a red stripe across the top.

"Here," she says, before moving around him to swipe the card. The door buzzes and opens automatically for us. Mila shuffles in, followed by Matt and my mom, before I step over the threshold and close the door behind me. It locks automatically, and lights flicker in the room.

Matt moves to the closest bed and lays my mom on top of the covers, before removing her jacket. I focus my gaze on everything else in the room, knowing what he's about to see, close up and in the light of day. My eyes connect again with Mila, and I notice the shine of tears in hers. "It's okay" I mouth to her. A small, reassuring smile forms on my mouth, even though it feels foreign to me. She nods and tries a smile of her own. My eyes track over her little face and down her neck to the stained red collar.

"Mila, let's take turns showering while Matt's helping Mom," I tell her, moving quickly. My skin crawls, and I'm suddenly very aware of the dried blood between my toes and caked under my nails. She doesn't answer but follows me into the bathroom. Matt doesn't comment, his eyes flickering to us then back to my mom. He's now pulling out bandages and another roll of tape. Once the door closes, I start the water for her and place the shampoo and soap bottles on the ground. We take turns showering and redressing quickly. By the time I step back out into the room, Matt has changed my mom's side of the bed into a makeshift hospital. I notice she's wearing a different t-shirt, a man's I'd guess by the size of it, and the television is on.

"It's not on the news yet." Matt nods toward the screen, where a woman is reading the events from the day. I catch the name Levittown and realize that must be the name of the town we're in. I wish I had my phone to google the city to see how far away we made it. Even if we drove thousands of miles, I think I would still be terrified of the boogeyman.

"I'm hungry," Mila's voice says from the bed across from where our mom lies. Thinking of food makes my stomach toss, but, I realize, it's been almost a day since she last ate.

"There's a sandwich in that fridge." Matt nods toward the mini fridge tucked under the desk. Mila gets up and opens the door. Waters, yogurt and four sandwiches line the shelves. She picks one out and tosses one to Matt, who catches it, before sitting back in the chair by the window.

"Want one?" she asks me, and I shake my head no. Nausea hits me full force just thinking about it. Instead, I join her on the bed and keep my eyes on the TV. Sure enough, the world news scrolling on the bottom touches on everything, but there is no mention of the violence in our Manhattan home.

A faint vibration pulls my attention to Matt, who picks up a cell phone. "How far are you?" The other line can't be heard: only Matt's side of the conversation.

"Green card," he replies to whatever the other person asks, before they hang up. The entire conversation happens in less than a minute.

"Who's that?" I ask, hating that, once again, distrust rises in my chest.

"My sister, Molly," Matt answers, tilting his head, eyes watching me like he knows I don't fully trust him yet. "She's a doctor. I need her to help your mom with some of her injuries that I can't take care of." Pain burns through my veins because I know what he's referring to. I know she was raped. Even though I tried to block it out, I knew what they were doing to her. I saw the evidence when I found her and when we moved her. There was so much blood. My breath hitches, and panic claws at my throat.

"Saylor," Matt says, he's moved onto the floor in front of me. His hands rest on his knees, so I can see them. "Breathe, kid. You're okay. She's going to be okay."

"I should have stopped it." The words fall from my mouth. The fear, from my inability to protect her, that I've pushed down until now comes out like word vomit. "I should have stopped them. I couldn't."

"No," Matt says. "She wouldn't have wanted that. She would not have wanted you to see or for those men to have found you. It might not feel like it right now, but she protected you both. None of this is your fault. You did exactly what you should have done." I believe him, even though it's painful. I fall for the words he speaks, and I clutch onto them, so I don't feel like a failure of a daughter.

"You both need to try and sleep." Matt's voice is gentle. "Molly will be here soon. You should rest while you can."

Mila shuffles under the covers, but I still can't move. "It's his fault," I say, my head raising to meet Matt's eyes. "I blame him. If he hadn't left us." My words cut off as my breath hitches. Ugly words I can't take back now hang between us. My dad is to blame for what happened to my mom. "They were looking for him," I tell Matt. Every word feels like small paper cuts in my throat. Matt doesn't blink or look away. There is no judgment or denial on his face, almost like he agrees with me.

"Get some sleep," he finally speaks, after several minutes pass between us. Our silent communication and loathing of the man who called himself my mother's husband is our new shared bond.

I slide under the covers next to Mila. I shouldn't be tired, after being knocked out for hours, but my eyes fight to keep open. I want to be awake in case my mom wakes up. I want to meet

Molly. All my wants are in vain, though, against the softest thread count sheets I've ever slipped into. The pillow cradles my head perfectly and the thick comforter is a shield of protection that lulls me into sleep, once again.

### ###

Hushed whispering brings me to consciousness, much to my body's dismay, my mother's voice among the plotting adults. I can feel Mila's form snuggled next to me and figure she must be asleep as well. They don't know I'm awake, so I keep my breathing even and my eyes closed, listening to them.

"No," my mother whispers adamantly, "no, I did not realize he was in that deep or how he was getting the money."

"You had to have known something, Kell. It wasn't usual for Cal to have that much money, right?" I hear Matt say accusingly. The casual way he uses my dad's name, as if he knew him, has my ears straining to hear more.

"No, Rogue," my mom sighs, "I promise I had no clue. Was it dumb of me not to question why all the sudden his small business firm was bringing in big dollars? Probably. I also had two little girls who were growing up and joining leagues and teams and wanting expensive things. So I guess I buried my head in the sand and went with it. Plus, you know Cal, Matt, he wanted desperately to get back what was taken from him when his parents died." Her voice wavers over the tears I can practically hear falling down her cheeks.

"No one is blaming you," another woman, who I assume must be Molly, answers. "What happened at that house is horrible. For you and for your girls."

"I didn't mean for it sound like I'm blaming you, Kelly," Matt's gruff voice interrupts, "I want to kill Cal for what he did. The position he put you and the girls in when he took off. You all could have died."

"I never wanted the girls to go through something like this. I can't believe he left us in danger." My mom sobs, and it takes all my concentration not to jump up from where I'm lying and hold her.

"He never mentioned he was back in contact with is extended family?" Matt inquires again.

"No," my mom chokes back a sob, "if I had known, we would have left. After everything, everything he went through as a child and losing his parents as a teenager, I never thought he'd be that stupid."

"Like you said, though, he's always wanted back what he lost. He always knew his life should have been different." Matt's voice lowers and actually sounds soothing for once.

"What are you going to do, Matt?" The other female voice, Molly, asks. My heart races waiting for his answer.

"I can hide you," he answers; yet, the hint of doubt in his voice hangs in the air.

"It's not your usual case." My mom points out to him. My head spins, trying to place a Matt or Rogue in my memory. I swear I've never heard of him until yesterday. This hotel, Molly, and now him saying he can hide us just leave more unknowns and more questions.

"No," he acknowledges, "but I can't not help you either, Kelly. I couldn't live with myself if I knew I could have tried and did nothing. I should have gotten in touch with you sooner, once I saw the news."

"How will this work?" My mom asks the question I'm dying to know.

"Identities are easy. I have a family willing to help. The only problem is that they know your family already." Matt's voice trails off. His thought process clicks in my mind. I know where he's going with this.

"They know to look for a woman and two girls," my mom answers, her voice breaking because it's making sense to her, too. "I can't do that. How could any mother choose?"

"I can't make the decision for you, Kell. I also have to give you all the facts. Everything is ready and set to go. We don't have much time," Matt explains. My mom silently sobs. A few tears escape my eyes, listening to her. I can't take it anymore. Adults and their secret plans never work out.

"It's fine, Mom." My voice hitches when I sit up quickly. Three heads turn to look at me. Matt is the only one who doesn't look surprised, almost like he knew I was awake the whole time. "I'll be fine on my own if it means we're safe."

Our eyes meet and hold. A million little wishes and thoughts pass between us. The strain and fighting over the past couple of days fade away, though. I can feel the courage and pain she pours into me. She's sorry, and I silently communicate my understanding and acceptance.

"Will you do it?" she finally asks. Her voice quiet. I spin the words over in my mind and realize I'm holding my breath, waiting for his answer, too.

"I can," Matt finally answers, "if that's what you want, I'll take her with me."

"If it can't be me," her voice breaks and her hands come up to swipe the tears off her cheeks, "there is no one else I trust more."

"I'll make the call," Matt says and gets up, before walking into the bathroom.

"Saylor," the woman next to my mom calls my name. "I'm Molly, Matt's sister."

"I know," I tell her, nodding my head.

"We have some errands we need to run. Can you help me?" she asks, giving me a conspiratorial wink. The woman must be able to tell I'm five seconds from losing it.

"Sure." I give her a small nod and swing my legs over the side of the bed. As I go to get up, everything hurts, and my vision swims.

"Let's get you some food, too," Molly suggests. "You look like hell, chickie."

I chuckle, the sound foreign to my ears. "I'll try."

Molly tosses me one of the sandwiches from the fridge, ham and cheese, before leading me outside. It's almost dark now, the last of the sun falling behind the clouds. I grip the sweatshirt I'm wearing tighter against my body.

"This way." Molly leads me to her car, and I hop in. She cranks up the heat, and I give her a small smile of thanks.

"What are we all getting?" I ask quietly.

"Just some essentials, for now. Once your mom and sister get to their family, they'll help them with everything they need. Same for you. Once you and Matt get home, you'll be able to get more clothes, shoes, jackets, whatever." She swings her hand around, before leaning forward and grabbing a stick of gum from the cup holder. I watch as she chomps the piece between her teeth fiercely. With the way she mauls the sticky piece, along with the stale smell of smoke in the car and the empty box of Nicotine patches on the floor, I'd say she used to be a smoker and quitting was a recent choice.

We drive ten miles down the road, before a neon sign for a Walgreens catches my eye. I stuff the last piece of sandwich in my mouth, just as Molly pulls off and parks the car. We get out, and I follow her inside the store. She turns down the aisle with hair products and stops in front of the coloring boxes. My eyes widen, and my stomach drops. "I thought this was something people only had to do in the movies," I say humorously.

"None of what you are going through right now is okay, and I know you want to hang onto anything of your old self you have left, but this," she waves her arm over the aisle, "is a necessary evil. Anything to throw whoever is after your family off their game is needed. They know what you look like. We need to change as much of that as we physically can."

I let Molly's words sink in. Instead of feeling enraged by the information, I feel a sense of calm. I know she's right, and at this moment, I don't want to be Saylor Torre anymore anyway. I reach for the different boxes, pulling different shades off the shelf that I think would provide the most drastic changes in Mom's, Mila's and my appearance. I'm about to leave the aisle and catch up with Molly when my eye catches on the silver boxes on the opposite side. Without thinking, I quickly grab the shade that calls to me and cradle it to my chest. When I meet Molly at the register, she has stacks of toothbrushes, toothpaste, feminine products, cotton balls, nail polish remover, and scissors.

"Here," she says, handing me an all-black baseball cap and nodding toward my head, as we walk out with our purchases. I rip the tag off the bill and slide my ponytail through the loop, before pulling it down low to cover my face.

"They already saw me inside," I remind her, and she shrugs.

"Worst case scenario, this is the last place you'll be picked up on camera," Molly tells me, before unwrapping a sucker and sticking it in her mouth. "Want one?"

I shake my head no and slump farther in my seat. My chest squeezes with anxiety, and I suddenly wish I had my magical, little, as needed prescription bottle. I had wanted to escape the house so quickly I forgot to grab the bottle out of my night stand.

"I'm going to have my hands full helping your mom when we get back, since she can barely move. Do you think you can take care of you and your sister?" Molly asks quietly, breaking my concentrated breathing exercise.

"Yeah," I respond, clearing my throat, "what do I need to do?"

"Color her hair. Cut off a little. Not so much that it's a monumental change or looks suspicious, but just enough to look like a natural length. Have her clip her nails and take off the polish. Change and pack. Do the same for yourself." Molly fires off the directions.

"Okay," my voice catches again. I'm starting to get annoyed with myself for sounding like I could cry at the drop of a hat.

Before I'm ready, we reach the motel. It's completely dark out now, and Molly walks at a fast pace to the room. Once we're inside, Molly helps my mom sit up, handing her a yogurt and water from the fridge to eat, then starts to move her to the edge of the bed to sit up.

"Saylor," Molly calls my name softly. "Help Mila." Sucking in a deep breath, I grab my sister's hand and lead her to the bathroom. With the door closed, I have her sit on the counter and face the mirror.

"What's happening, Saylor?" she asks me quietly. Our eyes lock in the mirror, and I try to paste on a calm expression.

"We're getting out of here and heading somewhere safe. I'm half convinced Matt and Molly are super spies." I crack a smile for her, and it works. Her own lips form a smile back at me. "Mila, we have to change how we look, so we're harder to track," I try to explain, while pulling her hairband out of her braid and combing my fingers through her hair. I've always envied the golden color of her hair. Some women try their whole lives to achieve this perfect shade of blonde and pay hundreds of dollars at their beauty salons to get it. Not Mila, though. She's never had a touch of color added. She's one of the lucky ones. Our eyes collide again. A sheen of tears shimmer in hers.

"I promise to make it look as beautiful as I can. It's not forever. It's just for now," I reassure her. She nods, unable to speak. "Work on your nails while I do this. Shove the clippings in this bag. You don't have to watch." She takes the nail polish remover and clippers from me and gets to work. Popping open the box, I swirl the color together and shake it, before slipping the plastic gloves over my hands. I work the black in, until I'm convinced every strand is covered. Mila avoids looking at the mirror the entire time, examining her fingers and hands over and over instead. While we wait for the timer on her color, I start stripping the color from mine. My brown eyes trace over every deep reddish-brown strand, as I coat them in bleach. Mila's breath hitches in her throat, and I know she's watching me.

When my color is setting, I wash the color from Mila's hair, until the water runs clear again. Before it dries, I use the scissors to snip a couple inches off the ends. Both of us have grown our hair out since we were little. The long tresses hung down our rib cages, and now, I've cut hers so that it lays flat against her chest. When I'm done, she sits on the edge of the tub and helps rinse my color out as well. The water takes on an orange and brown color that makes me sick to look at. For safety purposes I know I have to change the color, but I liked my hair color. I liked that the shade was darker than red and had chocolaty strands mixed into it. I got compliments from strangers on how pretty it was. Watching the color swirl down the drain is nauseating.

"Where are we going?" Mila's timid voice brings me out of my conflicting emotional thoughts. Looking at my reflection in the mirror, my head now looks like a combination of yellows with orange ends.

"I don't know," I tell her honestly.

"Mom said we're splitting up." Her eyes drop from mine. Her now dark head lowers.

"Hey," I say and lean over to wrap my hand around hers. "I'll be fine. Matt seems to know what he's doing. This is all weird as shit, but it makes sense. We'll be okay."

She sniffles, and my heart cracks again. "I want to stay with you, Saylor." Her words grip my heart painfully and shake it inside my rib cage. "What if I can't help Mom? You're the brave one."

"Mila," I wrap my arms around her shaking shoulders, "you are so strong. You saved me in that kitchen. You helped me get Mom to safety. Hell, you even had the guts to get to my room in the first place for help. You are strong, baby sis. Mom trusts Matt, and I...I do, too. We're going to be okay." I tell her anything to make the crying stop. I believe she is strong. The jury is still out, though, on if we'll be okay. My gut screams *yes*, but my mind tracks all the unknowns. So much has changed in the past twenty-four hours, and nothing is black and white. My whole life has been catapulted into a sea of grey, with no life preserver in sight. I'm literally treading water.

"It's not forever, right?" Mila questions. My grip around her tightens, and I nod my head.

"Right." I give her the only thing I can. A lie. Not to hurt her, but it sounds better than the truth. I have no idea if it's forever. I have no idea how Matt's job works. I hope it's not for forever, but there is no way to know.

"I'll cut yours," she tells me, pulling back and gesturing to my hair.

"Okay." I hand her the scissors and present my back to her.

"Why did you choose such an ugly color?" she asks, her nose scrunching up.

I laugh. "It's just a phase to help this color set in better," I answer and show her the silver box. I watch her eyebrows raise in the mirror.

"Well, Dorothy, we're not in Trinity Prep anymore," she jokes. Definitely not. No one in our school would be caught dead wearing this color in their hair. It would make them too unique. They would stand out, and, in their minds, being unique is not a good thing. Because if you didn't follow the social norms at Trinity Prep, you are automatically an outcast.

"That's exactly why I chose it," I tell her.

"Mom might kill you still," she points out, a little bit of her sass coming out.

"At this point, the more different I look is probably better. She'll get over it." I shrug and watch as more of my hair falls in front of me.

"Good?" she asks, gesturing to the length. She only cut the two to three inches off the bottom that were still brownish. I nod and start to dry the strands.

"Girls," Molly's head pops in, "you done? Matt's back. Mila and your mom have to go now." Her urgency sends us scrambling.

Mila braids her hair and tucks it into the hooded sweater she's wearing. I notice for the first time that the clothes she has on are baggier and not hers. It's hard to tell, looking at her frame, that she's a girl. The minute we step out of the bathroom, the room is in chaos. Matt is packing Mom's medical supplies. She is also up, dressed and leaning against a chair. The deep red I had chosen for her hair actually looks nice on her. I know it's not a color she would ever pick for herself, but it goes well with her freckles and skin tone. A floor length dress drapes her body but still hangs loose and a jean jacket covers the bruises on her arms. Our eyes meet across the room. She offers me a small smile that makes me want to wrap my arms around her and beg her to take me with her. Despite the tears in her eyes, the tension has left her face. She looks almost like my carefree mom. The mom I had before the Manhattan nightmare.

"He's here." Matt's voice chops through the moment, bringing us back to reality. The rumbling of a diesel truck can be heard from outside the door.

Mila flings herself into my arms, and I wrap her up one more time, breathing in her scent.

"I love you, Saylor," she whispers into my shoulder.

"Me too, Mi," I tell her, hating the scratchy way my words sound. My nose tingles, and I fight back the tears for her. "Not forever, remember that." She nods, before pulling away. Matt places an arm around her shoulders and guides her out the door to a waiting truck.

"Saylor." My mom steps in front of me, her body swaying slightly. I reach out and circle my arms around her shoulders, pulling her into me.

"I'll be okay," I tell her because it's what she needs to hear. "It makes sense this way," I say, even though the words hurt. After everything I've already lost, I feel like I'm losing them, too. A dark pool of dread starts to form in the pit of my stomach.

"I know you will be," my mom says, a sob hitching in her throat. "You're the bravest person I know, Saylor. I love you so much. I'll think about you every day. I'm so sorry, Love." She uses my childhood nickname. My eyes slam shut, my face turning into her hair, as I inhale her scent too--one of warmth, home, mom.

"I don't blame you," I tell her honestly. We pull back, and our eyes meet. Sympathy in her gaze collides with the rage in mine. We both know where I believe the blame lies.

"You have to go." Matt comes back in through the door and holds out a hand for my mom to grab. Our gazes stay locked, until she steps out the door, and I can no longer see her. I hear a door slam, and the engine fades away, before Matt comes back in the room. It's over and done. The tension I'd been holding onto leaves my bones, and I feel weak.

"When do we leave?" I hear Molly ask.

"In a few hours," Matt answers. He cleans up the trash that's scattered over the floor, shoving bloody sheets into giant pillow cases.

"Where are we going?" I ask. Both of them turn to look at me, but it's Molly who speaks.

"We can't say yet, Saylor. Even though we're safe here. Too many lives are on the line," she tells me. If that's not the most ominous answer ever, I don't know what is.

"Let's get cleaned up then we'll have time for some shut eye before we need to leave," Matt says.

I help them clean everything possibly seen by the naked eye from the floors, blankets and beds. Matt isn't satisfied until even the tiniest bit of lint is off the floor. He leaves then to shower, and I hear the sound of an electric shaver going off. Molly and I sit on separate beds and watch the news again. There has still been no mention of what happened. For some reason, this knowledge makes me uneasy. I can tell looking at Molly, it's the same for her, too.

She clears her throat before turning toward me. "Do you need help with the rest of your hair?"

"Sure," I answer, shrugging my shoulders. It's not that I don't like Molly or don't trust her; I just feel like it's a final piece of my old self that is going away.

"How about I just help rinse if you need it?" she replies, watching me. My eyes narrow at her perceptiveness and the way she seems to already know me.

She surprises me more when she laughs. "You remind me of my son," she answers, and I'm taken aback.

"I didn't know you have kids," I answer honestly.

"Just one." She faces me again. "He lives with Matt, actually. Being the medical professional, I'm usually gone a lot, so he lives with Matt for now. You'll meet him when you get home."

I bite my lip and ponder over her words. "Is it okay that he's home by himself when you and Matt are both here?"

Molly laughs. "He's just fine, Saylor." She continues to laugh when my mouth drops open. "Ciaran is eighteen. He's fine."

"You don't look old enough to have a son that old," I blurt out. My filter momentarily missing.

Molly's smile grows larger. "Thank you. I actually had Ciaran when I was really young. I had just started college when I found out I was pregnant. His dad and I tried to make it work, but we wanted different things. I moved back and have been in the family business since then," she explains. The family business is what I want to know most about.

Matt walks out of the bathroom then and I notice his hair is shorter and the facial hair's completely gone. "Finish anything you need to." He looks in my direction. "We leave in seven hours." I waste no time finishing up the color in the bathroom and cutting my fingernails down, after removing the pink birthday manicure Oaklynn had bought for me. Just thinking of my best friend brings on another wave of tears. Hopefully, one day, they'll all dry up. I dry my hair quickly and examine the purple shade in the mirror, twisting the locks in my hand. "Definitely not Trinity Prep worthy," I whisper to myself. Saylor Torre is gone.

# #Four

When Matt said seven hours, he really meant five. I feel like my eyes barely closed, before he had us up and out the door based on a gut feeling. Once again, my body is flying on autopilot, fueled solely by adrenaline. By now, I don't even question his urgency and instinct. Matt has been right about everything else so far. I quietly follow Molly and him out the door and into the backseat of a different car than the one we arrived in. Again, I do it without question. To any passerby, we look like a family of three, driving away from the motel we took a little vacation at.

Matt and Molly keep a silent conversation while we drive. I pay attention, for a while, before the scenery out the window starts to change, and my concentration is thrown off. I wish I had my phone. I wish I had my music and silencing headphones, so that I could stay in a happy place. The farther we drive, the more spread out everything gets, and I don't recognize any landmarks. From the last road sign, it appears we're going west. No one says anything, though. I lean my head against the window, and the glass is cool against my skin. It's comfortable. My eyelids flutter closed, just when the sun breaks the horizon.

"Hey, kid," Matt calls, while jostling my shoulder. My body jerks up, ready to run if need be. "Whoa, easy. We're getting gas and switching vehicles." His words register in my brain, my eyes opening wide. All I see is trees, dirt and this lonely gas station. It's dark again, which means I slept all day.

"Where's Molly?" I question, pulling myself upright. Somewhere on our journey, my body had sprawled across the whole back seat.

"She ran inside to use the bathroom. You should, too, if you need it. And get a snack." Matt nods toward the gray and red building, before turning back to the gas pump. I open my door and slide out, pulling the hat back down over my head, even though it's dark out. Walking quickly into the store, I pass Molly on my way to the bathroom. She smiles at me, even as worry lines crease her forehead. Shivers run up my arms when I slide into the single stall bathroom. The florescent light zings to life, while I splash water on my face, trying to force life into my pale features. I look sick. I look like a dump truck ran me over then backed up and did it again. My hair is a rat's nest, sleepers are crusted in my eyes, and my lips crack when I move my jaw because they're so dry. Fuck me. How long was I actually out for? My stomach rumbles under the baggy shirt I'm wearing reminding me I should eat again.

Sighing, I run a wet paper towel over my face and pinch my cheeks to bring some color to them. I pull my hair out of the ponytail it had been in and finger comb the strands, before adding a single braid that rests over my shoulder. I slide the black hat back on, as I leave the tiny room, hating that it brings me some comfort to wear it still. We might be far enough away from New York, but the fear of being chased is still too new. I don't want my face picked up on any cameras. I spot Matt waiting by the register; we make eye contact, and he uses his hand to gesture for me to hurry it up. I slip down a few aisles, before meeting him. He hides a grin while the attendant rings up my Pringles, sour gummy worms, Chapstick, a Red Bull energy drink and a box of Milk Duds.

"What?" I say, shrugging my shoulders at him. Everything sounded good, and I want to stay awake, instead of passing out, like I seem to keep doing.

"Nothing, kid," he answers, while his grin grows bigger. I follow Matt out the door and notice the chill in the air. Guess that blows my theory he was taking me somewhere warm and tropical.

I fling my purchases into the back seat and crack the energy drink open, before noticing that Molly is on the phone. She hangs up right as Matt gets in.

"Still same location?" Matt asks her.

"Yup, they made it to the first site. Andy said they'd rest, then do another couple hours tomorrow," Molly answers.

"My mom and Mila?" I ask, holding my breath and waiting for one of them to answer, excited to hear anything at all. My heart thumps painfully in my chest thinking of them.

"Yeah," Matt replies, "they're on time, and nothing looks suspicious." His words should make me feel better, and they do, but they don't take away the pit of fear that still exists low in my stomach. "We're going to drop Molly off then we're about eight hours away from our location," Matt says, making eye contact with me in the rearview mirror. My gaze flicks to Molly then back to Matt.

"You aren't coming with us?" I ask her, confused.

"No." Molly shakes her head and turns to look at me. "I got a call for a job while we were driving. I will be away for a while."

"Oh," I answer, starting to piece together what Molly's role is in their family business.

"We'll also switch cars again when we drop Molly off," Matt reminds me, even though I don't remember him saying this a first time. I nod, like it's old news, and glance out the window. The moon is full and high above us now. We're in the middle of nowhere. And I still have no idea where we are going. Unease starts to fill my chest, the unknown causing my anxiety to amp up even more.

Molly and Matt keep up small talk and include me, this time. In between their questions about my hobbies and school, I snack on my chips and a few gummy worms until my stomach hurts. My last real meal was days ago, and I just filled my stomach with junk food. A few hours later, Matt takes the exit for Chicago and recognition fires in my brain. I finally know where I am. As the city grows closer, skyscrapers lay out before us, the lights surrounding the city create a halo of yellow light. It's familiar and reminds me of better nights spent at home. Chicago is not New York, but it is a large city with people. A hum of energy courses through my veins, and my eyes eat up the chaos happening outside our vehicle. I liked that about living in New York. It was hard to feel alone when you stand on a street and are immediately surrounded by people.

Matt takes us a little ways outside the city to a development of apartments. The car comes to a stop outside a row of town houses. Molly and Matt climb out, before moving to the trunk. I follow, feeling unsure about my place at this moment. Do I hug her? Shake her hand? Wave? How do you thank the person who saved your mom? Just like before, Molly knows where my thoughts are going and how jumbled they are. Without speaking, she makes the decision for me and wraps me up in her embrace. I freeze for a second, before letting go and allowing myself to take a bit of the comfort she is offering.

"You're going to be okay, Saylor," she whispers next to my ear. "You're a fighter." My eyes squeeze shut while her words sink deep into my soul. Molly pulls back from me, before I'm ready, and turns to give Matt a hug as well. They exchange a few words, while my brain is still stuck on what she called me. I'm a fighter. Molly is amazing and comforting, and now, I realize how much I'm going to miss her, too. I attempt a half smile when she turns to wave goodbye to us. I don't miss the black duffle bag slung over her shoulder or the new surgical face mask she's donning as we pull away. These people, the secrets, this family business...I probably shouldn't be curious, but when have I ever run away from a challenge?

On the last eight hours of our trek, I learn two things. One, Matt sucks at small talk. Two, very few radio stations are coming in clearly, and the only ones Matt seems fond of are the country music ones. I'm even more agitated when my foot starts tapping on the floor board along with the song, while I shove the last remaining Milk Duds in my mouth.

"Are you going to tell me yet where you live?" I ask around the chewy caramels.

Matt's eyebrows raise. "You didn't see the sign back there?" he asks. My head whips around to look out the back window.

"No," I answer feeling anxious. "What sign? I didn't see one. What did it say? Are you sure?" My thoughts run rampant, while my neck twists at odd angles to see as far back as I can.

"Oh," Matt looks out his window as well, "well, maybe we didn't pass it yet then. It's pretty hard to miss."

"What are you---" My words die off when my gaze finally catches on to what Matt is referring to. There is no way to miss the giant stone statue in the shape of the state with bright red lettering across the middle. *Welcome to Minnesota.*

"Minnesota?" My memory scrambles to remember the geography tests from fourth grade, the ones where they make you memorize the states and capitols and where each state is located on the map. I haven't thought about it in years because, well, Google.

"Yup," Matt answers, turning his eyes to mine, a hint of a twinkle lights up his irises. "Home sweet home."

"To who? Eskimos?" I reply, my jaw hanging open in astonishment. What in the actual fuck? Matt laughs at my outburst, while my mind continues to whirl. Minnesota is up by Canada. Isn't part of it even jutted into the Canadian border? My mind hurts trying to remember all the specifics. I think it's located by the huge lakes that used to be glaciers, right? My stomach fills with dread thinking about the weather...lots of snow and tornadoes? I swallow past the lump of anxiety in my throat that's cutting off my oxygen.

"What about tornados?" I ask him, my mouth still gaping open.

"Okay," Matt turns to me, trying to keep a straight face, "First of all, yes, Minnesota touches the Canadian border. The Great Lakes were created by glaciers, and they're super cold. I don't recommend swimming in them unless you can stand prickling cold water. As far as seasons go, you'll get a little bit of everything here. It's fall for a few more weeks. They aren't predicting snow just yet. Tornadoes happen on occasion, but it's been years since there has been a really bad storm like the ones that people see on the news in Tornado Alley."

I swear my eyes go rounder with each question he unpacks from my brain. I hadn't meant to say all that out loud, but it sounds like I did. My eyes flick back and forth from the scenery outside the car then up to Matt's profile again. The grin he wears only grows bigger the longer I take to formulate an actual response. Minnesota. Fucking Minnesota. "Guess my mom's solution really was best. Dump her as far away from normal as possible. No one will find her here." I shrug, letting the sarcasm roll off my tongue.

"Believe it or not, Saylor, this will be one of the safest places you ever live. There may not be huge buildings and bars open until four am, but you'll go to bed every night not having to worry about the shadows and the boogeyman." Over the past few days, I've learned that Matt's voice hardens a little when he starts to get serious.

Still... "How did you know?" I ask. I've only been repeating that phrase to myself since we left New York.

"You talk in your sleep." Matt casts a glance my way. My body tenses. "You also snore and drool a little bit."

"Shut up!" I can't help the small twist of my lips. "I do not."

"She smiles," Matt adds, before looking back to the road. Miles tick by, and we pass a large city, I'm told is one of the Twin Cities, before we continue north for almost two hours. It's dark outside again by the time we pass a city limit sign, but I catch it briefly, Savage Lakes, population 723. My forehead taps against my passenger window as we pass through the smallest town I've ever lived in. We pass three churches before reaching the main drag. One side of the road is lined with brick and stone small businesses and shops. The other is fitted with two fast food joints, a gas station and Rogue's Car Repairs.

"Is that yours?" I ask, nodding to the car shop as we pass.

"Yup," Matt grins again, "It's my day job."

We travel another couple miles down the road and pass a local mom and pop restaurant with a sign for spicy chicken, and

I smile, thankful there is some country cooking up here. We wind around a lake, before making our way out of town. Huge pine trees line the roads, and what's left of colorful leaves are sprinkled over the tar.

"Why is it called 'Savage Lakes' if there is only one lake?" I ask, unable to keep still or quiet any longer. My knee bounces with apprehension, knowing we'll be to Matt's home soon. This is all too real now. It was easier, not thinking about it, when I had no idea where we were or where we were going, only that we were driving for a long time. With the road trip being over, my stomach summersaults and twists again. This is where I'll be living, on my own, without my family. Matt and my mom may go way back, but he is essentially a stranger. I have no idea what I'm expected to do or how to I'm expected to act now that I'm here. Matt seems oblivious to my discomfort.

"There are two lakes. The one we passed is the tourist one with the beaches and boat dock. The other is more a hidden gem the locals use," he explains. I nod, taking the information in and storing it for later use. The slower Matt seems to drive, the more my hands start fidgeting with the string on my hoodie. The road he turns down next has a few houses with enough yard space. My breath hitches in my throat when we finally pull up to the curb in front of a white paneled two story home. The only light on is the porch light. A driveway sits between the building and a smaller garage next to it. The backboard and rim of a basketball hoop hang over the garage door. My eyebrows raise at the sight. Matt gets out of the vehicle, and I follow, my knees wobbling and threatening to give out, as I try to get a grip on myself.

Tires screeching against the pavement pull my attention toward the road, right as an all-blacked out truck pulls up to the driver side of the car. Matt motions for the driver to go forward. Whoever is in the truck pulls ahead of us, leaving a few car spaces between us and it. I follow Matt to the trunk but can't take my eyes of the truck. Goosebumps rise on my arms and chase down my spine, before spreading over my legs. Even with the blacked-out windows, I can tell there is more than one person in the vehicle, and I wonder if they are watching me as intently as I'm studying them. Probably not, because I'm nobody to them. The bass coming from the truck's radio pulses in the night air and causes another round of shivers down my spine.

"Here ya go," Matt says, handing me my school bag and a plastic shopping bag from my trip with Molly. I take my bags and step away. "Go on in," Matt gestures to the front door, "I have to take care of this quick."

"Okay," I mumble and walk on shaky legs toward the house. I keep my back to the truck, even as I feel it. Heat, scorching hot attention, slithers up my spine and bores into the back of my head. Awareness of being watched and studied flushes my cheeks red. A window cracks, and Wiz Khalifa's "King of Everything" leaks out, the lyrics wrapping around my body and compelling me to turn and look. Guess they have more than country music here. My gaze focuses on the window I know I'm being watched out of, staring back just as intently, searching for a shape, a profile, a face, anything, like an obsessed creep.

"Ready?" Matt asks, suddenly in front of me. I blink and bring his face back into focus. The volume on the bass turns up, and I want to look again. Something tells me that whoever is in that truck wants my attention, too, or else why would they be stalling to leave? Keeping my attention on Matt pushes my limits, causing my eye to twitch as I force myself to nod and answer him.

"Yeah." My voice sounds pinched in my throat, so I clear it, right as the engine revs and tires burn rubber on the pavement, before launching forward, speeding down the road and out of my peripheral vision.

"Fucking-A, Ci," Matt mutters. He turns to watch, and I finally let myself look, too, knowing that they're gone. Did he say key?

"Who?" I ask, my brow furrowing.

"My nephew. Ciaran, or Ci. You'll meet him tomorrow," Matt says, while turning the lock and pushing open the door.

Just inside is a small entryway with a staircase going up to the second floor. To the right, the room opens to a dining room and kitchen. The left side of the house holds a couch and two recliners, along with a huge TV and sound bar.

"On the second floor, there is a spare room, third door on your left that is for you. A bathroom, the laundry room, and Ciaran's room are also up there. Hope that's okay. Kitchen is over there, feel free to make anything you want to eat. I grocery shop on Sundays, and there is always a running list on the fridge. The only rule is that if you're up first, you make the coffee." Matt lists everything off, while I follow him around the house. "Also, my room is in the basement, as well as my other projects. Nobody goes down there, okay? So when you have friends over someday, act like that level doesn't even exist, got it?"

I fight the urge to roll my eyes. One, I doubt I'll make friends here or be here long enough to make friends, and two, the last thing I'm going to say to anyone is 'hey check out my basement.' Sounds like a B-Horror movie plot line. "No worries, Rogue," I reply, taking it upon myself to use my mom's nickname for him, hoping it will make things less awkward. Sure enough, it earns me a crooked smile.

"Okay, your IDs will be ready in a few days. If there are any names you're fond of, let me know ASAP, or else I'll be forced to make something up. In the meantime, if you need a vehicle, use any in the garage. They're all chipped with tracking devices. You have a bank account opened already and can use this card," he explains, handing me a silver piece of plastic. I turn it over and read the name on the front.

"Rogue's Car Repairs?" I question, looking closer.

"I give all my employees cards for their expenses," he answers without blinking.

"I don't work there, though," I point out, getting ready to hand back the card.

"You're still an employee. Use it until your new ID comes in, and you can set up your own card with the bank," Matt instructs, and I nod. Just one more thing to add to the ever-growing list of things I do not understand.

"Thank you," I mumble anyway.

"Since tomorrow is already Friday, I told the school you'd start bright and early on Monday morning. That gives you time to get settled and get anything you may need, sound good?" He asks and that pit in my stomach stretches a little wider.

"Sure," I tell him, pulling my eyes away from his. With a town population of a little over 700, I know, for sure, the student population at the high school is not going to be huge. All these kids probably grew up together since diapers, and, once again, I am going to be the new girl, just bulldozing my way into junior year. Reflexively, my fingers find the end of my braid. For the first time, I almost regret my decision to color my hair purple.

I catch Matt's eyes flicker over me in my peripheral. "You okay?"

My shoulders lift. "It's a lot to take in. I have no idea what half of the things you just said mean."

He laughs. "I'm not good at the orientation part. It's been a long time since I've personally hosted anyone here. There is a lot to know and adjust to. I'm sorry. We'll just take it one day at a time. If you have questions, ask."

I turn to face him, feeling marginally better. I nod in response but stay silent.

"See ya in the morning, kid," Matt says, before heading back down the stairs.

I listen until I hear the basement door close, before exhaling. For the first time, since the incident at home, I am alone. The silence buzzes around me when my reality starts to sink in. I turn to the closed door Matt had pointed to, and with one twist of the knob, the door glides open, without making a noise. My hand searches the wall, before landing on the light switch. Thankfully, the light is attached to a ceiling fan and is bright enough to surround the whole room in a warm glow. My eyes travel over the plain wooden dresser, the standing mirror, twin doors that open to a two-rack closet, and finally land on the queen size bed with a wooden headboard. A dark blue and forest green comforter lays across the top of the mattress. The design in the middle has me curious and inching my way closer.

"No way," I mutter to myself, taking in the profile of a man hunting with a black lab sitting next to him. My hand reaches down to pull the comforter back, and, sure enough, the sheets are flannel and printed with ducks. I sigh and pinch the bridge of my nose between my fingers. The walls are bare; yet, it looks like someone cleaned in here recently. My mind drifts toward the blacked-out truck from earlier, and the nephew I have yet to meet.

Exhaustion seeps in as a yawn is torn from my throat. I let my bag drop by the side of the bed and place the toiletries I picked up on top of the dresser. I have no pajamas, and, despite being on the top level of the home, the air feels slightly cold. There is one window in my room that overlooks the road in front of the house. The whole block is silent and dark. I pull the shade down, before moving toward the light switch. I hesitate, hating to plunge the whole room into darkness. There are no lamps or those plug-ins my mom used to get with the oil diffuser on them. If the light goes out, it will be pitch black. I won't be able to see anything. Frustrated, I shut the door and turn the lock, before slumping down onto the bed. I move my body under the covers and pull them up over my head. My eyes close, and I try to breathe normally, only I feel suffocated and confined, which brings me back to the space under my bed, listening while those men beat and tortured my mom.

"Ugh," I moan into my arm and swing the blankets off my body. I curl to the side where I can keep my eyes on the door and angle the hood, on the sweatshirt I'm wearing, to block the light. My fingers tug at the extra material around my arms while I make plans. Tomorrow, I'll venture into town and look for a small lamp or a night light and get some new bedding. If I feel up to it, I'll even think about doing some laundry and figure out what clothes and jackets I'll need. I know nothing about Minnesota and its weather, except that it's cold, and it snows the majority of the year.

It isn't long before thoughts of snowflakes and cold weather calm my brain down, and I'm able to sleep. The light behind my eyelids eventually fades as well. I'm thousands of miles from the boogeyman tonight. I'm finally safe.

# #Five

A door closing and the sound of water running pull me from sleep. My eyes crack open, and I'm happy to see the sunlight filtering in behind the curtains. Rolling onto my back, the bed creaks slightly, and I pause, needing a few more minutes to myself, before facing my new life here. I can smell coffee being brewed from the kitchen while someone moves around the space. The water from the bathroom next to my room turns off, and the sound of an electric toothbrush buzzes next.

I sit up slowly, stretching my arms and legs. My sleep was so deep last night that I didn't move from the spot I balled up in all night. There was no way to tell the time without a phone, so I add an alarm clock to my list of things to get today. Quickly, I peel the clothes off that I slept in, making a face. I really need a shower and to wash my clothes. I grab the clean jeans and hoodie that sit on top of my bag and pull them on. Glancing down, I realize it's the same outfit I escaped Manhattan in. Examining the cuffs and sleeves, I notice that the dried blood has all been washed out. There isn't even a stain left behind as evidence. I quickly throw my hair up in a top-knot on my head and glance around the room again. The silver bank card that Matt gave me last night rests on the nightstand. I grab it quickly and shove it in my back pocket.

With no more reasons to stall, my shaky hand reaches out and twists open the door. Stepping out into the hallway, I can hear voices coming from the kitchen.

"It's not just me." The voice I don't recognize, but assume is the nephew, reaches my ears. "You know she's different. This isn't what we do." The edge in his voice makes me pause mid-step. It's cold and harsh; at the same time, it's deep and powerful. His animosity toward me does not go unnoticed. My stomach swirls with annoyance. What the hell is his problem?

"Silas needs to get over it. You both do. She's staying," Matt bites out, his voice lowering, as if he doesn't want me to hear their private conversation. Doesn't take a mind reader to know they're talking about me.

Holding my breath, I make my way down the stairs and let them know I'm awake and present. The last thing I want is for them to keep arguing about me like I'm not here. The air crackles with tension the minute I step foot in the kitchen. Two sets of eyes turn to look at me. Matt's gaze drops back to his coffee while he handles the introductions.

"Saylor, this is Ciaran. Ciaran, this is Saylor," he says, almost sounding bored.

My mind freezes, and my heart squeezes in warning. My body knows, even before making eye contact, that this Midwest Boy is going to ruin me. I can feel the waves of hostility rolling off him. Slowly, my eyes run over his perfectly white sneakers and black track pants, before moving up to his black sweatshirt with white writing across the front. I take in the way the material stretches across his broad shoulders. A mess of white, blond hair sits on top of his head, the unruly white locks clashing with his sun-kissed skin. Not many guys can pull off that look, but, on Ciaran, it works. He has sharp cheekbones and a square cut jaw that tightens when my eyes flick over it. He's beautiful in an avenging angel sort of way. I blink before sweeping my gaze back up and locking with his blue eyes, the same color as the center of the hottest flame. Ciaran's gaze singes my skin while he stares back at me with open disdain. A slight sneer pulls at his perfectly plump pink lips. I've never felt dislike so strong before. I want to take a step back. Somehow, though, part of me believes he'd see retreating as a sign of weakness, and Ciaran is not a person I want to be weak around.

My spine straightens as I stand a little taller. It's harder to do with my five-foot four stature, but I try. My chin lifts in rebellion. "Hi," I throw out casually, as if this battle of dominance isn't happening.

Without speaking or acknowledging me, Ciaran moves his gaze over my shoulder, as if I'm invisible, and walks right past me. Standing frozen, I hear keys rattle, followed by the front door slamming shut. My lungs pull in air slowly, trying to relax. That was intense.

"He seems nice," I spit out, turning to Matt, who finally lifts his head from the newspaper article he's been studying so intently.

"He'll be fine. Just give him some time," Matt grunts, turning the page and bringing his cup of coffee to his lips.

With Ciaran gone, I feel more at ease, so I move farther into the kitchen and grab a cup of coffee for myself. Eyeing a banana on the counter, I grab that as well.

"What do you want to do today?" Matt asks me, even while he continues reading.

"I was hoping to go to the store in town. I have a few things I want to get," I tell him, watching his emotions play over his face.

"You want me to go with you?" he finally asks.

I shake my head. "No. I want to go on my own. I need to figure this place out."

Silence stretches between us, and I think he's about to say no, when he sets the paper down and turns to me. "Get what you need and talk to people as little as possible," he instructs, before digging in his pocket. Matt pulls out a cell phone and hands it to me. "There is no internet on here. A tracking system is installed, and our numbers are already programmed," he tells me.

"Thanks," I nod in understanding, before pocketing the phone.

"Don't be gone too long," he says, standing and heading out the same door Ciaran left through moments before.

Part of me wants to rejoice at being alone and another part of me craves to have someone to talk to. Standing alone in the kitchen, it's easier to take in the details I missed last night. Like the mile-long grocery list Matt mentioned that is filled with red meat, pizza, and other junk food. Wrinkling my nose, I take the dangling pen and scribble chicken breasts and veggies on there. I chuckle softly to myself, imagining Matt walking up and down the produce aisle. Judging by the list and what's on the counter, these guys don't eat healthy very often.

Not wanting to wait around any longer, I run back upstairs and throw what's left of the items in my old school bag, before slinging it over my shoulder and running outside to the garage. I hit the key fob and watch lights flash on the bulking tan 95' Ford Bronco. I make my way over to it, even though I'm not sure how I'm supposed to drive it. The thing looks like a square box on wheels and probably doesn't handle that well on the road. I barely passed my driver's test, and I took that with a car half the size of this thing. For a second, I contemplate calling Matt and asking him to trade with me. My neck cranes out of the garage toward the street, looking for the car we arrived in last night; only, it's gone. The curb is completely empty. "I don't want to know," I mutter to myself, and decide I could care less if anyone is around to hear me.

Backing the huge end of the vehicle out of the garage seriously takes all my concentration. I'm going to have to talk to Matt about it when I get home. Somehow, though, I figure out how to maneuver it down the driveway and onto the road. I travel by memory back toward town, paying attention to road signs and street names, just in case. I turn on the radio and find the only station that plays actual music. I wouldn't pick country to listen to by choice, but I do recognize the song as Blake Shelton's "God's Country" after it played everywhere earlier this year.

The drive into town is shorter than I remember, and before I know it, I'm coming up on the main drag. I make the quick decision to park now, since I'm not sure where all the different stores are. It's a nice day out, so walking won't hurt me. The minute my feet hit the pavement, the world seems to slow down. People who are rushing by stop to look. Cars stop honking and even the wind turns to barely a breeze. At least some of the gawkers have the decency to hide their mouths behind their hands, even though I know I'm the object of their whispered conversations. Too bad for them I'm used to gossip and stares. I plaster on my fakest Miss America smile and make my way to the store that caught my eye last night. Rad Radioz appears to be the only electronic store on this strip. The banner advertises Beats, sound bars, dock stations and even records and turn tables in bright neon writing. Since my phone has no internet or apps, I look high and low for a device where I can download music.

"Ah, excuse me." I lift the box to the guy a row over, wearing a green vest and holding a stack of boxes.

His head lifts up, as his eyes examine the product I'm holding. "That's a great model. Can hold up to 4.7GB."

"Do I need to have an email to download or access anything?" My eyebrows lift in question.

"How do you not have an email address? Do you live under a rock?" His mouth gapes at me, and I really can't help but pull comparisons between him and Anthony Michael Hall's Farmer Ted from *Sixteen Candles*.

"Does this state count?" I ask and get a grain of satisfaction when his eyebrows pinch together, as if he's in pain, and wondering how I manage to function through the day. Carefully, he sets the stack of boxes he was holding down on the shelf, before running long fingers through his short, sandy brown hair and walking over to me.

"Hand it," he says, holding out a hand. I set the box on his hand and watch as he pulls a smaller iPad from his vest pocket and starts looking up information for me.

Up close, I notice the name Reed sewn on his vest. I then take in his appearance. He's taller than me but not taller than most guys. Light green eyes scan over the screen, while he reads the information, scrolling quickly. He looks book smart in his white Vans, khaki pants and white shirt that hangs loose on his lanky frame. I'd bet my left arm he'll be the class valedictorian someday. He must sense me studying him because his eyes snap to mine, and he takes a hesitant step back, before handing back the box.

"The manufacturing site says you can use it without buying the subscription, which you would need an email to do; you just won't get the perks of having the subscription, so like ads and stuff will run in between every couple songs." He shrugs, keeping his gaze averted.

"Okay," I tell him. turning to the front of the store. "Can you ring me up then?" My head whips around the store, looking for other employees, but he's the only green vest I see.

"Sure." He walks quickly to the counter, continuing to ignore me, while ringing up my purchase. When I hand him Matt's business card, I swear he stiffens, before swiping the card and handing it back to me as if it's on fire.

"Here you go." He hands me the plastic bag and is careful not to let his fingers touch mine when I take it. The old Saylor would have laughed and maybe flirted, just to make him more uncomfortable. The old Saylor would have taken a small piece of happiness that she made a guy this nervous. Not now, though. I have no email, no contacts, no social media, and I am getting a new identity. All the fire and last bubble of happiness in my chest fizzle and pop.

"Thanks," I mutter, slipping the bag up my arm, before I head toward the door. At least, if the rest of my shopping day is a bust, I was able to get the one thing that matters most. I glance back over my shoulder and find Reed still watching me. Something like fascination or fear crosses his face, before he tears his gaze from mine. Suspicion and unease settle in my gut. Something about that kid is familiar. I swear I've seen his face. Remembering him feels like a nightmare or a ghost story told by adults to little kids to keep them on the straight and narrow.

Frowning, I make my way down the block, hitting each store that calls to me as I walk by. Along the way, I start to notice a pattern. The checkout clerk does a double take, shakes their head, then rings me up. When I hand over Matt's card, three out of the five times, I get the stare at you under the eyelashes' look.

It's bizarre, and I'm going crazy, because by the afternoon, I've started doing it, too. I finally cave and call Matt to see if there is a larger store in the area. He tells me to try Wal-Mart, which is in the next town over. Following his directions, I make it in under half an hour. I breathe a sigh of relief at the much larger selection and patterns than the antique store had back in Savage Lakes. I finally have a new bed spread and sheets, alarm clock, backpack, and I also pick up a hat and glove set. Slowly, I make my way through the clothing section. Nothing is jumping out at me, though. I add two pairs of jeans to my cart and another hoodie.

"You look lost, Hun," a voice calls to me from a rack over. My head zips back and forth, trying to locate the source. A tiny woman moves forward from behind the large mound of clothes she is holding. "Can I help you find something?"

"No, I think I have the basics," I tell her, shrugging and attempting a neutral smile. When I look back at her, our eyes clash, and her mouth drops in recognition.

"Oh, my!" She moves closer, examining me from my shoes to the top of my head. "You look exactly like your mom."

"Uh, do you know my mom?" The question squeaks out of my lips. After everything that has happened, I was starting to wonder if I even knew her.

"Oh darling, I used to go to Savage Lakes High with your mom. We were thick as thieves back in the day. We haven't spoken now in, oh my, probably eighteen years," the woman continues to explain, her eyes still roving all over my face.

"Until she moved to New York." I nod in understanding.

"You betcha. She moved right after graduation. I hope now with you being here, maybe I'll get to see her again," she continues, completely oblivious to my comfort level dropping dramatically.

"Maybe," I agree, noncommittally.

"Well, what are you shopping for? Anything I can help with? Hunting season is almost over, but there is still some camouflage and orange gear in the back if you need it." She points to the other side of the building. My mouth drops for a split second, before I have to bite my lip to stop from laughing. A mental image of myself dressed in bright orange and camo floats through my mind. If Oaklynn was here, she would probably die laughing with me.

"Just some essentials for school," I tell her, pointing to the items in my cart.

"Clothes for school? Did Matt send you here?" she asks, eyeballing my cart and snorting behind her smile.

"Yeah," I nod, looking along with her.

"Men," she huffs out, "look, I'm not knocking our products, because we have some cute things, but most kids your age go to the mall for their clothes. It's just on the other side of town."

"There's a mall?" I ask, again wanting to make sure I heard her right. Stupid Matt.

"Yup." She smiles. "It's not going to have the same stores you're used to; those are probably closer to the Mall of America, but they will have a better selection for school. It's hard enough to be the new kid, I can't believe Matt told you to come here." She shakes her head, her black bob haircut bouncing with the movement.

"Men," I agree with her and shrug my shoulders. "Thanks, though," I tell her.

"No problem, sweetie," she chuckles. "Hope you have a good first day."

I smile again and push my cart back between the rows and racks to the checkout counter. Once my bags are in the trunk, I find my way to the mall, and I want to smack my forehead, for not noticing it before. Almost another hour later, I pack more purchases into the trunk and suddenly feel a lot calmer about starting school on Monday. Even if I have to be the new girl again, at least I'll feel a little more like the new me.

By some miracle, I manage to find my way back to Savage Lakes. Before hitting the far end of town, I notice a brown sign instructing drivers to turn left to go to the water access. I lift my brow, my curiosity piqued. This must be the other lake that Matt said was for locals. Without thinking, I turn down the dirt road and drive until I reach the parking lot. Jumping out of the car, my feet make their way to the start of the sand, and my breath catches. It's beautiful. I now understand why the locals keep it to themselves. Stepping onto the sand, I notice it's solid from the cold weather and frost. I make my way to the edge of the water. Ice has started to form on the edge of the banks, and orange, red and gold trees line the water. A series of cliffs are farther down, on the opposite side from where I stand. My stomach does a little flip, imagining climbing those rocks and jumping into a freefall from the top. I wonder if the water is deep enough over there. A boat lift is nestled off to the left of where I'm standing. Closing my eyes, I picture how summer could look here. My smile thins when I realize I don't even know if I'll be here this summer or what will happen to my life.

Casting one last glance at the water, I head back to the Bronco and lift myself inside. I have no reason to stay; yet, the thought of returning to a home I'm not sure I'm wanted at makes my insides twist. Reaching into the glove compartment, I pull out my new iPod touch and start clicking on the music from the store that Reed had set up before I left. I find Ed Sheeran and click on "Antisocial" before leaning my seat back. Closing my eyes, I concentrate on breathing and let the lyrics and melody dance in my blood.

I'm so lost in my own private concert, I don't hear the truck pull into the parking lot a few spaces down from me. I don't notice their music over mine. When the sudden honk from a horn goes off, I jump, and my body slams against the seat, my nerves automatically on edge. The sunlight dances over my eyes, momentarily blinding me while I fight to keep them open. Squinting, I raise my head over the edge of my window and immediately lock on the grey truck with its tinted passenger window half rolled down. My eyes widen when my brain clicks with what I'm actually seeing. The blonde girl's head is thrown back, her mouth open, while her breasts jump from the impact of the solid looking body crouched behind her, pumping his hips into her. All I can see of him is tan skin stretched over rippled stomach muscles. One large hand grips the window, and I don't know where the other hand is. My voice squeaks in my throat, as I slump back down in my seat, shifting to my side, and turn my own music up louder in my ears. My heart hammers in my chest, hoping they didn't see me, and don't bother to look to see if anyone is in this vehicle.

I'm not sure how long I keep my body balled up and eyes slammed close. Close to ten songs have played in my headphones so that should be enough time, right? Hesitating, I slowly turn, so I'm laying upright, and raise my seat back to its normal position. The minute I do, I wish I hadn't. The truck is still there, with the passenger window rolled up this time, only my brown eyes clash with an angry set of forest green ones. Destroyed blue jeans hang off his lean hips, while he slips a black Henley over his head, not breaking eye contact the whole time. A blush spreads over my cheeks and the need to avert my eyes and cower is strong. *Please don't think I spent the whole time watching.* My mind races while this stranger continues to stare me down. My throat goes dry when I notice the muscle in his square jaw jump and his lips thin in disgust. If I thought Ciaran's scowl is painful, this guy's artic glare is brutal. I can read the hate in his eyes when it dawns on me he didn't care that I could see. He wasn't hiding. With one last sneer, he turns away and disappears inside the truck. My chest heaves while he backs up and guns it out of the parking lot. Sucking in air, I struggle to bring my racing heart back under control. I'm at a loss as to what that dude's problem is. If he is going to get it on in public places and doesn't want people to see, he should probably check to make sure he's alone or keep his windows closed. Not my problem he's a dumbass. Shaking my head, I twist the keys in the ignition, and that's when I see it.

"No fucking way." I open my door, stepping out, and walk to the hood. A condom. A dirty, used condom is plastered to the hood of the Bronco. Matt's Bronco. "Agh!" My head falls back as a yell is forced from my throat. Who does that? Jackasses do, apparently. A gnawing in my gut has me guessing this was no accident. That asshole threw it on my vehicle on purpose. The hate in his eyes went way beyond just being upset someone might have seen him humping his playboy bunny in a parking lot. He knew me. He clearly has a problem with me. Popping the trunk, I grab a plastic bag and slide it over my hand like a glove and peel the tainted condom off the hood, flipping it into the bag. Hustling over to the garbage, I slide it in, before racing back to my vehicle and tearing through my other bag for the hand sanitizer I bought earlier. "Crazy rednecks," I grumble and curse that giant Neanderthal. Without waiting another second, I back up and screech my own tires to get out of the parking lot.

Cruising back through town on the main drag, I keep my eyes peeled for the car wash and gas station I saw earlier and pull in. The sun is starting to sink into a cotton candy pink sky, and a chill hangs in the air. I had no idea so much time had passed while I was at the lake. Checking my phone again, I'm surprised to see Matt hasn't tried to contact me or check in. He clearly is way more laidback than my mom would have been. I decide to fill up the tank while I purchase a car wash. My eyes wander over the shops and the restaurant across the street selling that chicken. Whipping around, I notice that most places look dark and closed up. An almost eerie silence buzzes around me. I didn't remember if Matt said there was a curfew in town. Another glance at the phone tells me it's only half past six. Is this a Minnesota thing?

The pump clicks when it's done, and I grab my receipt for the car wash code and drive around the building. Twenty minutes later, I pull the Bronco back into the garage and park it. I load my arms up with all my bags, refusing to have to make more than one trip. The sun has officially set, and it's freezing. My hoodie no longer provides enough warmth against this temperature.

"Oh, hey." Matt glances up at me from his spot at the kitchen table when I walk in the door. "You just get back?"

"Yeah, I got a little distracted," I tell him, gesturing to my many bags. His eyes widen, but he keeps his mouth closed.

"Okay. I'm getting ready to head to the garage. I have some work to do. Ciaran already left. There's some left over frozen pizza in the fridge if you're hungry. I usually get Mama G's, but with the game tonight, they closed early," Matt explains.

"What game?" I ask, remembering how shut down the town is.

"Football," Matt explains. "Big game tonight. Winner goes to sectionals next week."

"Everything closes down for a high school football game?" I question, making sure I heard him right the first time.

"Yup. Whole town really gets into it. We have a great team this year. The quarterback is being scouted by top tier college teams," Matt answers, while pulling on his jacket and shoes. "Did you need my help setting up anything in your room?"

My mind blanks for a minute, still digesting what he told me, before his question fully registers. "No, I got it," I reassure him, shaking my head.

"Make sure you eat," Matt instructs, before heading outside.

The silence echoes in the home as I make my way back up to my room. I throw my bag on the bed, before heading to the kitchen. Armed with a couple slices of pizza and some water, I start tackling my room. I make a wash pile with the sheets and blankets then a separate one for my new clothes. I quickly find the only power outlet in the room and plug my new lamp into it, before turning it on and testing it. It's bright enough to keep the demons at bay, but not overpowering where I won't be able to sleep.

Putting my headphones in, I take my first load of laundry to the washer. I lose myself in the rhythm of Mako's "Breathe," singing and swaying my body to the beat. After days of being scared and unsure, it feels good to be doing something normal. Laundry isn't exciting; it's mundane, which is exactly what I need to feel like a regular teenager. Smiling, I shimmy my way back down the hallway, before sliding to my door Risky Business style. My glide is halted, though, when my body crashes into an immovable object, bouncing and stumbling backward. Catching myself, I straighten and come face to face with an unamused Ciaran. His glare travels over my body, and I become painfully aware that I'm only in a pair of sweats and my sports bra. Heat blooms in my chest followed by splotches of red over the exposed skin.

"I'm so sorry," I say, my eyes widening, while I watch his glare turn from disgust to rage.

"Watch what you're doing, Princess," he practically hisses, "and put some clothes on. You may be a charity case but have some decency to act appropriately, okay?"

Heat flares in my cheeks. "What the hell is your problem?" I spit the words out, matching his glare with one of my own.

"You, being here." He steps farther into my space. My body fights the instinct to back up. Instead, my head tilts back, never breaking eye contact with him. "I don't like you. You're only here because of Matt's loyalty to all things Rogue. There are other people out there who deserve our help more than you and your family." Each word from his mouth is like a sucker punch to the gut. My body literally folds in on itself in order to stop the painful verbal blows.

"You have no idea—"

"And I don't give a fuck," he cuts off my words, refusing to even hear my side of the events, which, these days, is typical.

"You're an asshole." The words are bitter as they fly from my mouth.

He smirks. "Yeah okay, Roxanne," he says, before shouldering his way past me and into his room. His door slams shut, and I'm still frozen in place outside my room.

Sighing in frustration, I open the door and close it behind me. My good mood goes from ten to one within a five-minute time span. Adrenaline fuels my anger. My body is alive again. Resentment, frustration, and pain swirl inside and pump into my veins. He called me *Roxanne*. I know the song he's referring to and I hate that he thinks that of me. I need to hit something. I want to run. I crave the sting of the pain to wash away the feelings I'm experiencing. Pacing in my room leaves me breathless and fighting for air. My body sinks to the floor while my traitorous memory plays over every detail of the past few weeks like snippets and screenshots in my mind.

Ciaran's words mold their way into my conscience. And I hate that he's right. Matt even said himself this isn't a case they'd normally take on, but he did for my mom. Because of their history. Not everyone will agree with him, though. My dad destroyed lives. The news covered stories of the victims affected. One man even committed suicide after losing all his family's money because of my dad. Other families lost their homes, or they were going to lose their long-time family businesses because my mom and I were too naive to open our eyes, and he was too much of a greedy bastard to stop. The worst story, the one that will haunt me until they find him, that was in the news after my dad's arrest was the mother who killed her entire family after they lost everything. They lost their money, her position of employment was terminated for making a bad deal and signing with my dad, and their friends turned against them for bringing my dad into their lives as well. Tears spill down my cheeks, remembering that family's photo when it had flashed across the television screen.

Ciaran is brutal yet honest and the sudden realization that Monday is not going to be a walk in the park for me becomes real. These kids are going to know who I am or at least have heard of my family and what my dad has done. All the fight and strength leaves my body. Sagging onto the bed, the tears start again. Starting over is no longer appealing. Monday will be the same story as before, just a new state and a different area code.

# #Six

*Ciaran*

Monday arrives before I know it, and I really have to pretend to have my shit on lock down today. It was easier over the weekend. I worked during the day, Saturday and Sunday, and at night, we partied at the beach with a bonfire. Kai knew both Silas and I needed a distraction and needed to let loose, so, for once, he let us, keeping it under wraps from Matt. Needless to say, I avoided the house and *the disaster*. That's what she is. A disaster that is going to bring havoc to the town. It doesn't matter that her mom used to live here or that she and Matt used to be friends. Kelly almost destroyed Rogue when she left and married that prick. Her husband, though, is responsible for much worse. He's an international criminal. He ran instead of facing the charges. This is *not* how we operate. No matter how Matt tries to spin it, Saylor is still an outsider, and her family is currently leaching off the company he claims to be so proud of. The company our families have built to save those who need and deserve our help. Not to be a shelter for an entitled, spoiled princess, who couldn't be bothered to try and preserve an ounce of discretion. Who the fuck has purple hair anyway?

"Straighten your shit out today," Matt warns, peering at me across the kitchen. "I mean it, Ciaran, she's staying, so you and Silas need to move on. Even if we talked about it beforehand, it wouldn't have mattered. I'd still had helped Kelly."

"That's so fucked up after everything her family has done," I shoot my mouth off, resentment pushing to the front. "You know

65

what he was like when she left, and now, you've invited all those memories back."

"Ci," Matt's voice lowers and deepens. "What happened was horrible and tragic, but they didn't ask for this either. Despite what you and Silas think, Kelly has always been my friend, too. Hell, she was an original, so, no, I'm not backing out of this because Silas has his head up his ass. You will drive her to school today, and if I hear otherwise, you can kiss your social life goodbye."

The finality in his voice eats at me. I glare daggers at his back as he walks out the door. Matt may be my uncle, but his perception is seriously skewed if he thinks for a minute that I'm going to be welcoming to the princess. As if my thoughts summon her, just like a demon, heeled shoes hit the wood floor. It's a train wreck I can't keep my eyes off as more and more of her comes down the stairs. Bare legs followed by a dress of all things and a denim jacket. It's a sexy as hell combination. Since running into her last night I haven't been able to get over the fact that Saylor is beautiful. Not in the made-up and fake way either. She's short, sexy and sassy, making her a deadly combination in my book. My mouth drops for a second, and heat flares in my gut when I also remember who her parents are and all the reasons I hate her. "You look ridiculous." She comes to stand in front of me, a small dose of embarrassment flashes in her eyes but disappears quickly.

"Luckily, I don't care what you think," she sasses back and that thread of anger coils tighter in my stomach. A dull flush heats the back of my neck. My eyes rake her up and down, until she grips her fingers together to keep from fidgeting. A thrill zips through my body, knowing I make her nervous. She should be. She should be fucking scared to enter into *my* world.

"Maybe not, Princess, but you should damn well care about protecting your ass and your family. The idea is to blend in. To hide. If anyone has any idea who you are, you could be found like that." I snap my fingers in front of her face, bringing those brown liquid pools back to mine. She's breathing harder, and I know my words are affecting her, even if she won't admit it.

"What good is it to save you if you plan to destroy the whole operation by standing out? As if your hair wasn't enough." My lips form a sneer when my eyes dart up to the purple waves around her shoulders. It's the most ridiculous thing I've ever seen, yet somehow she makes it look natural. They'll never find her, but she still needs a healthy measure of fear.

"I just wanted to feel like myself today." She shrugs, giving me a challenging look. Her expressive eyes are not as innocent as her words.

"Princess, being yourself is what got you here," I remind her, and, sure enough, an ice bucket of reality hits her head, instantly dousing any fire she had in her. Seizing the moment, I step closer to her, ignoring her sugary, sweet scent, forcing her head to fall back, and our eyes hold. "Here's the deal, at school and out there, you're under my watch. Keep your head down, don't draw attention, and don't talk to me. I don't exist to you, got it?"

"Got it," she grits out between clamped teeth. A nice red flush sits high on her cheeks while her nostrils flare. If she could breathe fire, I have no doubt my little dragon would right now.

Smirking, I check her shoulder with mine while walking past her to the door. "Let's go," I call out. Half a second later, I feel her behind me, a silent shadow, trailing in my wake. Glancing down the street, I notice Silas' truck still sits in the driveway, and I can breathe easier, knowing he hasn't seen her yet. Except for that first night when Matt dropped her off, anyway. It took half a bottle of Jack and two hits of a blunt in order to calm him down that night. And he's usually the calmer one of the three of us. Just having to bring her to school feels like a betrayal of our friendship.

She's silent during the drive across town. I don't engage, and she doesn't dare to open her mouth. My music blares through the speakers, effectively eating up the space and silence. Whether she hates it or loves it, Saylor remains quiet. As we get closer to the school, my muscles start to loosen, and the tension lessens. Without hesitating, when we're a block away, I slow down and pull off to the side. Her raspberry lips part in question when she turns to look at me.

"Out." The command rolls off my tongue. Confusion, sadness, then anger flash across her features. Saylor's face is an open book, and each emotion sends spikes of pleasure through my veins. A horn honks behind us before she moves, hesitantly, to grab the handle and open the door. The minute her feet hit the pavement, I grin and snap my gum. "Better hurry, Princess," I call to her, right before the door shuts in my face. Laughing, I drive off, watching her frozen frame in my rearview mirror.

The student parking lot is crowded, like always, when I maneuver my truck to the back, pulling in next to Kai's car. The only car, for that matter, in a line of all trucks. Some people have their tailgates flipped down and are chilling while waiting for the warning bell. Others cross the lot to head into the school. I'm in no hurry, so I flip my own tailgate down. In seconds, Kai and a few other kids we go to school with make their way over. Everyone wants to talk about the parties this weekend and our win over one of our rivals, the Mountaineers, football team last Friday. Kai gives me a knowing look, while I keep my eyes focused on the entrance. Silas could get here at any moment, and, of course, the Princess is taking her sweet time walking here. My mind begins to spin and pictures her walking on her own. She wouldn't get kidnapped, right? I grimace and contemplate if I need to go back for her or not. With just a sweatshirt and jeans on, I'm not freezing, so she won't die of hypothermia or lose any toes and fingers to frostbite before she gets here. My eyes jump from one direction to the other, waiting.

"Didn't hear from Si yet this morning, did you?" Kai questions, flipping his hair back from his face.

"Nah," I reply, shaking my head, "his truck was still in the driveway when we left." Kai grunts in answer, before turning back to join the conversation around us. His eyes flick, every once in a while, to where I'm staring, but he's better at hiding it than I am. We've been on edge about this day for a week, though, it feels like it's been years in the making.

Time continues to pass and looking at my phone is starting to annoy me. "The bell's gonna ring any second," Kai says, while sitting straighter then hopping off my tailgate. My eyes dart around the crowd that is gathering and shifting toward the doors.

"Let's head in," I tell him, lifting my chin toward the building. Kai's eyes roll, but he follows my lead anyway. Right before my feet hit the curb, a flash of purple catches my eye. I feel Kai tense next to me and hear his intake of breath. Saylor has no idea she is suddenly the object of everyone's attention. More than a few heads turn to watch her walk by. She passes us with her eyes down, ears covered with her headphones, and hands tucked into the pockets of her jacket.

Kai moves from my side, with an extra jump in his step, until he lands right in front of Saylor. I notice the way her body freezes, and her hands jerk inside her jacket. *Ready to fight or run, Princess?* My lips pull into a thin line, while I walk up to them.

"Hey there, Gossip Girl," Kai's voice carries. Saylor's eyes dart up to look at him, and a small smile tugs at her lips. Until she sees me, that is, and then her eyes drop back down to her feet.

"I don't know if I should be intrigued or frightened that you know a New York reference." Saylor's words slide past, quiet enough that only we can hear.

"Oh, I know many things." Kai leans over, so his face is hovering in front of hers, and winks. My eyes narrow while my hand makes contact with the back of his head.

"Chill, bro," Kai states, turning to me. His eyes invade my privacy, giving me a knowing look. I keep my gaze averted, passing it off as Kai being the flirt he is and chatting up the new girl, while I stand aloof and ready to play wingman if needed. My stare levels the crowd, before colliding with Bentley Rhodes'. His eyes flick from me and back to Saylor, before traveling from her head to her toes. She has his attention, and she doesn't know it. When I see the smirk on his lips, my fists clench. He then leans over to one of his football buddies, nodding in Saylor's direction. Two more sets of eyes flick over her while they talk. Fuck, of course, she'd gain his attention. Rhodes isn't a bad guy. He makes our school proud every Friday as the team's all-star wide receiver.

He leads the team with the most points earned and is close to breaking a state record. It's the baggage he carries that concerns me. He and Saylor are more alike than he realizes.

"Here are your new IDs and bank card for your new account." Kai's voice yanks my attention back to them, as he's reaching into his back pocket and depositing the plastic squares into her hands.

Excitement flares behind her dark irises while she scans her new identity. My smile grows while her lips morph into a frown. "Ariel Waters? I thought I got to pick my name?" Her voice is barely above a whisper, while her eyes dart between us and the crowd. I'm aware some have stopped moving to watch us now, while others shoot looks over their shoulders, before continuing their way inside. Kai and I are used to the attention. We've had it since before we reached puberty. This school is our playground, and we know it. They all know it, too, which is why I avoid almost everyone like the plague. There is too much riding on my shoulders, too many innocent lives at stake for me to mess up. Aside from the guys, I don't build connections. I observe and report, just as I've been trained to do.

"You took too long," I answer her with a shrug. Her eyes snap to mine, red flags brush the edges of her cheeks, and the darkness inside me enjoys watching her feel defeated. "Besides, it's a name for a princess, right, Princess?"

"Stop calling me that," she grits out, her teeth slammed together, and her jaw locked.

Such a fighter. I let the emotion slide off my face and step into her, until my lips graze the outer shell of her ear. "It could have been worse. You could be Roxanne." She sucks in a breath while I continue past her. A moment passes, before Kai joins my side. His eyes are glued to the door, and his face is blank.

"Not cool man," he mutters, once we're inside the building and heading toward the locker bay. I glance at him in my peripheral and shrug. I know he's talking about the ID, but I don't give a crap. My chest still tingles where it brushed Saylor's shoulder. I got too close to her, and everyone saw.

"I don't give a fuck if her feelings are a little hurt because she can't pick out a name," I clip out, "Si is our friend and that's what matters. Not her or her feelings."

Kai's head shakes next to me and a few beats pass before he answers, "Yeah. Okay. It just didn't feel right, though." His shoulders shrug, and I fight to ignore the tightening in my chest. There is no reason I should feel guilty. The name isn't that terrible. She'll live.

After throwing my bag in my locker, we breeze easily through the senior wing, before dropping into desks. I have calculus first hour and dread it every day. If it were up to me, I'd be taking study hours and office assistance work with a late arrival built into my schedule. Unfortunately, my mom and Matt dictate what I need for classes, and insist, I be here every day, just in case. In my entire school career, the dooms day event they planned for has never happened. The school days would continue, whether I was here or not. My mom keeps saying it's part of our training and that continuing to have some normalcy is good for me. Being born into Rogue automatically gave me status to help others. It was explained to me at an early age about the good things we do for families and individuals who need help. Every day is something new and the adventure of the unknown working with Rogue is both intriguing and exhilarating.

"One year left, Brother," Kai mumbles under his breath next to me. I cock my eyebrow at him. He's scarily perceptive and has a really freaky way of being able to read Silas and myself. He shrugs, in response, while a lopsided grin pulls at his lips. If I comment, I know I'll get a smartass remark from him about being superior at reading people due to the Chinese blood flowing in his veins. The first day I met Kai, he introduced himself with both his first and last name. Kai Liu. What first grader does that? One who wants you to know his last name literally stands for kill and destroy. He became Silas' and my best friend after that, and it's been just the three of us for the past ten years. Matt and Jason, Silas' dad, took notice of our friendship early on. It didn't take long after that for Kai's family to be inducted into Rogue. His family is another safe home in our town. I want to take over for Matt and my mom someday, just like they did for my grandparents. Kai and Silas are on board already, too. For Kai I think it's the possibility of danger that intrigues him while Silas is cataloging all the changes to technology and policy he wants to make.

"Thank fuck for small miracles," I mumble back, before yanking out a textbook. Unlike other schools across the country, who are supplying their students with Chromebooks and the latest technology, our school insists on keeping it old school with massive textbooks and a blackboard. As Matt likes to say, more teens with technology, the riskier a chance we could be discovered by anyone paying attention. I always wonder why other students never question it. It's been brought up at a few parent-teacher meetings, but it's always quickly squashed by our current principal.

A commotion at the door in my peripheral pulls my attention. Silas slips into class, right as our teacher, Mr. Nelson, goes to close the door.

Silas smirks while Nelson huffs. "Try to be on time tomorrow, Mr. Montgomery."

"Yes, Sir," Silas responds. The sarcasm in his voice slides right over Mr. Nelson's head, and I bite back a grin. Kai is already turned sideways in his desk, facing our pissed off looking friend.

"You saw her already, didn't you?" Kai prods. He always knows the right buttons to push when necessary. Silas' head rises, and their eyes clash right before he turns to look out the window. The only acknowledgement he gives is the slight tilt of his chin.

Kai turns to me, nodding his head in Silas' direction. The mask he's worn since we were little, the face he gives the world when he doesn't want them to know he actually gives a fuck about something, is firmly in place. His shoulders tense because he knows I'm studying him. To an outsider, Silas may look like a moody teenager who didn't get enough sleep, who dropped his Pop-Tart, and who realized his gas tank was on low all in one day, but we know better. When you've been friends since elementary school, you pick up on the things others wouldn't. When you're trained to study human behavior and dissect their cues, there is no mistake that my best friend is royally pissed off and hurt. Years of resentment simmer right beneath the surface. A sense of justification fills my chest. I don't care if I hurt Saylor's feelings, or if she cries herself to sleep, after her first day, when she realizes she has no one in her corner. It will be bros over hoes any day.

# #Seven

*Saylor*

**W**ell, *that could have gone better*, I think to myself, sighing in frustration. Tears prick at the corners of my eyes. Hot, angry, violent tears. I'd love nothing more, right now, than to wipe that smirk right off Ciaran's face from earlier, preferably with my fist. He's made it more than obvious, he won't be my welcoming committee, and fine, I can deal with that. But his blatant disregard for even the smallest piece of me that I wanted, I can't handle. It's a name, yes, but it was something that was supposed to be my choice. It was my decision, something I will be stuck with for maybe the rest of my life. Now, I'm named after a land-loving mermaid, who wants to be a human princess. No disrespect to that Ariel, it was actually my favorite Disney movie when I was younger. It just isn't what I wanted. New hair, new town, new home and a name that doesn't fit me. Princess. I can hear the way his voice rolls around the vowels and deepens when he says it.

The buzz in conversation continues around me, and I'm determined to tune it out. I've done the 'new girl' thing, so the whispering and eyes roaming me up and down, sizing me up, doesn't faze my anymore. Pushing my shoulders back, my fingers spin the combination on my locker, until the door pops open. So far, I've made it through two class periods, and things continue to go smoothly. As I grab my book for third hour, I'm so far in my own head that I jump when a body lands right next to my locker.

"Hey!" she says, when my gaze turns toward her. My head whips to the side, looking around.

"Me?" I ask, not sure why her smile gets bigger.

"Duh." Her gray eyes sweep over my face. "You're new, right? I'm Winter, yes, like the season. I saw what happened outside. You were talking to Kai and Ciaran, right?"

My eyebrows raise. "You usually introduce yourself like that?"

Her shoulders lift as a soft chuckle leaves her lips. "You always avoid saying hi to people?"

"If I can," I throw back, enjoying some banter. Almost every person so far today has either smiled politely or politely acted like they were ignoring me as they shuffled on past. "Winter?" I ask, and she nods her head, her long black curly hair bouncing around her shoulders.

"My parents clearly weren't very creative." She shrugs again, and this time, I crack a smile.

"I'm Ariel Waters." I try out the new name and hate how it sounds coming out of my mouth. It's foreign and not at all me.

"Guess your parents weren't very creative either," she jokes, only she has no idea how close to the truth she is.

"They definitely weren't," I agree, frowning at myself, thinking of the lengths Ciaran went to, to pick out my new identity, and wondering how Kai fits into all of this. He had actually seemed friendly, making jokes and smiling, while Ciaran stood off to the side brooding.

"Although, I do agree with Ciaran, it's better that any reference to a song about a materialistic girl who will only love a guy to elevate her status," she says, and my face pales.

"You heard all that, huh?" I turn back to my locker and shove my book in a little harder than necessary. Should I go tell Ciaran? My mind reels, trying to figure out what to say. Winter doesn't come off as vindictive, but for all I know, she could be the loudest mouth in this school. As much as I don't want my identity known, I don't want to be associated with Ciaran even more. I'm almost thankful the jerk let me out before we got to school this morning.

It doesn't take a genius to know that Ciaran is a big deal at Savage Lakes High. I felt the shift the minute those boys approached me outside. He wears his crown in the form of messy blonde locks.

Instead of answering directly, she winks. "You are definitely attracting attention on your first day." Her eyes glance past me. My eyes follow hers and collide with a pair the color of caramel. White teeth are framed by pouty lips and set in a narrow, bronzed face that is surrounded by waves of an even richer, chocolate brown hair. He looks like a damn dessert served on the beach. My eyes travel over him, picking up on the confidence he carries, before pausing when I notice the letterman jacket folded over his muscled forearm. My eyes narrow.

"Yup, not doing that again." I whip back around to face her and laugh.

"Bentley Rhodes," she sighs his name, as if it's a curse and a prayer in the same breath. "Have you dated a footballer before?" Winter grins conspiratorially.

"Kind of," I shrug. "It's a long story."

"Good thing we have lunch together then." Winter smiles, and I find myself letting my guard down a little. I really hope my decision won't kick me in the ass later, but something tells me it won't. I get a vibe from Winter that she knows more than she lets on and that she'd keep the darkest of secrets for her best friend. My heart flips under my ribcage when Oaklynn's face flashes in my mind. I bite my lip to distract myself from the pain it causes.

"See you later," Winter calls, as she heads into the classroom across the hall from mine. My head nods to acknowledge her. I'm not even sure how I made it to the classroom, but I did.

It's chemistry and pairs of two are already set up around the room at the various lab tables. I find the only empty station in the back and set my bag down. My eyes widen when I notice Reed, from the electronic store, sitting at the one across from me.

"Hey," I call out to him. His eyes dart to mine then back down, without saying anything. "Okay," I mutter to myself under my breath. I'm not really surprised, though. There was nothing about Reed that screamed friendly and outgoing.

"Don't take it too hard," a smooth voice sounds next to my ear. My eyes turn and land on the guy from the hallway, Bentley, I think Winter said his name was.

"Do you see tears in my eyes?" I ask, not bothering to mask my hostility. Red flags jump around in my brain. He reminds me of Nash, which is something I want nothing to do with anymore.

A smirk kicks up his lips, and his eyes gleam like I just threw down a gauntlet. "Not yet, but I can think of a few ways to have you crying for me." Great. He's one of those guys.

I feign my most innocent face. "I—"

"Bentley!" A shrill voice calls out from the other side of the room. His body doesn't move while my eyes peek over his shoulder. The Queen B of the school stands by an open lab table, one hand on her hip. Her jeans fit tightly, the top barely brushing a cropped Country Girl, teal long sleeve tee. She's pretty, with her make up done up. Her blonde hair is pin straight and falls just above her collarbone. It's her emerald eyes, though, as they shoot daggers at me that really let me know she thinks she rules this school. And, if I had to guess, she also believes I'm trying to move in on her boyfriend over here. At this point, everyone in the classroom has stopped what they are doing and are now paying attention to the three of us, just confirming what I already knew.

Shaking my head, I lean closer to Bentley. "She looks pissed. If I had to put money on it, you'll be the only one crying tonight," I tell him, before sidestepping and sitting at the empty chair next to Reed. I could care less if he talks or even acknowledges me the rest of the school year. I keep my gaze trained forward, on the chalkboard, ignoring the chatter and curious looks, and pretending not to see when Bentley sneaks another look at me.

"I don't want a partner." Reed finally opens his mouth.

I shrug. "Me either, but I also hate sitting alone," I tell him. His lip jerks like he might crack a smile, before he turns away from me. Not until the teacher walks in and goes through attendance, do I feel like my body finally relaxes.

The hour passes by quickly, and I hardly learned anything new. Some of the classes here are covering material I learned earlier in the year and some of it is material my school covered last year. I spend the majority of my time discreetly watching everyone else. Almost the entire class is football players or cheerleaders. Except for myself and Reed. I now understand why he has been flying solo.

After waiting for the class to empty, I finally pick up my book and head back to my locker. Winter is already leaning next to the door when I walk out. "Took you long enough," she mutters, while drifting next to me.

My eyes dart around the halls, taking everything in. "It was crowded," I shrug, "Might as well let them all out instead of getting smashed in the door."

"I heard you pissed Cassidy off already." Winter smirks and turns her face toward me.

My eyebrow lifts. "Is that the blonde with Bentley on her shit list?"

Winter laughs. "I think he's always on her shit list."

"How romantic," I reply, shoving my books inside the cramped space.

"Lunch, right?" Winter asks, and I nod. She leads me back through the hallways to an open area in the front of the building. I'm pretty sure when I passed this space earlier, it was set up for a study hall. We get in line, and I stack my plate with salad, Cutie mandarins, and broccoli cheddar soup, before following Winter across the room. A few other students are already there, sitting at the table. They give me the same polite smile as everybody else. One of the girls asks Winter a question about their English project, and I take the time to survey the room. I immediately pick out Reed. He's, once again, sitting by himself at a table, his leg sprawled out, and he's reading a book. I chuckle to myself, before moving on. The loudest table, of course, belongs to the football crew. Bentley sits next to Cassidy and all their friends are hanging around. A few people are even standing and eating because there aren't any chairs left.

My eyes drop down to my food, and I take a few bites before it starts. Warm currents of energy course through my body, and a flush heats my cheeks. I'm being watched. Closing my eyes, I take a deep breath before lifting my head. Ciaran's eyes meet mine, and a tidal wave of emotion crashes against my chest. His gaze is hypnotic. I meet his challenging glare with a tilt of my head and watch his nose flare slightly. He's thoughtful while he studies me, and I don't miss the flash of heat in his gaze either. It causes another round of fiery tingles up and down my spine, curling my toes inside my boots. When a girl with cherry red lips leans over and whispers in his ear, that flicker of heat vanishes along with any warmth I was feeling. My eyes drop from his, but not before I see the victorious curl of his mouth.

"You okay?" Winter asks quietly, nudging me with her arm.

"Yeah," I answer, looking up and noticing the others are all staring at me.

"Addy asked what side of town your family moved in to." Winter repeats the question that had been directed at me while I had been in a sexy stare down with Ciaran.

"Uh, the other side of town," I half answer to be safe. It's not technically a lie.

"Same as me then," Winter answers, before asking one of the guys about the game this coming Friday. I send her a small smile, thanking her for taking the focus off me. I'm in no way ready to open up and start divulging my life, especially if it means people knowing I'm living with Ciaran.

My spoon dips into my soup right when the energy in the room shifts again. The buzz quiets down, girls turn to look and a few people hunker down lower in their seats. I can feel it, too. Anger rolls through the cafeteria in the form of a bulked-up, dangerous looking guy with a head of black hair in a crew cut and a gaze that could kill. Chills run down my spine. My eyes meet Ciaran's again briefly, before he turns as the other guy approaches his table. It's then I notice Kai is also with him. Without meaning to, I'm pulled into his stare. I can feel the hatred in those orbs as they pierce my face. Recognition suddenly hits me full force. "Condom guy."

"Wait," Winter whispers next to me, "You know Silas, too?"

I turn to face her, right as the guy, Silas, turns toward Kai and Ciaran. I'm forgotten for now. My body sags a little from the tension dispersing. "Not really," I answer. Her face morphs with confusion, so I quickly tell her about my lake side run-in from last week. By the end of my story, Winter is howling with laughter.

"It was not that funny," I chastise her, while trying to keep my mouth from smiling. "It was disgusting."

"Oh my lord," she breathes heavily and fans her face, "I wish I could have seen that."

"You're no help," I tell her and turn back to my food.

"I'm sorry," she chuckles again. "It's just so damn hilarious. You do realize who they are, right?"

I turn toward her, and our eyes meet, but I refuse to answer. I know who they are, but I don't exactly know everything about what they do.

Winter sighs. "Have you ever been to juvie?"

I laugh. "What? No."

"Watched *Orange is the New Black*?"

"No," I answer again, smiling this time.

"Okay, well we're going to use jail as a metaphor anyway. Just like on TV. We're all the inmates. Some were born to be here, and some were placed here for being in the wrong area at the wrong time. There's a hierarchy system inside." She points toward Bentley's table. "They're like white collar criminals who are here to do their time and are most likely leaving here without worry. Almost like royalty." She lifts her chin to another group. "Those guys over there would be your cyber hackers. Anything with electronics and gaming, they're you're go to. And those couple tables in the back are the everyday civilians who are here for petty crimes or sleeping off being intoxicated. Our table would be gang related. We do better in a group and have each other's backs."

"What about him?" I nod to Reed, right as he walks past us to dump his tray. The sharp intake of breath across the table puts me on alert.

"Reed is..." Winter's voice trails off, "he's the Hannibal Lector of the place. Insanely smart but very, very scary."

"He won't actually eat you, though," the girl from earlier puts in. I should probably learn her name.

"Okay and what about Ciaran's table?" I finally ask.

"They don't belong in the jail," Winter tells me, her eyes hardening a little. "They're the wardens."

"What?" I question, chuckling.

"I mean it, girl, their job is to make sure the school runs smoothly. Their parents and families pretty much own and run the town as well. They're the originals in the families who work for Rogue," she answers, scooting closer to me, so that only I can hear.

"I call bullshit but thanks for the tour." I laugh again.

She shakes her head. "Listen, Ariel." I can't help but notice the way she drags my fake name out, and her voice lowers. "Ciaran, Silas and Kai are best friends. Their families are really important in the community and to a lot of the kids who go to this school. No one messes with them. They literally control everything here. If they told me to stop talking to you, I would have to."

"They can really do that?" I ask quietly. I'm already isolated and alone. I don't know what I would do if Ciaran actually did that.

"They won't, but they could," she answers. "They can act sweet as pie to your grandma then turn around and be a deadly force to an enemy and that's why we call them the good ol' Midwest boys."

My eyes fly around the room, taking it all in. Winter's words have shaken me, and I'm starting to really wonder about where Matt has brought me. The days we spent in the motels and on the road flitter through my mind. Pieces of conversation mingle with memories, and the walls in my chest feel like they might close in.

"You're like me," I breathe out, so that only Winter can hear me. I barely notice it, but her head moves in a silent yes. "Is everybody?" I ask, picturing all the people I've met today already.

"No," she answers, a small smile pulling at her lips. "You're not supposed to be able to tell who is or isn't."

"Why are you telling me then?" I ask, turning to face her again.

She shrugs. "Let's talk later, yeah?" Her eyes slide to the others at the table, and I fake a smile at them, before tilting my head in a nod to her.

The rest of lunch passes in a blur. My mind scrambles to accommodate my new reality. I knew Matt was bringing me some place safe. I knew it was also the location of his business. Ciaran, right away, warned me about keeping a low profile, and Kai handed me fake IDs and a bank card. All of that should have been warning enough that I was stepping onto dangerous ground. I feel like I landed on a mine field with no way to navigate to safety. Except, I also don't know what safety is.

Without my permission, my eyes find Ciaran in the crowd, as he's walking away, flanked by Kai on one side and Silas on the other. The girl with the red lips and one of her friends also trail behind them. A surge of possession crawls in my chest. I push it down and squeeze my eyes shut. He hates me. Ciaran knows about my family and why I'm here. Even though I catch fire whenever we look at each other, he will never see past my family, and I shouldn't want the attention of another boy who can't do that. I learned my lesson with Nash. All that relationship got me was shunned by my peers and alone on my birthday.

With only three more classes left after lunch, the afternoon creeps by. My knee bounces under my desks, and I spend most of my classes doodling in my notebook. I can't concentrate and won't even pretend that I'm trying to. I think about everything Winter told me on loop. My head is a broken record that I can't fix. I need more answers.

When the final bell rings, I bolt from my seat, ignoring the people around me, and book it to my locker. Quickly, I shove a few books and papers into my bag, before racing to the front entrance. I have no idea how Winter gets to and from school. I stand on my tiptoes, trying to find her in the crowd. My body gets jostled and bounced around a few times, and I'm apologized to again and again, even though I'm the one holding up the flow of traffic. I'm about to admit defeat when I finally catch sight of her raven curls. She soon sees me and waves over her head, motioning toward a different door. Right as I change direction, my body collides into a mountain of muscle. I jump back, ready to apologize, when he cuts me off. "Watch where you're going, Trash," Silas grits out between his teeth.

"I'm sorry," tumbles out of my mouth before I can stop it. He just insulted me, and I apologized. "Look dude, I'm sorry about the lake okay. I didn't see much. Next time, don't pick a public place if you plan to be naked," I rattle off, proud of myself for my voice not shaking. In my peripheral, I see Kai turn his head, choking back a smile. The two girls from earlier both wear angry frowns, before turning to each other, probably trying to figure out who the girl was at the lake, since it wasn't either of them. I can feel Ciaran burning a hole in the side of my head with his gaze, but I refuse to look away from Silas. Judging by the intensity of his gaze, he has no idea his buddy and I already had one run in.

Silas' face masks any emotion, his eyes narrow, and he bends down to look me straight in the face. "I could care less about what you saw at the lake. The only problem we have right now is that you're in my way, taking up air, and doing what you do best... being a waste of space."

My heart tightens at his words. He shoves past me, soon followed by Kai and the girls. There is no other way to describe Silas other than evil. What I have seen so far of Ciaran is mean and cold. Silas is in his own bracket of uncaring. My cheeks turn pink, and I have to bite my lip to distract myself from the tears that are gathering in my eyes. Where did all this hate and hostility come from? I turn to face Ciaran. I want to ask about the damage my dad created for Silas' family. Nothing else about his actions makes sense otherwise. He won't meet my gaze, keeping his eyes on Silas and Kai. And with Silas' hateful words and Ciaran's glacial demeanor, another crack in my armor forms.

I'm vaguely aware of the snickers and oohs that sound around me. I'm already a spectacle, and it's only day one. So much for laying low. I wonder briefly if this is what Ciaran meant when he told me not to draw attention. It isn't other students I have to watch out for, though, it's Silas.

"Let's go." Winter takes my arm and leads me to the parking lot. My lungs take in the fresh air greedily. My hands wring together while I fight to keep an anxiety attack at bay. I hate this. I hate feeling weak.

"Can you take me home?" I ask her, the minute we get to her car.

"Of course." She nods, and we both get in. We sit for a few minutes while I fight to get my composure back.

"Sorry," I tell her.

"You don't need to apologize." She shakes her head smiling. "I can't believe that just happened. They aren't supposed to engage. Silas made that way too personal."

"He pretty much just made me the least liked person in school, didn't he?" I ask, even though I already know the answer. The tight pull of her lips is all the confirmation I need. "How is that even allowed?" I say more to myself than her.

"It won't last," she replies. "Matt will intervene, and you'll just end up being invisible rather than rejected."

I blow out my breath. "I'm not sure that's any better. I just wanted to make it through the rest of this year and get my life back." I also didn't want a repeat of my previous school, but I'm already heading down that same path. I didn't intentionally set out to provoke Silas.

"It will get better," Winter promises. "You have me and Jamie, Addy, and Ella."

"Are those the other girls we sat with at lunch today?" I question, suddenly feeling bad I didn't make more of an effort. I can tell from the side-eye that Winter is throwing that she is thinking the same thing.

"Yes," she answers with a laugh. "Let me know if you need a ride again. Okay. Where am I bringing you to anyway?" She scrunches her nose.

My head turns toward the window while I rattle off directions. Her head whips to look at me, before glancing back at the road. "Are you kidding me? You live with Ciaran and didn't say anything?"

I scoff. "Like I want people to know that. It's complicated. My family knows Matt. It's the other reason why I'm here." My shoulders sag.

"Well, holy fuck. I was wondering, but now it all makes sense."

"Can we not talk about it right now," I request quietly.

"Yeah," she nods in agreement, but I can still hear her wheels turning. "I was very young when I entered Rogue without any other family and I grew up idolizing what my foster family does. Matt reached out and offered me a position once I was old enough. He thought I acclimated well to my situation here. To answer your question from before, it's my job to talk with new hidden children when they come in. All of them. Little, big, if they're new, I'm their first stop. I explain the rules and help them figure out school life." Her eyes cut to mine, and she has my full attention.

"What rules?" I ask, my throat sounding scratchy.

"You asked me if everyone is hidden, and I said no. Which is true. To help us blend better, we're expected to follow some rules. We're not supposed to form relationships with each other. We can't date each other or non-hidden people. It sounds harsh, but it gets messy. You can't tell who you really are, so, essentially, you're lying to everyone. Why would you want a relationship built on lies?"

"Can you tell me who else is hidden?" I have a few guesses.

Winter shakes her head. "I can't unless you're breaking a rule. There are under twenty-five of us here, though, if that helps. Just like you, we have new identities and everything. Matt keeps the electronics and internet use to a minimum. Once you've been here and, essentially, prove you aren't going to compromise yourself, you'll get internet. It's still monitored, though. Most of us live with a host or adopted family. You're the first person in direct care of the Jakobes. If I was you, I'd keep that under wraps."

I nod in agreement. "I was already planning to."

"I'm not sure what's going on with you guys, but that was not cool. I don't care about policy right now. You're my friend, and Ciaran can suck it." Winter laughs, and I laugh with her.

"Will you get in trouble?" I wonder. I do not want to be on the other side of Ciaran's wrath yet again.

Winter shakes her head. "Nope. I can handle it."

Before I'm ready, she pulls up in front of the house. It looks empty. Ciaran's truck is not in the front or even by the garage.

"Thank you," I tell Winter, before unclipping my belt and getting out.

"See you, Babe," she shouts and waves, before pulling away from the curb. I watch her drive off, before glancing up and down the street. An eeriness settles around me, as I turn and book it to the house.

Silence greets me. Pulling my headphones from my pocket, I put them on and head up to my room. My bag falls to the floor before I drop to the bed. My eyes close from exhaustion. Events from today play across my eyelids. My stomach cramps reliving Silas' accusations and the emptiness I felt from Ciaran. Turning to my side, I pull my legs to my chest and hug myself. I'd give anything to go back in time and change what happened and stop my dad from stealing that money. Renewed anger consumes my body. I choke back the sob that wants to escape; squeezing my eyes tighter, I breathe in and out through my nose. I'm not alone here. Ciaran may run the school, but I am not the only hidden student. Screw him and his rules.

# #Eight

*Ciaran*

Turns out keeping her head down is something the demon princess is actually good at. It's been four days, and she still hasn't ratted us out to Matt, like I expected her to do. Thanks to Winter, Saylor now has a new ride to and from school every day as well. She leaves, comes home, and then locks herself in her room all night. I know she's eating at least. Every day some of the leftovers of her weird tropical fruits go missing from the fridge overnight. That's probably the only reason Matt hasn't intervened yet. Saylor has followed all of our rules to the T. Gone are the skirts and heels, too. Since that day, she looks like a shadow, moving around in all black. Hoodies and sweatpants that swallow her whole. If it wasn't for the hair, she would be unrecognizable to others. I could pick her out in a crowd anywhere. No matter how dressed down she gets Saylor would stand out to me which is irritating. She avoids me and that makes me happy. Except at lunch. The only time our paths cross is in that box-sized cafeteria. She ignores everyone around her, except Winter and Reed. She sneaks glances at him, studying him to the point that a line of concern etches across her forehead. If he notices her, which I know he does, then he doesn't let on. He's following the rules. Unlike Rhodes, who openly glances at Saylor, and keeps attempting to make conversation. Points for Princess, though, she keeps blowing him off, which, for some reason, appeases me.

"You should quit staring," Kai says under his breath, just loud enough for me to hear.

"I'm surveying," I answer back, really not giving a crap.

"You both did enough damage." Kai looks between Si and myself. "Try to play it cool, alright?"

"I'm not looking. I'd rather shove a ball point pen in my eyeball and wiggle it around, before looking in Trash's direction," Silas grunts out. I eye him. It still bothers me he didn't tell us he ran into her at the lake or what happened there.

"Relax, Kai," I say. "Everyone, besides Rhodes and Winter's freak table, are ignoring her and keeping their distance. Mission accomplished."

"We aren't supposed to isolate her, Dick," Kai bites back. "Just do our job and make sure no one pays any attention to her."

"Same thing." I shrug, before bringing my Gatorade bottle to my lips.

"It's still not on the news anyways," Silas point out.

"Yeah." Kai turns to me. "Matt say anything about that to you? That's not normal."

I shrug again. Matt frequently checks the news but hasn't resorted yet to checking online. Fear that their names or anything related to a missing family in New York will trigger a hack. "Not yet," I respond again. My gaze shifts over to Saylor right when she throws her head back laughing. It's the first real emotion I've seen from her since she got here. She looks happy, and I want to wipe that smile off her face.

"I'll reach out again," Kai responds, even though I'm only half paying attention. Kai is our tech guru. A name he made for himself when he "accidentally" hacked into a government server with my video game counsel when we were thirteen. Silas' hand fists on the table. He isn't watching her, but he heard her laugh, too.

"You both need to get a grip." He shoots off, head flying back and forth between the two of us. My gaze turns to Silas who is openly regarding me, waiting for my direction. My eyebrow lifts, challenging him to make a move first. I'm not happy she's here either. I know the pain it's causing my friend. Silas made a critical mistake the other day, though. We do not engage unless forced to. We do not make friends with them. We do not acknowledge them. Matt only requires us to act if their lives are in danger. Calling Saylor out for bumping into him and calling her trash put a huge bull's-eye on her back for almost a week.

"Fine," he concedes, leaning back in his chair. "I'll lose the nickname. It won't be hard to pretend she's invisible because, to me, she may as well be. She's nothing."

"Do we have that covered now?" I turn to Kai whose mouth, if possible, frowns further.

"I give up." He throws his hands in the air, before getting up from the table. I watch as he makes his way out of the cafeteria toward the lockers, eyes flicking one more time over the purple head only feet from me.

"Why didn't you say anything?" I ask Si, before looking back to him. His jaw ticks.

"Why are you so concerned?" he questions back. "Yeah, I saw her. Didn't know it was her at first. There was an empty truck, and Beth wanted to ride my dick. Didn't know it was her in the other truck until after."

"That's it?" I ask, my jaw clenching slightly. I remind myself that I don't care. I just need a story to answer for in case the demon Princess quits being such a good girl.

"Yes," Silas grits out. I nod, before standing and grabbing my trash. I need out of this small space. The cafeteria has got to be the most poorly designed room in the entire school. It's made to look open concept, but it's so packed with tables and students, it would make a claustrophobic nauseous.

Walking past her table, I notice her body stiffens, and I grin, but my eyes are on a different prize this time. "Hey Rhodes," I yell for him, and, as expected, he stops and looks around. Good thing Kai already left. "Good luck tonight. Keep your head in the game." I slide my gaze to Saylor, before walking around Bentley's frozen form and heading off in my own direction. If he's smart, he'll listen to me. Tonight's game is a big deal. Winner goes to the State Championship. I also have some money riding on his win.

The rest of the day passes uneventfully, and, once again, I silently curse Matt and my mom for keeping me here.

"Hit the drive thru?" Silas asks, rounding to the other side of my truck before getting in, and I nod.

"Better hurry before they close," Kai throws in, grinning.

I take off down the main street of town, passing and waving at a few people here and there. Tonight's the game of the year, and this place is about to shut down completely. The whole town is expected at the game tonight. A quick check in my rearview mirror, and I can see that Matt is already at the shop. He'll be running surveillance from there, while we handle the in-person at the game. Adrenaline spikes in my veins. Most of the people in town are oblivious to what we do to keep them safe. With the media coverage and a spike in audience attendance, we're all on edge. Purple hair floats in my mind, and my jaw clenches. If she's smart, she'll stay home tonight. It's bad enough that so much attention will be on Rhodes already. Not that anyone should recognize him. He's been in Rogue and under our protection for the past nine years. My mom reconstructed his nose after I broke it, in order to help change his physical appearance, and his hair has darkened on its own. Someone would have to look really close to recognize him.

After grabbing some burgers, fries, and drinks, I head back toward the field. The lights are already flipped on, and a few die-hard fans have already crept to their reserved seats in the stands. The sun has started to sink, giving the sky a pink and orange glow, that quickly fades into blue. Matt said to expect overcrowding tonight. With that in mind, I swing my truck into the last row, closest to the nearest exit, yet still allowing us to survey the whole field and the visitor stands. We get out, and Silas pushes down the tailgate. Kai jumps in and positions his backpack. It's sporting a hidden laptop that is taking photos of everyone entering through those gates tonight. Silas leans against the hatch, one leg crossed over the other. I can see his eyes moving rapidly over the cars already in the lot, the three yellow buses lined up in the front, and the cars that never left the building. He's cataloging the layout and license plates. His mind is a jumble of letters, numbers, and codes for him to remember it all. Shaking my head, I climb all the way in and take a seat on top of the cab. The added boost allows me a visual of the whole crowd that is starting to form a line to get in. Pulling my phone from my pocket, I call Matt.

"We're all set," I tell him, my eyes scanning entrance to entrance and back again.

"Looks like a nice night," he acknowledges, giving me a code that he's all set on his end, too. Everything on Kai's end must be working. All the licenses Silas pulls are also checking out.

"Make sure you keep an eye on Ariel tonight." Matt's voice is gruff when he says her name. My body stills, and anger sweeps in.

"Not happening," I answer back, a new bite in my voice.

"Wasn't a question," he answers back, before hanging up the phone. I glance at the blank screen like it's laughing at me. My jaw ticks in frustration. Matt knows this will piss Silas off, and, obviously, he doesn't care anymore.

The announcer's booth fires up the sound system; AC/DC's "Back in Black" blasts through the air, right as our team takes the field. My gaze almost becomes frantic as it bounces over the now full stands and over the players lined up on the side of the field. Shiny black and silver uniforms look dangerous. The growling savage bear, on the front, claws at the school name. My eyes drag over the student section, looking for those offensive purple locks, only to come up empty. One whole row is blocked with a sign meant for the other team. I chuckle and read it out loud, "Tell your girlfriends you'll be free next weekend."

"At least they're more creative this year," Kai responds laughing. Silas cracks a grin, but it vanishes in an instant. The air crackles, and the wind sends shivers down my spine. I know, without even having to ask.

"She's here," I say, even though it's obvious. I can feel it. The change in the surroundings and the tight punch in my chest.

Silas looks to me then back to the vehicles, doing his check again. Kai sighs, but doesn't turn around. He just checked her identity on his laptop.

My head snaps up, right as she steps into the ticket line, along with Winter and one of the other girls from their lunch table. She's smiling at something Winter says. I know she can sense she's being watched from the hard line of her back. The purple head looks casually around. If it weren't for the way her fingers grip the edge of her jean jacket, I'd swear she was only taking in the crowd. My lip curls when she finally finds me. That dark, curious look in her eyes draws me in. I pin her in place, conveying a message between her and me only. *She better, if she knows what's good for her, go in, not cause a scene, and go straight home afterwards.* Her chin lifts in acknowledgement. I tilt my head studying her. Her mouth is set in a firm line, a pink tinge sharpens her cheek bones. Her eyes stay wide open, watching me, the color deepening to almost black. I wink at her just to mess with her more. Her mouth drops open in surprise, before smashing back together. The urge to laugh sits on my lips.

"No fucking way," Kai breathes out, looking back to his screen, while scrambling to get to his knees.

I break eye contact with the demon to look at what he's showing me.

"Is that who I think it is?" I take the phone and switch the angle mode. It's blurry, but the height and shaggy hair is unmistakable.

"What?" Silas asks, his eyes still on the not crowded parking lot. His body tenses again, preparing for a fight.

"The fuck is he doing here?" Kai questions.

"Who?" Silas barks out, turning to face us.

"Anderson," I mutter, my eyes tracing over the screen again.

"Reed?" Silas says his name, his face paling. "He never goes to these things." Kai and Silas stare at the screen transfixed. My eyes flick back up to the crowds. The stands are too full to support all of the spectators, so many of them are lined on the outsides of the fence. I find Saylor, right away, leaning against the fence, her arms propped on top. The girls around her chat and laugh. She only has eyes for the field, though. My jaw ticks, and I keep moving over the spectators. Twelve people down from her, Reed slides up to the fence. Everything slows down. The crowd and the noise become a low buzz in my ears. Reed turns to look at Saylor, at the same time she looks at him. She waves and seems confused when he looks away again. Only I caught it. He may not have waved back, but his head inclined. He acknowledged her. It was a barely there gesture, and if you didn't know Reed, you'd miss it.

"Interesting," I mutter, slinging my eyes back to Saylor, who is completely oblivious, while she cheers for the team.

"What do we do?" Kai asks. My poor friend looks unhinged and confused, like he was just told his answers on his calculus test were wrong.

I shrug. "It's a free country, and he can be here."

"But why is he *here*?" Kai's gaze darts from the screen to the crowd and back again.

"Who cares," Silas mutters, leaning back and finally sitting on the tailgate. "As long as he watches and doesn't do anything shady, it's fine. Maybe little Reed finally got tired of sitting in the shadows."

"That's creepy and fucked up," Kai interrupts.

"It is what it is," I tell them both. The clock on the score board runs out finally, signaling the end of the first quarter.

"This is going to be a long game," Silas states. His words hang in the air, with all of us in silent agreement. Too many of the hidden are here. One in particular continues to hold my attention, making this even more dangerous. I can't get sidetracked.

"Don't forget we have that meeting after the game," Kai reminds us.

My eyes close, my fingers pinching the bridge of my nose. "Who's up tonight again?"

"You," Silas grunts. "But I'm ready to go, if you want."

"Nah," I exhale, "I need this one." My body is packing enough extra energy to unload on a few tonight. The need to hit something is strong. The bones in my fists crackle from the tension.

When the final seconds count down on the clock a few hours later, I'm practically bouncing in place in the truck bed. Sure, the game had been good, our team barely scrapping by, only it wasn't the game that had me on pins and needles. Every time Saylor moved, Reed moved. She laughed, and he watched. She yelled and cursed when our team lost the ball, and Reed couldn't keep his eyes off her, studying her, those empty eyes of his cataloging all her responses. Tension was thick. It took everything inside me not to advance on him and start the interrogation process. For the past thirteen years, Reed has never done something so out of character, and it doesn't sit well with me.

"If it wasn't for Rhodes, we would have lost," Kai announces, shaking his head and putting the laptop away.

"States, here we come!" Silas yells, his head thrown back. A few people who pass by laugh and cheer along with him.

"Yeah," I answer, "Matt's going to love this." Matt likes control and keeping an eye on the situation. We were able to get this game on our home turf but that won't work for a state championship game. We'll be traveling to the city to keep surveillance.

"It's going to be a long ass week," Kai gripes. My sentiments exactly.

"She's leaving." Kai nods over my shoulder. I turn and watch as Princess gets in Winter's car. I turn back to Kai and raise an eyebrow. A shit eating grin is already on his mouth, though.

"Wow," he says.

"Shut up." I shake my head, annoyed with myself that I can still see the car in my peripheral. "What's the deal tonight? What are we fighting these punk ass kids about?"

"Uh huh," Kai laughs, then clears his throat once Silas reaches us. "Ahh, tonight are those fools from Carson."

"Are you serious?" Silas laughs and shakes his head.

"Didn't we square them away already?" I question, running through the reports in my head.

"Oh, we did." Kai grins wickedly. "They think they know better than us, though. Same jackass as last time. Thanks to those missing signs, we received that last shipment to the garage late and....Mama D did not get her chicken shipment in on time."

"Messing with the damn chicken." Silas shakes his head. I scoff.

"What's fuckface's name again?" I ask Kai. I only remember his face broken and bleeding from the damage Silas handed him.

This guy is either an idiot, or he just enjoys being degraded in front of his boys.

"That would be Jaxson Matise," Kai answers, before sliding his phone back in his pocket.

"What are we waiting for?" Silas asks, hopping into the cab. The crowd has dispersed by now, and the last bus is leaving.

Kai and I jump in as well, and I fire up the engine. We take the back roads until we get to the city limit lines. I roll the wheel right and onto the dirt path that takes us into a secluded area hidden by trees. It used to be a park but has since been abandoned. Cops don't patrol this far out and wouldn't interfere even if they did. When you work for Rogue, this is how we handle business.

A crowd has already formed by the time I pull up. A few cars face the lone slab of tar, where the old basketball court was, their lights fired up. A circle of spectators has formed to watch, and in the middle is Matise, bare chested, with his jeans hanging from his waist. The psycho smiles when he sees me approaching.

"I was hoping it would be you again, Jakobe," he says, that smile growing wider while his eyes take on an almost dead look to them.

I look over my shoulder at Silas. His own face cracks before him and Kai almost fall into each other laughing. I shake my head.

"What's his damage?" I ask Kai, who is currently trying to pull breath into his lungs.

"The sign was one hundred and seventy, our late shipment bill was one hundred and twenty-three dollars and eighty-five cents, and Mama D's chicken set her back two hundred dollars roughly," he answers, pulling out his phone to scan the details.

While Kai talks, Matise hops back and forth on the balls of his feet, jumping up and down like he's preparing to get in a ring, which causes sweat to drip down his forehead. The manic look on his face never leaves. He's proud of himself. I fight the urge to laugh. This isn't fight club or a boxing arena. I blow a whistle out between my teeth.

"Yikes, man." I walk unto the old court, dropping my jacket behind me. "That's roughly five hundred dollars in damages that are owed."

He laughs and his gang of goons behind him nod and shake their heads. I bet they think they have it made, that their ruler knows what he's doing. Blind trust in the dumb is just that, though.

"You like pain, Matise, or do you just enjoy public humiliation?" I cock my head to the side, studying him. Arrogance pours off him. He has no idea I already know he's using some type of substance, that he jumps lighter on his left leg that the right. Probably due to an old injury or broken bone, making it his weaker leg. Last time we met up, I broke a rib on his right side. That was less than six weeks ago, so there is no way, it's healed already. A faint yellow bruise still dusts his skin. One of Matise's buddies has already inched closer than the others, and his right hand is shoved inside his sweater pocket. Could be a weapon or keys if he's the sober driver. The others' eyes are glassy. They've definitely been drinking.

Matise spits on the ground between us. "You stalling, Jakobe?"

I grin, stepping closer, as the crowd starts to chant and cheer. My adrenaline kicks up, my body becoming hyperaware of the movement around me. Years of learning grappling and self-defense through martial arts, along with boxing stance and footwork, have been drilled into me by Matt and a few master combative trainers from the military. All in preparation for needing to defend myself and the hidden families, should the need arise. It also came in handy when dealing with scumbags who try to cause issue in my town. My fists come up, ready to punish, but not kill. We aren't there yet. Matise swipes out, and my head jerks back. His eyes widen for the fraction of a second it takes me to jab at the vulnerable area he exposed to my fists. The first sting of losing skin on knuckles is satisfying. Matise hops back. Uncertainty crosses his features, before he lets out another unhinged laugh. He's so messed up, even his brain can't keep up to kick in his survival instincts. He lunges again, and my arm loops over his, pulling him forward, before slamming his body to the ground. I hear a snap, and he cries out. I don't stop, though.

My foot connects with the same broken rib as last time, before I disengage and walk back. Fucker is slower to get up this time, but he does. A few of his friends behind him are starting to look worried. Of course, the crowd is only getting louder. Someone fired up their sound system, and Brantley Gilbert's "Take It Outside" blares from the speakers. I advance first, threatening, causing him to react by racing toward me. My feet are lifted from the floor, before my back hits the ground, exactly how I want it to. I lock my legs around his back, forcing his arms to brace, leaving his face open. I get three good hits in, before he yanks himself out of my grasp and stumbles backward. I surge forward, tackling him to the ground, delivering punch after punch, until the twisted smile on his face is gone, and fear flashes in his eyes. He tries to crawl away from me, but I stop him, pressing my heavy combat boot on his ankle. He howls in pain. Two of his friends advance toward him but are stopped short by Kai and Silas.

"Done already, Matise?" I grin, taking in his swollen eye and split lip. Blood gushes from his mouth where a tooth is now missing. Red splotches cover his abdomen and sides. He'll be nice and purple tomorrow. "Here's the deal." I lift my head to address his buddies, too. "Hand over the five hundred, don't step foot in Savage Lakes again, and I won't bust his leg. I heard you have scholarship to the U for track, right?" I peer back down at the idiot in front of me and don't miss the way he turns paler at my words.

"How did you--" He starts to ask, but I cut him off.

"I don't miss anything, Matise. You fuck with my town and your whole life becomes my business. You pull this shit again, and I'll follow you to your town. You won't be able to walk away if that happens," I warn, adding more pressure to his ankle. One more push and his Achilles will snap.

"Okay, okay, okay," he starts to panic, finally starting to figure out the danger he's in. The darkness inside me takes satisfaction at the wet spot forming on the front of his jeans. I step off his foot and kick his leg out of the way.

He shouts in pain and cradles his leg. The crowd erupts in cheers, mocking these idiots. Silas and Kai step aside, letting

Matise's friends haul him up. They start pulling him back to their cars. I bend down and swipe my jacket from the ground where I left it.

"Get it?" I ask Kai, who nods, holding out five crisp hundred dollar bills.

"Fucking cake eaters," Silas mocks next to me. I check out the crowd around us. Another win under the belt, and now, it's turned into a party. A few spectators are tilting back bottles and flasks. Some of the girls start dancing in the circle. A quick flash of purple hidden by a black hoodie catches my eye, sending a current of energy through my bloodstream, while she hurries away with another figure camouflaged in black. Fucking Winter. My fingers flex and burn from the open and bleeding gashes across the knuckles. I'll take care of it when I get home, I decide. Thankfully, neither Kai nor Silas seem to have noticed her. My jaw clenches, thinking about Saylor. I knew before the fight started, and I didn't make her leave like I should have. Something about her calls to me, and it pisses me off. I'm glad she knows now how we handle business here.

"Drink?" Silas offers me a flask that was handed to him, and I shake my head.

"Driving, you dick," I respond.

"Oh yeah." He tilts back for one more drink, before handing it to Kai who also takes a pull. I plop down on my tailgate and relax while they enjoy the party. My mind swirls with ways to punish the demon princess for stepping out of line. She shouldn't have been here or seen what she did. My chest thrums with energy, remembering the way her raspberry pink lips slam together when she thinks she's being defiant. My knee bounces with renewed energy to get home. Things are about to get really interesting.

# #Nine

*Saylor*

My body is wound tightly after being out all night and witnessing what I did. After the game, Winter was adamant I see something that would help explain the control Kai, Silas and Ciaran have on the town. She drove us to a clearing in the woods, almost out of town, and parked away from the other cars. We waited until the guys showed up, before moving closer to the crowd. The minute I spotted Ciaran step onto the old basketball court, I could read the tension in his muscles. His opponent never stood a chance. I watched in fascination while the guy turned pale from whatever Ciaran was saying to him. Then it was over. Winter explained that the guy, Jaxson Matise, and his friends had stolen some road signs in town, which caused some financial and business issues for the city and, most importantly, Rogue's Car Repairs. Matt's business. She also said this wasn't the first time that Ciaran has had to deal with Jaxson.

When it was over, we sprinted back to the car and took off. Everyone else who was there were Rogue employees. We could get in trouble for being here and breaking Ciaran's rule to stay under the radar and out of his way. I wasn't clueless, though. I had felt the searing heat on my retreating back. He knew I had been there. Nervous energy had coiled around my muscles the minute I stepped through the front door. I'm on edge, wondering when Ciaran will get back. Frustrated with myself and my feelings, I crank up my music and bounce around my room, throwing moves

I haven't practiced in weeks. It doesn't take long for sweat to coat my skin and my damp hair to cling to my neck. At least the nerves have settled. In all this time, Ciaran hasn't come home, which is a good sign. I decide to take a shower, needing the hot water to ease the rest of the tension out of my now sore muscles.

Once I'm clean and feeling more relaxed, I turn the water off and wrap a towel around my body. The florescent light hums and the mirror has fogged up. The rest of the house remains quiet, though. Quickly, I brush my teeth and rinse with mouthwash, while towel drying my hair the best I can, before running my brush through it.

The hallway is dark when I step into it, taking long strides to reach my door. Unease trickles down my spine, creating goosebumps across my flesh. Twisting the knob, I cross the threshold and smack right into the solid wall of flesh waiting inside. The material on his jacket feels rough against my bare skin. Ciaran steps closer, until my back hits the cool surface of the door, sending another round of shivers over my body. Slowly, I lift my gaze to his. Black pupils expand in the crystal blue irises, and his eyebrows lower, while he scans me from head to toe, before bringing his eyes back to mine. I hug the towel tighter to my body. A calculating smirk forms over his puffy lips, and my stomach tightens in response.

"What are the rules, Princess?" Ciaran asks, leaning into me, folding one arm over the other. I notice his knuckles are caked with dried blood. His fingers graze across his bottom lip, contemplating and waiting. I'm so distracted by the small gesture that it takes my mind a few minutes to catch up with what he's saying.

"I don't follow your rules, Ciaran," I answer, challenging him. "I stayed under the radar at the game and didn't cause any problems."

"You shouldn't have been there," he growls, moving in closer.

"I don't know what you're talking about," I lie and push off the door to move around him. Ciaran's arm shoots out, blocking me in. I turn back to face him, forcing my body to relax, and put a bored expression on my face to mask my real emotions.

"Don't lie, Say." Ciaran dips down, his voice gravely, and heat coils low in my stomach. My name on his lips keeps me locked in. If I moved my head, even a little, my lips would rub against his. For some reason, that thought makes my chest ache with excitement. My stomach clenches in response. Our eyes lock. I pull my bottom lip between my teeth, unsure what he wants me to say. I want him to say my name again. My body is his hostage, hovering and waiting for him to make a move or at least put me out of my misery with cruel words. Having all of Ciaran's attention is almost more painful than being ignored, because when he takes it away again, the loneliness may swallow me whole.

Ciaran's gaze drops to my lip that is gripped between my teeth. His shoulders tense, as if he's fighting an internal battle of his own. Just like me. My heart races to the point I'm positive he can see my pulse throb against my skin. Words hover on my tongue, until the front door slams shut downstairs. Startled, my eyes flash up to Ciaran's in panic. He steps back and holds a finger to his lips, telling me to be quiet. We listen as booted feet walk to the kitchen. Bottles clang in the fridge, and my heart finally comes to a rest, realizing it's Matt. A cupboard opens and closes, before he walks toward the door that leads to the basement. Only when the door clicks shut, am I finally able to release the breath I've been holding.

"Get out," I demand of Ciaran, while I move away from the door, heading deeper into my room. Having some space between us allows air back into my lungs and my thoughts to get control of themselves. I wanted to kiss Ciaran. I wanted his eyes on me and that is not something that can happen. Without another word or glance, he exits my room, barely making a noise when he slips out the door and down the hall to his own room. It's creepy how he moves almost ghostlike.

My legs shake with adrenaline while I throw on some sleep shorts and a t-shirt, before crawling under my covers. The whole day flashes through my mind in a series of pictures and clips. Even when I attempt to distract myself, I'm caught up in the past few minutes. My eyes slam shut, as if that will make the mental images go away. Even behind my eyelids, molten blue irises burn into me. Once again, I wish Oaklynn was with me. Where I am fire and easily pushed to anxiety, she is calm and cool. She would know how to navigate this world where I feel like I'm floundering.

### 

Nothing changes over the next few weeks. Thanksgiving came and went. I had no contact with my family over the holiday and an ugly ball of resentment started forming in the pit of my stomach. There is still no news about my dad, and our family's disappearance from New York has still not made the news. My hate for him festers and bleeds all over my life. Ciaran has gone back to ignoring me, for the most part. When he isn't bossing me around to stay in line. Matt remains oblivious to the tension between his nephew and me.

We are a few weeks into December, and I'm dreading the week long break over Christmas. Thinking of spending another holiday without my mom and Mila is enough to make my eyes sting with unshed tears. Tears, I have become really good at faking don't exist. The only small escape I have from my reality is school. Winter and I grow closer over our love of dance videos and pizza. She also likes photography like me, and her dream is to go to college at the University of Minnesota and get her degree in journalism. The girl is an adrenaline junkie who is looking forward to traveling to exotic or hostile environments to take pictures. I'm in awe of her and at the same time jealous. I no longer have any control over my future and that is a tough pill to swallow.

Winter does her best to shake me out of my bad thoughts. She promises parties and ice skating over the holiday break. Sure enough, two feet of snow have been dumped on the town in the past few weeks, and the temps have fallen drastically, some days barely making it to double digits.

"I'm telling ya, Cassidy is a horrible human being, but she throws the best New Year's Eve parties. We have to go." Winter is on a roll again, lips and hands moving a mile a minute while I stand next to her, putting my books in my locker.

"I'm not against going," I remind her.

"You just look like you have period cramps anytime I mention it," she points out. My eyes flick over to Cassidy and the others. Her arm is wrapped around Bentley's, even while he keeps his body angled away from her. "Oh my god, are you, like, into Bentley?"

"No," I almost snap, looking around to make sure no one is paying attention. "She thinks I am, though. I don't want it to be awkward or have there be any drama if I show up at her party."

"Oh," Winter flips her hair over her shoulder, "I wouldn't worry about it. As long as you don't go dancing up on him, she should be fine."

"Yeah, right." I laugh and roll my eyes. I have zero interest in Bentley, and yet, that does not stop him from trying. The boy is persistent in getting my attention. Sometimes I give in just so he'll leave me alone, and sometimes, it's to draw the attention of a different boy with cobalt eyes and blonde locks that constantly fall over his forehead from his fingers running through them. It's shameless and my newest obsession. I come alive the minute I have Ciaran's attention.

"Well, think about it some more," Winter says, while wiggling her fingers goodbye. I watch as she makes her way confidently down the hallway like she owns it. I peer down at myself, wondering if I'll ever find that level of confidence again. I feel like all I wear is leggings and jeans with hoodies or Henley's. Anything to make me feel invisible and swallow me whole. It's depressing.

When I reach the biology room, I slip into my seat next to Reed. Over the past few weeks, I haven't had any real conversations with Reed, but he does ask me to pass the syringe or ask what measurement is needed to go into the test tube. Baby steps. My fingers pull restlessly through my hair, as I tie it in a top-knot on my head. It's grown longer since I arrived at Savage Lakes, almost back to its original length. I wonder if Matt will make me cut it soon. I have recolored my roots a few times to keep the color up.

"You missed some." Reed's quiet voice makes me jump in place. My head swings in his direction, but he isn't looking at me.

He's simply drawing in his notebook. My fingers dance around my neck and clasp onto a strand I missed.

"Thanks," I offer, while winding the stray piece around the already formed knot and tucking it into my hair tie. Reed doesn't reply, not that I expect him to. I steal another glance at him anyway. There is something about Reed that is so familiar. I want to know his story, but I know he won't share. I've asked Winter about it before, and she clams up immediately. Apparently, his case is one where it's only safe if no one knows. I wonder if Reed's story is like mine and if he has a boogeyman of his own. Thankfully, the past few weeks, my nightmares have been lessening, they're almost nonexistent. At least I'm not waking up from them anymore.

Bentley and company file through the door, and I pretend not to notice the chin nod he gives me. My head ducks down to avoid any accusations in Cassidy's eyes. Reed snorts next me. I glance back at him, appalled and wanting to laugh at the same time.

"What's wrong with you today?" I question, raising my eyebrow at him.

His mouth clamps shut, and he tilts his head.

"Don't pretend," I smirk. "You never talk to me, Reed, unless you have to. Now today, you've corrected my hair, and you almost laughed. What gives?"

Instead of answering, of course, Reed just stares at me with those vacant eyes. When he refuses to say anything, I turn back to face the front of the room. There is no reason to be upset, but, for some reason, his silence hurts me. Not Ciaran level hurt. More of a mild sting. The only time I can relate to the same feeling was the first day Oaklynn moved away in Elementary school. Just like that, my mind drifts to my best friend again, and my heart squeezes. My eyes drop to the cell phone between my legs. My fingers wrap around the device. Even if I wanted to call her, I don't have her number memorized. Matt still hasn't given me permission to use the internet either. I have no way to reach out to her unless...

"Hey, Reed," I ask quietly, looking around to make sure no one is watching or listening. "You work today?" His green orbs slide to mine. Questions dance behind his gaze, but he doesn't voice them. Instead, he shakes his head yes, and that's all the info I need.

Instead of waiting for Winter after school, I shoot her a quick text that I'm staying behind to study. I sneak out the doors and through the parking lot, keeping out of any of the Midwest boys' view, and jump the fence around the football field. Once my feet land on the other side, I trudge through the snow, until I hit the gravel road in a nearby neighborhood. The street will eventually lead me to the dirt path that goes behind the main road, on the backside of the businesses. I pull my black stocking hat lower over my ears and hitch my hood up. My fingers wiggle deeper inside my gloves, before I shove my hands into my pockets. The wind is against my back, thankfully, during the walk there. It takes close to half an hour for me to reach the store, thanks to the snow drifts. By the time I step into Rad Radioz, my legs are frozen, and a touch of windburn stings my cheeks. I spot Reed instantly, as he is slipping on his green smock toward the back of the store. My feet shuffle across the floor to get to him. His head snaps up and surprise crosses his features.

"Hey." I wave my gloved hand in his direction. He doesn't answer, but his eyes dart to the front of the store and back to me, before his arms cross against his chest. "I need your help. As crazy as it sounds, I think I can trust you. I also think you are the only person who could actually help me with this," I explain the best I can. Truthfully, I have no idea if Reed will know what to do. I just know a part of me, deep down, knows he is the only person I can ask.

Reed stays silent, quietly observing me, his eyes becoming curious the more I ramble.

"I need a burner phone. Something untraceable to here or to me. I need to get it to someone." I get out my words quickly. Reed's mouth opens at the same time he reaches for his pocket.

"Wait! Wait!" I hold up my hands, my voice pleading. "Before you call the cavalry or whatever, just hear me out. I have no plans to give away my location or anyone else's. I'm not even going to put a number in it. Well, not really anyway. It's not a phone number per se. You can even watch me program it if you want to. Please, Reed, I'm begging you. I would never purposely hurt anyone. I just need my best friend to know I'm alive, that's it."

Heartbeats pass while Reed studies me. His eyes probe mine, peering into my soul and making himself comfortable. After a while, the corners around his eyes soften. Whatever he is seeing in me, I'm hoping he understands. Without hesitation, Reed walks past me to the back shelf, an area I did not browse the last time I was here. On the very bottom, he bends down to grab a small bulky device, similar to an early two thousands flip phone. Reed takes the package and leads me to the cash register.

After ringing it up, he takes a box cutter from his pocket and tears into the plastic. I reach into my wallet and extract the card Matt had previously given me. Before I can swipe, Reed's hand lands on mine and pushes it away. His fingers dance over my wallet, before taking out my new bank card for Ariel Waters.

"This one's better," he mutters under his breath. "This person doesn't actually exist." Our eyes connect again when he says it. Reed has known all along about me, just like I've known about him. I swipe the card and go through the questions while Reed plugs the phone in to get a charge and turns it on. My breath hitches when the little screen flares with light.

"Thank you," I tell him. Reed pauses, before entering the contact screen, and offers it to me. My fingers fly over the keyboard before I hand the phone back to him. He glances at the screen then to me, without asking questions, before holding it out to me. I throw it in the manila envelope that I swiped from a teacher's desk and shove the phone and charging cord inside.

"Can I print an address label?" I ask, looking over to the office supply wall. Reed leads me over and pulls up the screen. After I print one off for Oaklynn, I realize, for the first time, a small flaw in my plan. My head falls to my hands, shudders of sobs threaten to spill over. "I can't believe I forgot a stamp would need to go on this. If someone were to take it, they would see it was mailed from

Minnesota." My chest deflates; my good intentions are effectively squashed. I want to cry and have to resist the urge to slam the phone against a wall.

"Here." Reed takes the bundle and disappears in the back. When he returns, there is a mail stamp across the front from New York.

"How?" I turn it over and over, examining it.

"Don't ask. Just let me mail it back there." He nods to the back. I hesitate, before handing it over to him.

"You promise you'll send it, right?" I ask, my gaze focusing on his. "You won't turn it over to Ciaran or Matt?"

Reed allows me a few more minutes of eye contact before he drops his gaze and shuffles. He shakes his head no. If I blinked, I would have missed it. Nevertheless, he promised and that means more to me than anything right now.

"Thank you, Reed," I tell him again, giving him a small smile, before heading to the door.

I leave the same way I came and hop the fence again when I reach the school. I'm practically Elsa at this time, I'm so cold; yet, I can't bring myself to care. I finally have a shot at reaching Oaklynn. Every time I think about it, my smile widens to the point my cheeks hurt. There is an extra lightness in my chest, which makes the long walk home easier. Phase one of my plan is complete.

The house is dark when I finally get back, and Ciaran's truck is not in the driveway, which makes me sigh in relief. I pretty much run up the front steps and let myself inside, stomping snow off as I go. My heart races, fearing I'll be caught.

In the safety of my room, I pull off my jeans, the ends are now soaked from melted snow, and pull on my favorite pair of deep maroon leggings, followed by a pair of fuzzy socks from my drawer. Standing on my tiptoes, I reach for my favorite hoodie, the only one I took from home, and throw it on. The end hits almost to my knees and the sleeves hang a few inches over my fingers. It's loose and broken in, the collar slightly frayed, exactly how I like it. Once I'm warm, the knots in my stomach dull.

Heading downstairs, I start in the kitchen and make myself a quick sandwich and some chips for dinner. The silence in the house feels comfortable, for once, even though I'm jumpy. I need to talk to Matt, if I ever want the next part of my plan to work. Pulling out my phone, I hit his name on the contact list. Right when my line rings, I can hear his ring tone below me. Standing from the chair, I move toward the door to the basement. The ring gets louder. I pause, unsure if I should knock or just go down. My hand reaches out before I can stop it and twists. The door opens, and I take a breath, before descending the stairs.

Until this point, I have never ventured into Matt's space, respecting it as his. When I first arrived, he told me it was off limits. Butterflies dance in my stomach, wondering how mad he'll be if he finds out I was down here. As my feet hit the bottom step, my eyes grow wide, and my breathing stops. Maps line every wall, making up the entire United States. Colorful tacks are stuck randomly in cities on each one. Realization hits that these must be other safe houses and hidden families. My body moves on its own, curiosity winning over self-preservation, farther into the spacious room. A steel door is on the right and on the left is a desk with a simple monitor on it. The screen is black, even though it hums with energy.

"What are you doing?" Matt's voice sounds behind me. I whip around to face him, shame and embarrassment flooding my features.

"I'm sorry. I tried to call you, and I heard the phone ringing and thought you were down here," I ramble. "I know I shouldn't be here, but I just had a real quick question."

Matt's face cracks into a smile, a laugh escaping him. "Easy kid. It's not the end of the world."

"Oh," I frown, halting my words and apologies, "I thought I couldn't be down here."

He shrugs. "There is a lot of sensitive material, but, most of it, is behind that door," he says, pointing to the steal slab, and my eyes roam over it.

"Want to take a look?" he asks casually.

I nod my head and follow him over. Matt opens a panel and lays his hand across it. A green light flashes and is echoed by the sound of a lock clicking. Matt pushes the door open, and I follow him into the darkness. The minute we step in, automatic lights flare to life. My ears ring from all the chatter in the room. Four television monitors are anchored to one wall, each with a different news station recording. On the opposite wall is another map of the United States, only, this one, is electronic. Little red and yellow dots flicker in different cities in various states all over the country. Moving closer, I scan Minnesota and pick up a cluster of red and yellow dots. A number sequence is located off to the side.

"That's me and the others here?" I question, only going off my assumption.

"Yup," Matt answers, watching me thoughtfully.

I step back and scan the map again. There are thousands of lit up lights. My breath hitches in my chest. Matt's operation is larger than I had expected. It's not surprising he has as many people working for him as he does.

"Want to see your mom and Mila?" he asks, turning to me. My eyes widen in surprise.

"Yes!" I rush back over to the map where Matt has moved to. He points to a group of clusters out in Arizona.

"They're here. Red dots are high priority and yellow indicate the ones who have been hidden for over ten years. Not that they aren't high priority, but there is a greater chance that what they've been doing is working. No one is actively looking for them."

"What are the green dots?" I question, noticing those are few and far between.

"Open houses or families," Matt answers. I nod in understanding, my eyes moving back toward the cluster mom and Mila are in.

"At least they got to be somewhere warm," I say, more to myself, smiling slightly. My mom always liked the hot temps. I wish I could see them. See their faces to know they're okay.

"If the lights aren't flashing or on blue then that means everything is okay. Each home has a panel of lights that can be hit for our system. I know it's not like seeing them on surveillance, but at least you can see that they are okay," Matt continues speaking. "Over here is a file of incoming cases. And these radios are pretty much a giant walkie talkie system. We only use them for a check in, which happens once every month. The day varies, though. If anything were to go wrong, each family also has one of these in the home and could call for help if they can't reach a phone."

"I don't know why, but for some reason, I imagined huge computer monitors running surveillance or something," I tell him laughing.

"That's at our other location," Matt answers, turning to face me. My mouth drops in surprise.

I walk toward the television screens and scan over the news. "Did our story ever break on the news?"

Matt's brow furrows; I can tell it bothers him, too. "No. I haven't been able to pick up on it, and no one else has either. I think whoever hit your house that night were professionals - ones with friends in high places who are keeping it quiet."

Memories haunt me, and I have to close my eyes to fight them off. "I'm not dreaming about it as much anymore. Sometimes, though, if I'm alone or smell something in particular, it hits me all over again. I feel like I'm still trapped under that bed."

Matt's gaze travels over my face, offering silent support. I know it will get better someday. There really isn't anything else he can say. "Can I come down here sometimes?" I ask. "Not all the time but just once in a while to check on their dot." My voice sounds young and vulnerable, and I hate how childish it makes me feel.

"Yeah," Matt answers, scratching his head with a free hand. "Preferably when Ci or I am here, though, okay? Just in case you did accidently hit something, we can correct it right away, okay?"

"Okay," I respond, a small speck of happiness bursts within me.

"What did you want to ask me about in the first place?" he questions, while propping himself on the edge of the desk.

I swallow. "I was wondering if I could possible get internet on my phone yet?"

Matt studies me, tossing the idea around. "I guess you have been here for about two months now, huh?"

I nod again. He sighs. "That shouldn't be a problem. You know the rules, right?"

"Yup," I answer quickly, "Winter explained them to me already."

"Okay, I'll have Kai enable your phone." Matt nods and stands straight again. "I have to head to the garage again. Now that you'll have Wi-Fi and all that good stuff, that also means you're ready to start working."

"Working where?" I ask, turning toward him.

"I need some help with orders, emails and bookkeeping at the garage. You can start there next week," he answers, before leaving the room. "Don't forget to close the door all the way!" he yells. I listen as his heavy feet sound up the stairs. I greedily run my eyes over the dots and televisions one more time before I decide to leave, too. I got what I needed, and in a twist of events, I found Mom and Mila, too. The excitement takes away some of the guilt I feel over lying to Matt.

"Bye Mom. Love you, Sis," I whisper to the board, before closing the steel door behind me. I wait for the lock to click back into place, before racing up the stairs. By the time I reach my room, my phone chimes with a text from an unknown number.

Unknown: Your Wi-Fi capabilities are programmed. Use responsibly. Also, this is Kai. Save my number ;)

I shake my head at the last part. Like I'd ever reach out and text Kai. Sure, he's hot as hell, but he's also Ciaran and Silas' best friend, which means he probably hates me, too. I let his mild flirting slide, content and happy that phase two is complete. Tomorrow at school, I'll talk to Reed about setting up the final step of my plan.

# #Ten

*Ciaran*

I wasn't surprised when Matt announced that the demon Princess would be working at the shop next week. I was prepared for the rage that would flicker behind Si's eyes. Matt didn't know it, but I heard his conversation with Saylor. I heard the way her voice cracked when she asked about her mom and sister. I saw the way her shoulders caved in, protectively, when she talked about her nightmares and the boogeyman, as she refers to the men who broke into her home.

While I was prepared to hear she would around a lot more, and knowing the agony it would have on Silas, I didn't fight Matt's decision. In the past weeks, since that night after the fight, the night I had Saylor against a door, completely at my mercy, I've become more aware of the monsters haunting her. She thinks she's over it, and it's getting better, but it's not. Every night, like clockwork, her body thrashes hard enough that the headboard hits my wall. By the time I reach her bed, she's twisted in her sheets, face pulled into a grimace, mumbling about the boogeyman. Sometimes, she outright screams. Every night, I lay a hand on her arm and tell her she's safe. Every night. I can't figure out why I care. I try to tell myself she deserves it, that her family brought it upon themselves, but something has me coming back to her room each night to soothe her and ease her pain.

Now after hearing their conversation, I realize how fucked I am. My head is all over the place. Anytime I think of the demon, all I can see is her skin with water droplets sliding off into the towel she held protectively against her. A thin barrier, really, if I had wanted it off. Her skin glowed and took on a pink hue. She smelled like raspberries that I wanted to take a bite of. I fight myself not to go to her again. I get a sick satisfaction that she quiets the minute I touch her, and she never moves the rest of the night. It's addicting. Saylor has become an addiction; she's in my veins, in my blood, and I don't know how to stop it from spreading. And, part of me, maybe even all of me, doesn't want it to stop.

After Matt's announcement, Silas stalks out on us, and then I hear the engine of his truck fire up and tires peeling out.

"That's surprising," Kai states and turns to look at me.

"You're the one who enabled her Wi-Fi," I respond, keeping my gaze averted.

"True," Kai admits, "I didn't know it meant she'd be working here, though. What is Matt thinking?"

I shrug in response, still lost in my own traitorous thoughts.

"How come you're not more upset?" Kai questions. Once again, I hate his ability to read too much into things.

"I heard Matt talk to her about it last night," I answer, keeping my voice neutral.

"Did something happen between you two?" Kai keeps going.

My head snaps up. "Jesus fuck, you're irritating!"

"It's a viable question," he shrugs. "Usually, you would have been hightailing it out of here with Si, ready to drink your problems away. Instead, you're over here, sorting parts like nothing happened."

I turn to face him. "I don't care what the demon Princess does. I heard them talking about it last night, so I guess I've had more time to get used to it. Not like Matt has listened to us this entire time anyway. She's been here for two months. And it's almost winter break, so we can use all the help we can get."

"Yeah, okay, Ci," Kai chuckles. "I guess I don't care about Ariel either. I'm just saying, she may not be that bad. And if you decided that, too, then Si is just going to have to put on his big boy pants on and get over it. Girl can't help who her parents are."

"Are we done gossiping now?" I question. I'm over this conversation. My mind is already in pieces over Saylor, and I don't need Kai's acceptance of her on top of it. He waves me off, and I give him my middle finger in return.

Taking the steps two at a time, I search out Randy to get the list of jobs that are needed by tonight. "This it?" I ask him, scanning it over.

"Just the one," he responds, flicking his eyes at me. Any hopes for a good night just went to shit when I see the name on the clipboard.

## JASON MONTGOMERY

Slapping it against my hand, I shoot a text to Matt, before working on setting up the truck.

Me: Does Jason know yet?

I wait while the dots jump on the screen.

Matt: Yeah.
Me: Does Si know that Jason knows?
Matt: I told him already.

I blow out the breath I had been holding in, feeling slightly better that Matt already broke the news to Si. But Jason being back here with Saylor also here is not going to go over well. In some delusional part of his brain, probably the part that's been soaking in whiskey for the past thirteen years, I believe Jason wishes he had been Saylor's father. If he's back in town, it is not going to be good. Any progress Si has made regarding Saylor over the past couple months is about to go up in flames.

I shove the last bolt in place on the exchange car when Silas' truck whips back in the lot. His face is blank on the outside, even when his body is vibrating with pent-up energy.

"Ready?" He asks, even though it's obvious.

"Hey," I lower my voice, "you don't have to go. I can do this one on my own or see if Kai has time."

Silas' stare jumps to mine. "I'm good."

"You sure?" I question, following his lead and climbing into the cab.

"We're extraction," he answers. "Let's go extract the motherfucker already."

"Okay," I respond, before starting the engine. Silas shoots Randy a text with our set arrival time, while I hit play on the Bluetooth. Future's "Codeine Crazy" bumps through the speakers, as I navigate us toward the main highway. We're picking up Jason a few miles south of Minneapolis. I can already tell the ride will be shorter than I want it to be. Tension is thick inside the cab. Every few miles, Silas checks our surroundings and reports our location in thirty-minute time frames. He's precise and professional, even with his hand balled into a fist resting on his leg.

The miles fly by, and just before seven, we pull into a parking lot off the interstate. Jason is already waiting for us. A slow smile forms on his mouth when he sees us. Silas jumps out of the truck before I can stop him.

"Are you drunk?" he demands, stalking closer to his dad.

"I had some time to kill." Jason shrugs, smiling larger. His eyes are bloodshot, and I can smell the alcohol on his breath.

"How are you going to drive the extraction vehicle then?" Silas asks, getting up in his dad's face.

Jason places a hand on Silas' cheek and tilts his head back. "I'll ride with you clowns. I told Randy I didn't need it. He probably forgot to pass the message on."

"That's not how it works," Silas reminds him.

Jason swallows, his eyes fighting to pull his son into focus. "Don't you tell me how things work," he slurs.

"We should go. We can all just ride up front," I cut in, placing a hand on Silas' shoulder, preventing him from doing something he'll regret, like punching his dad in the face.

I climb in the driver seat, and Jason climbs in next to me. Not even a minute passes before he asks, "Have you seen her? Does she look like Kelly?"

"Jesus Christ," Silas mutters. "Shut up."

"What's wrong with you?" Jason questions. "Ciaran, does Matt think he's going to bring Kell in when this is over?"

"No!" Silas growls. "She's not coming here. Get over it. She didn't want you nineteen years ago, what makes you think she'd want you now?" He swings the door back open and hops out, before Jason can yell, leaving him fuming in the spot that Silas vacated.

Silas starts unhooking the car from the back and lowers the lift. I get out to help him. We work in silence, until it's unloaded, and my trailer is ready for travel. When I get back in the cab, Jason is passed out with his head against the window.

"Fuck," I mutter to myself, while shifting the gear into drive. Saylor's face flashes across my mind, and I see red. My conversation with Kai from earlier vanishes and so do any feelings I was starting to have toward her. Seeing Jason tonight is just another reminder of the damage done to my best friend. No girl is worth ruining a friendship over. I've seen Si go through hell and back because of her family. I was crazy to think I could ever feel anything toward her besides animosity.

### ###

That one night was all it took to solidify the side I stood on. It would always be us against her. The quicker she realized that the better. I stopped helping her at night, taking a sliver of satisfaction when she woke up with her same old nightmare. For years, I watched Silas escape his house at night, fearful of his dad, and snuck him into my room. Saylor deserves that now. I ran isolation on her the last few weeks of school before break, making it difficult for her to have any interaction with anyone. The best part was watching Winter explain it to her. She felt me watching, and when those almond eyes swung to mine, they were filled with tears. I winked at her and went on with the rest of my day.

The holiday season and New Year came and went along with our break. My mom made it home for a few days. She fawned over

Saylor, and it took all I had not to snap at her. I didn't understand why everyone was so willing to forget her dad was responsible for ruining lives. He was the offender. He was not a victim this time.

Saylor started working at the garage and kept out of our way. Her interactions were limited to the bits of conversation she would have with Kai when she stepped into the office they shared. He was still a little friendlier to her than I was comfortable with. He wasn't there that night, though. He didn't witness the devastation and years of pent up hurt that flashed in Silas' eyes that night when Jason mentioned Kelly.

I told Matt about what happened. He shook his head and told me he would talk to Jason. He warned me not to take it out on Saylor, but it was too late. Nothing he could say would stop me from destroying her little bubble of happiness. The light dimmed in her eyes a little more every day I antagonized her. Purple bags were forming under her eyes from tossing and turning in the night. I waited for her run to Matt and tell him what was happening, but just like before, she didn't. It was almost like she knew she deserved it.

I let her go out once with Winter. They spent a few hours getting ready, doing their chick thing. By the time they got to the party and made it through the doors, they found out plans changed and Saylor, or *Ariel,* was actually not invited. I watched her break from my position in the main room. Her eyes frantically searched for me. Right as Sophia was taking my tongue down her throat, our gazes locked. The hurt expression on her face was all the high I needed the rest of the night.

"I think you need to tone it down a bit," Kai finally breaks his silence at lunch on our first day back after break.

Slowly, I turn to face him. Gone is his usual easygoing demeanor. He looks pissed, and if Kai is pissed, you should listen up. I was going to have a hard time letting him have this, though.

"He's right for once," Silas chimes in next.

"Da fuck?" I swing my gaze to look at him. "You of all people?"

He shrugs. "It's almost sad really. And the teachers are starting to notice. If they say something to Matt, we could lose privileges."

"Privileges?" Kai scoffs. "We could be spending spring break in the barracks. No, thank you."

Man has a point. My fingers steeple in front of my chest and my eyes flicker over to Rhodes. Even with the freeze out in place that jock strap still can't keep his eyes off her. I hope he puts a condom over his eyeballs for how hard he's eye fucking her.

"Rhodes!" I yell across the lunch room. His head swivels to me, and I see him visibly swallow. I look to Saylor then back at him and motion that the freeze is over. Busted for staring, Rhodes turns back to his table, keeping his head down.

"Couldn't have been more subtle, could you?" Kai smirks and shakes his head.

"Everyone is already here, why make multiple speeches?" I explain my logic. Si snorts into his drink next to me.

"Anyways, remember that cousin of Aiden's who was visiting last year? She had the huge party at his house while he was on vacation with his parents?" Kai asks.

"Oh yeah!" Silas answers. "The one where she had the slide from the roof into the outdoor pool. She heated it up, so it was a giant hot tub!"

"Now I remember," I nod.

"Well, Aiden let it slip in English that he's going out of town with the family again this weekend for another ski trip and guess who is house sitting?" Kai high fives Silas. They both grin and laugh, figuring out how they can approach her ahead of time to set it up. I'm half listening while the other half of my attention is focused on the back of the purple head in front of me. She and Winter are close together. Whatever Winter is telling her, I see hair move with every shake of her head. My eyes narrow. Her body tenses when she feels my glare; yet, she fights the urge to turn and look. I run my fingers across my lips, thoughtfully. With her new found freedom, I wonder if the little demon Princess will find her way to the party this weekend.

Kai does not disappoint, and, before the end of the week, we have a party set up, thanks to Aiden's cousin, Brileigh.

"Apparently, she does homeschool and never has the opportunity to make new friends." He shrugs.

"And you volunteered to be her new friend," Silas states rather than asks.

The smug smile that plants itself on Kai's lips is answer enough. I could care less about his conquest or his new friend. As long as we have a place to party is all that matters. The need to see how this plays out is driving me insane. Will she go, or won't she? By now, Saylor has heard all about it. The epic stories from last year don't even do justice to having actually been there. Brileigh may be homeschooled, but she sure has a wild side and spared nothing of value in that house or on the property.

"Everyone received an invitation, yeah?" I inquire again, making sure the job was done. Spinning my pen between my fingers, I make eye contact with Kai who nods, while Silas avoids me. My conscience bounces back and forth between good friend and bad friend. I want to punish Saylor for the way she's weaving herself into my veins. At the same time I crave to be around her, to see her face and hear her speak. She's all I think about, and I can't let the guilt from that go.

# #Eleven

*Ciaran*

Kai was right as always. Aiden's cousin did not disappoint. Once again, a plastic slide has been fitted to the upstairs balcony, and it flows right into the underground pool that is rocking a temperature of one hundred and two degrees, or so I've been told. The game room is decked out with drinking games, a bar with every liquor imaginable and bags of chips. I shake my head when I pass by the supposed snack stand, knowing right away whose idea that was. I head toward the basement where the majority of people are. The minute my feet hit the bottom step, a hazy cloud of smoke, from the copious amount of weed being smoked down here, hangs in the air, engulfing me. One of the tech kids, who I believe is a sophomore, has a table set up where he's playing music. He's playing decent tracks, so I won't correct him, for now. Travis Scott's "Highest in the Room" bounces off the walls. Girls grind their hips to the rhythm, leaving their guys to join in or watch. Aiden's house is perfect. The walls are thick and barely any noise, besides the chatter from the pool outside, can be heard. I almost feel bad for him being gone on vacation with his parents when his whole house is being used like an episode of a MTV reality show.

Almost.

It takes a few hours for Saylor to arrive. Just like the first night she showed up at my house, I sense her presence before my eyes discover her. Tight black jeans mold to her hips like a second skin. The knees are ripped, feeding my imagination with ideas to make those rips big enough to expose the skin and rub it red. A white shirt, if you can call it that, fits tight against her chest then flares, before stopping right above her navel. There is a whole lot of smooth skin showing between where that shirt ends and the top of her jeans begin. My fingers twitch. Her purple locks hang straight down. It's longer than when she arrived, almost brushing against her stomach. She follows Winter over to a group of girls on the dance floor, my eyes tracking her movement. With her back to me, I finally see why they took so long to arrive. Her worn and faded jean jacket now sports a large painted white square on the back. WHAT DOESN'T KILL YOU MAKES YOU WEIRD AT PARTIES is written in black, glittery letters. I smirk. *How very morbid of you, little demon.*

She moves at ease around the room, which means she's either oblivious to the fact that I'm here or she's trying really hard to pretend she doesn't feel the pull that always backfires against us. Either way, the easy smile her lips form is pissing me off. I take another drink of the bottle in my hand, trying to force my attention to the Tippy Cup game in front of me. Kai is playing, his arm thrown around Brileigh, although he still looks completely sober. Another quick scan, and I locate Silas, sitting on a couch, straddled by a blonde, who's on a mission to swallow his mouth whole. He's distracted and hasn't noticed Saylor yet.

Her little group moves to the center of the room and becomes the focus of everyone close by. Her hips sway side to side with the beat of the song, while her hands roam up her thighs to her hips. She clinks glasses with Winter and that's the first time I realize she's drinking. As far as I know, she's never drank at any parties, not even when she lived in New York. I search her face for a tell, a clue, anything to know what is ticking in that pretty purple head of hers. Her eyes are closed while she shimmies and sways, absorbing every rift and beat in the song, oblivious to the eyes that watch her. My jaw clenches, and I narrow my eyes, meeting a few gazes of the brave souls still ogling her. Once they're aware of me, they back off and turn their attention elsewhere.

My neck flushes red and hot. So far this is not going how I planned. I'm not even really sure what I wanted. I want her to suffer. I want her to pay. I listened to Kai and lifted the ban. I purposefully made sure she was invited tonight and made it known the doors were open to her. Seeing her, though, only angers the darkness inside of me. He's out for blood and wanting a taste of the demon princess.

I turn back to the game and force myself to concentrate on anything but her; instead, I designate her to my peripheral vision, stalking her movements that way. She dances, has a drink, dances some more, and has another drink, before her group moves over to the dartboard. The bottle in my hand crushes under the pressure when I notice who is also there. Bentley Rhodes. My head snaps in their direction so fast, there is no way Kai didn't see. His head swivels between me and her then over to Silas. The wheels in his brain are flipping over the different scenarios of how this is going to play out tonight. I know because I've been doing the same thing. No matter how the chips crumble, a clash is inevitable.

My feet move on their own, before I can even process what this means or how this is going to go. I do know for sure, though, that Bentley's hand on her waist is pushing my limits. The dark and ugly I keep locked down is threatening to push to the surface, and right now, it would like nothing more than to see red painted across our state football champion's face. Not even the silent headshake Kai is giving me is enough to halt my movements.

He leans closer to her ear, so she can hear him over the music. My fists clench at my sides. She slips her hair behind her ear and smiles.

"I appreciate the offer, but I'm not interested," I hear her telling him, which does nothing to deter the determined look on his face. Bentley knows the rules. We know he and Cassidy hook up, but have never made things official, which makes it acceptable. His disregard for the rules and pursuit of Saylor does not.

"You'll go out with me eventually, Waters," he tells her, authoritative certainty thick in his voice.

I see red.

Something snaps in my brain like a rubber band.

The minute my hands connect with more force than intended, Bentley's body is shoved to the side. His drink sloshes over his hand and his fists come up, ready to throw punches, before he realizes who knocked him in the first place, and that it wasn't an accident.

"Are we really going to have another talk about the rules, Rhodes?" I bite out, using my other arm to shove Saylor behind me and away from his view. His head tilts to the side, silently defying the question. His refusal to fall in line only makes things worse. The darkness starts to creep out. This is what she does to me. The need to hit, destroy, decimate hisses and stirs under my skin. A thick fog clouds my mind. I advance, ready to go head to head, when a tug at the back of my shirt makes me pause.

"Ciaran." My name out of her mouth is a warning, with a hint of fear attached to it. I glance back at her; my eyebrow raises when I find her dark gaze has been on me the whole time. Her concern is for me. Saylor's hands clutch the fabric of my shirt until her knuckles turn white; all the while, she never stops staring at my face. I allow my body to take a step back until her arms are resting against me.

"Walk away while you still can," I tell Rhodes, my gaze hardening. He's getting tiring. Always ready to push the limits like he needs the world to acknowledge him one more time. Trying his best to recreate that survival high. But Bentley can be smart, too. With one more attempt to look over my shoulder at Saylor, he walks away with his group of jock buddies in tow.

Once he's far enough away, the realization of what just happened comes back to smack me in the face. I can feel Silas and Kai hovering on the edge, while I fight to pull myself away from the raspberry scent at my back. Always fucking raspberries.

"Are you done now?" I ask, loud enough for her to hear me, my voice cold and void of all of the emotions I just shoved back in their bottle. Her grip on my shirt loosens, and I can feel them drop away from me.

"I didn't mean—"

"You weren't thinking is what you mean," I fire back, turning to face her, letting my monster out again. She flinches when I let her see the disdain in my gaze. "You gotta think smarter Princess when you start making up excuses."

"I'm not making excuses." Her head shakes in denial.

"You just enjoy playing with people's emotions then?" I bite out the question, enjoying the struggle of her chest while she fights to stay calm.

"No," she answers, "that's not it at all."

"Are you a cock tease, Waters? Is that it?" I goad her, finding the right button when her chin tips up.

"Screw you, Ciaran."

I laugh. Her words are tough and pack a punch, but there is only one of us walking away from this without leaving blood. "I get it," I shake my head, "you just like playing with people's emotions. You like seeing them dangle, putting everything out there, only so you can yank it back and set their world on fire? Because let's face it...he's at more of a risk than you are. I almost just rearranged his face for breaking the rules. Is that what you get off on?"

Her eyes shine and fill with clear liquid. That dark pink bottom lip slips into her mouth and is held in a vice grip by her teeth. The urge to deny what I'm saying is on her tongue.

"Like mother, like daughter, I guess." I lean toward her until we're face to face. "Must be a family trait. The not caring about who suffers because of you, huh?"

My gaze stays locked on hers, watching, while her mind goes over every word I just told her. I hope they cut. I hope it hurts like hell. Her face loses its natural pink coloring. She backs up from me, ready to flee, ready to run from her nightmare in the flesh. Those salty, liquid tears finally free fall from their holding place to paint wet streams of rejection on her face. She lets me have it. I see all of her pain, before her pride can't take it anymore. Saylor whips around, purple strands almost smacking my face, and dodges past the remaining gawking bodies and up the stairs.

Once she's out of my sight, the air rushes back to my lungs. I can breathe evenly again. My mind clears, the darkness retracts, and my adrenaline calms in my veins.

"What the hell, Ci!" Kai pushes at my side. I can hear the disappointment in his voice, without even having to look at him. "You better go fix that. I know you and Si got beef with her but for fucks sake that was uncalled for. In front of everybody, too."

My head lifts up, his eyes are darting around the room, and, sure enough, the crowd didn't get smaller when Bentley left, and now, everyone is attempting to not look like they didn't just witness my conversation with Saylor. Fuck. I got emotional. In my need to hurt her, I drew attention. Sure, I beat people bloody every other week, and I'm not afraid to put anyone of them in their place, but this deal with Saylor is different. I actively engaged with her without mercy. I slipped up and mentioned her family even. Shrugging out of Kai's grasp, I head toward the stairs.

There is no way I'm going after her, but the sudden pressure of everyone's expectations weighs on me. My feet hit the first step before my eyes connect with Silas'. Unlike Kai, he didn't crowd me right away. He held back. His expression is like stone. I didn't expect him to look grateful, but I also didn't anticipate to see disgust flashing at me. Looking away, I stalk up the stairs and make my way out of the house.

# #Twelve

*Saylor*

Twisting what's left of the crusty, brown leaf in my fingers, I hold it close to my head and throw my other hand up in a peace sign, silently counting down the seconds until the timer ends and the picture is taken. My eyes close, inhale, exhale, and it's done. Picking my phone up off the hood of Matt's Bronco, I examine my work. All that's visible in the shot is the open area covered in snow, long purple hair, the leaf and my fingers. Not my eyes, not my body, not my face. It's perfect. My fingers fly over the screen before I hit share.

Once the shot is posted, I scan over the twenty-five other ones I've collected. Just like this one, nothing except my hair and a hand gesture is visible. That was my deal with Reed. After I begged, pleaded and shed a few tears, he was willing to be my accomplice and help set up a secret Instagram account for me. Since Matt and his good ol' Midwest Boys supervise all contacts, internet use, and apps that are downloaded, I knew I had to go to someone just as smart and savvy as them to help me. To his credit, Reed did turn me down countless times, before I finally wore him down. After that horrible confrontation with Ciaran at the party, I pretty much ugly cried all over Reed at the store. Poor dude had black mascara streaks on his shirt for days after that, and he caved.

I remember watching his fingers scramble over the screen. It was a process of finding a real person and duplicating her account to create a second Instagram account under that person's name, then changing the settings, so it was hidden from her. The fact that Reed pulled it off makes me both amazed and fearful. I didn't care, though. #MNGirl was up, running, and waiting for Oaklynn to find.

My heart falters a little when I realize again how much time has passed since Reed mailed that burner phone. As promised, I didn't leave a number to call. I only programmed #MNGirl. He assures me, in as few words as possible, that it's fine. I shouldn't worry... but I do. If Matt finds out, or worse, if Ciaran finds out, I'm dead. They won't understand. He'll only see it as a breach of security and all his reasons for not wanting me here will be justifiable.

Heat sears my cheeks and tears threaten to spill just thinking about Ciaran. I barely survived the night he destroyed me in front of everybody. I'd like to think that after New York my skin was thick and words couldn't hurt me. I was wrong. His words beat me down that night. It was brutal, and I left feeling shamed and humiliated. I can't deny what my dad did. The whole world is aware, and the fallout wasn't pretty. Having to hear it from Ciaran, for him to fold me in the same cloth as them, and to make assumptions about me, hurt more than anything I'd experienced yet.

Two weeks have passed, and we continue to exist around each other. I don't see him when he's home because I try to be gone or asleep when he is there. It's a stroke of luck we don't work the same shifts either. When I am at the shop, I'm in the office with Kai. Ciaran and Silas are runners and are usually chasing down vehicles, getting rid of vehicles or helping with extractions in this state. He hasn't approached me. I'm not even sure if I want him to. Words can't heal what happened at that party. There is something wrong with me to crave his attention while he lives to wreck my life.

Matt doesn't know, or if he does, he hasn't said anything to me, which just goes to show how far of a reach the guys have on the students at school. They're gods, wardens, and their word is law. If I didn't understand before, my eyes are wide fucking open now. The last thing I want to do is let Matt down. He took me in when he didn't have to. He saved us from that house, so we could survive. I fear the storm brewing inside me, though. Most days, I'm steady, barely rocking, but some days, I want to hide under the covers and give myself over to the waves of grief and pain. I can't outrun the monsters in my sleep, and I pay the price during the day.

"Please find me, Oak," I whisper to the universe again. Wrapping my arms around myself, I walk back to the Bronco and slip into the driver's seat. I left it running to keep it warm. We're nearing the end of January, and the temps continue to dip lower. Winter constantly tells me it's not the temps that are bad, but the wind that makes it worse. It's freezing. The air, the wind, all of it.

When I pull into an empty parking spot at the repair shop, I sigh in relief that neither Silas nor Ciaran are here. Jogging quickly across the lot, I slip in the doors and race up to the office I've slowly started to claim as my own. After some convincing, Matt finally caved and let me get a Keurig in the space and color-coded folders for my desk. Once he saw my system, he complained less about it. As long as I unplugged the Keurig after my shift, he didn't care. I make myself a small cup, before sitting at my desk. One more look at my phone indicates no new notifications. Blowing out my breath, I toss the phone into my drawer and promise myself I won't look again until after my shift. Before I can open my files, the adjoining door to my office opens. Kai steps into the room, his eyes searching me out, biting his lip.

"Hey," he says, approaching carefully, like I may attack him. He's around six foot two, and while he may be leaner than Ciaran or Silas, Kai is still muscled. His forest green long sleeve shirt molds to his torso. His black hair is longer on the top and often falls into his eyes. Eyes that are a few shades darker than mine and tip up slightly at the corners. His eyebrows are as dark as his head, and they create intimidating slashes across the lightness of his skin. Winter has mentioned that Kai's grandparents are from the Guangdong province in China. He's beautiful and very flirty.

My eyebrows raise in question when he approaches. Kai never actively seeks me out. "Me?" I ask, suddenly unsure.

"Yeah," he answers, walking to my desk. His hand reaches back to scratch his head. He looks like he's in pain. "You know what I do, right? For Rogue?"

I nod, my heart rate increasing, wondering where this is going. "Security and IT stuff."

"IT stuff," he scoffs offensively. Kai walks over to the window that looks down into the shop. My stomach plummets, terrified that Ciaran or Silas may be down there, before he strides back over to my desk. "Come with me."

"In there?" I question, pointing to his office. I've been told by Matt, under no circumstances, can I go in there. He may trust me around his small set up at home, but I do not have the clearance for whatever is behind that door.

"You scared?" He smirks, tilting his head to the side.

Hook, line and sinker, he lured me right in. I stand from my chair and follow him. "Matt will kill you," I warn.

"They're all out on runs tonight," he assures me, before placing his palm on the scanner.

The door clicks open. Kai walks through and stands to the side to let me enter. Taking a deep breath, I step over the threshold and into a scene from every movie with a NASA or Matrix set up. The farthest wall is a giant screen, similar to the one in Matt's basement, that is lit up. Thousands of red, green, and yellow lights flicker all over it. Small screens and monitors are surrounding it, scrolling news and footage from aerial views from all over the world. Kai sits at a desk with three monitors running numbers. Another has social media open on it and another is flashing red.

"This is what I want to show you." He motions to the flashing frame.

A number scrolls across it with an envelope that is waiting to be opened. "What is it?"

"I intercepted a message from this number earlier. It only flagged it because of the content," Kai explains, never taking his eyes off mine. Blood pumps in my veins so fast and hard, it's almost painful.

"What was it?" I ask, even though I know the answer.

"Saylor, question mark, question mark," Kai answers, his Adam's apple bobs visibly while talking. "The number is untraceable. California area code. The reply was to a comment on a duplicate social media account for an Annika Dowing in New Hampshire. It's registered under a different email, even with an encrypted domain. Hashtag M-N Girl."

My stomach drops. I have to look away, too scared for Kai to see my face.

"Is it your dad?" Kai asks, cranking his head, so that our eyes meet, bringing my gaze back to his.

I shake my head. "It's Oaklynn."

Kai blows his breath out while his fingers drum against the desk. "Who helped you?"

"I did it myself," I answer. If Kai reports it to Matt, there is a good chance I'll have to leave. I can't let that happen to Reed.

Kai nods, as if he isn't sure what to believe at this moment. "Why?"

"Are you going to tell Ciaran?" I ask hesitantly.

Kai raises his brow. "Shouldn't you be worried about Matt?"

I shrug. "He's the lesser of two evils."

Kai laughs. "Oh, you have no idea, Gossip Girl. Matt may seem like an old dog, but his bite is a hell of a lot bigger than Ciaran's. Matt built this empire. He didn't do it by being a push over for teenage girls."

I can feel a band closing around my neck, cutting off the air to my lungs. The light dims, and words become nonsensical. "I did everything I could to not give away who I am or where I'm at, Kai."

My gaze swings to his, he's watching me intently. "I would not purposely put myself or any of the other hidden kids here in danger. I wouldn't do that to Matt. Not after... not after that. He saved me."

"You need to give me a very good reason why I shouldn't say anything, Ariel. I'll give it to you that this was high level secure. I just have your name flagged everywhere and probably read through thousands of messages a day, or else this would have slipped by. Once I flagged it, I had to encrypt it again and cover my tracks. It was a freaking headache," Kai rants, and I let him.

"I'm sorry," I offer. "I am, Kai. I just, I need my best friend. That night was the worst thing that's ever happened to me. I didn't get to process it. I lock it down, and it makes me sick and scared. That man...his face haunts me. What they did to my mom...I can't erase her screams from my memory. They're there every day. I can't sleep. I'm trying really hard to move on, stay under the radar and blend in when all I want to do is stand in the middle of the room and scream until someone looks. Oaklynn would look. She'd never leave. You guys, Ciaran, Silas, and you...that's what she is to me. She's my other half, and I'm so lost and scared. I just wanted a piece of my old life back. I know it was stupid." My voice cracks and breaks. I wasn't even aware I was crying until the tears hit the backs of my hands that are resting on the chair. I never wanted to break down like this in front of any of them.

Time passes slowly, and Kai gives me my moment to let it out and unbottle that fear. It's therapeutic and calming. Not something I expected from Kai, even though I should have. His whole demeanor is relaxed. The entire time I sob, he stays silent, clicking away on his keyboard. I don't know where we go from here. Staying quiet seems to be the best option at this point.

"I replied back, yes. I secured a line to this phone. You can't use it without me opening it. The phone won't let it. I won't say anything right now. That's on you. If for some reason you use this recklessly, I will shut it down fast." Kai's voice is calm and precise while he talks to me. The harsh lines around his mouth have disappeared.

"Why are you doing this?" I question, not believing he actually did something nice for me.

"I understand trauma. Plus, I'm pretty impressed with the extent you went to for this. I've seen some hack jobs over the years, but this was professional level. Make sure you tell Reed he should take me up on my offer to run this next year," he laughs.

My mouth drops open. "You knew? Wait, where are you going next year?"

"Curious about me, Gossip Girl?" Flirty Kai is back. For the first time, I notice a small dimple in his right cheek.

I shrug. "I just figured you'd be here helping Matt, I guess. I forget you're seniors."

"We'll be back eventually," Kai responds, nodding his head. "Part of the requirement for Rogue is that we enlist in the military."

"For real?" I ask intrigued.

"Yup," Kai laughs. "I'm excited, actually. I can't wait to blow some shit up."

This time, I laugh in response. "What branch?"

"I'll be Army. Doing more cyber warfare training. Ciaran is also Army, but Silas is still undecided," Kai answers my question. His words are enthusiastic, and again, I'm reminded how different he is from his broody counterparts.

"I better get back out there." I stand and point to the door. "I. Thank you again, Kai. I don't even know what to say."

He shrugs. "Just be smart, Gossip Girl. This better not come back to bite either one of us. And you will tell them."

"I know." I wince and nod in agreement. The mental image is too painful to think about right now.

"Get to work," he orders and spins back to his station.

My legs are unsteady and shake as they carry me out of Kai's office and back to my own desk. So much for getting anything done tonight.

### 

Another week passes without any further contact from Oaklynn. I want to ask Kai what he did or for help, but he hasn't been alone at school. Even at work this week, he wasn't alone. Matt has been spending copious amounts of time in that office as well. With Kai knowing Reed helped me, I'm freaked out to bring him into this any further.

Winter can tell I'm preoccupied, but she doesn't pry. I would feel guilty telling her about my plan as well. I'm grateful for

Winter, and I'm happy we're friends. I just hope she can meet Oaklynn someday. Winter knows my life now, and Oaklynn has known me since I was seven.

Listening to Winter, I put a strained smile on my face and hope it looks legit.

"It's in March," she states, while looking through me.

"I'm sorry, Winter," I shake my head, "I'm really trying to stay focused; it's just extra hard today."

"It's okay." She lifts her shoulder, while biting into the banana in her hand.

"What's in March?" I question, turning to face her this time.

"The talent show." Her eyes brighten when she says the words.

I cough and choke on the water in my mouth. "Is that a thing here?"

"Only the second biggest school event next to prom," she answers. I feel as if she's barely contained in her seat, ready to bounce right out of her chair. The whole table nods in agreement with her.

"Oh, okay." I smile. "Are you entering?"

"We usually do a dance routine." Winter nods to the others around the table. "Do you want to do it with us this year?"

"Uh," I hesitate, "I'm not a good organized dancer. The whole counting steps thing throws me off. Seriously, I'd ruin it for you."

"Everyone can dance." Winter gives me a lopsided smile.

"Oh no." I hold my hand up. "Don't try to Footloose me. I'm not the Willard to your Ren. We're not getting matching shirts that say 'Dance Your Ass Off' either." I point a finger at her accusingly. Knowing Winter, that is exactly where her mind would go.

She laughs, until she's in tears, and people are eyeing our table. My cheeks are pink from the attention, but she finally calms down.

"Fine," she huffs out in between giggles. "Be a fun hater. But seriously, though, is there anything you can do for a talent?"

I pause. The old me would have jumped at this opportunity. Trinity Prep did not have a talent show, but they did do productions and musicals.

"I, ah, I used to sing," I answer, keeping my voice low, for only Winter to hear.

Her smile turns mega-watt bright. "This is perfect!"

"What? Why?" Her smile is freaking me out as much as that calculating look in her eye.

"Ah, because, Cassidy and her cronies usually do a song set, and they always win, because nobody is brave enough to go against them." Winter rushes through her words. Her eyes get even bigger, if possible, the pupils stretching until they're barely rimmed in grey.

"I don't think I'm going to enter," I tell her gently, letting her down easy.

"Think about it at least." Winter's smile is small this time. I want to tell her it's too close to home. That my vocal cords haven't been used like that in months, but I don't. I should tell her I used to practice with my mom and that, without her, I don't think I could carry a tune, but I stay quiet.

I continue eating my lunch while their conversation goes on around me. I'm lost in the past, soaked in the lies I find there, now that I know what I'm looking at. Sharp pain pulses against my temples. Using my pointer fingers, I massage in circles, until it lessens. Warmth touches my skin and tingles rise from my chest to the roots of my hair. I hesitate before lifting my head, knowing what or who is waiting for me. Taking a breath in, I lift my face to the challenge. The minute my eyes look up, they lock with Ciaran's from where he sits across the lunch room. He just arrived, judging from the snow still on his jacket. His blond waves are damp and pushed back from his face. His gaze roams my face, almost caressing it, which is the most contact we've had in weeks. He holds me captive, even when I want to look away. He doesn't deserve my time.

"Are you going tonight?" Winter leans in to whisper, finally freeing me from Ciaran's hold.

"Where?" I ask, turning to face her.

"The lot," she answers and tilts her head back in Ciaran's direction.

The lot, the fight, the place Winter took me after the game weeks back. "He's fighting again?"

"It's a monthly thing, usually," Winter answers, shrugging, "It keeps the peace and stops people, without this town's best interest in mind, in-line. Ciaran is up again tonight, though."

"Oh," I respond, still feeling shaken. "I have a lot of homework. I'll probably stay in tonight."

"Same girl," she responds. We share a smile, before going back to eating our food. I keep my head down or only look at the others at the table. I continue to feel the heat from Ciaran, but I ignore it. He doesn't get to win; I tell myself over and over, even when I'm tempted to take just a peek.

The rest of the day continues the same as always. I'm more aware now of the neon colored posters that read Talent Show in the hallways. After school, I work a few hours at the repair shop, before heading back to the house. Matt lets me know before I leave that he'll be home late tonight and that Ciaran may not be back either. I nod and smile but I also feel guilty. Kai's words echo in my head, and I know I'm on borrowed time to come clean to Matt.

I'm not even hungry by the time I get home. My anxiety is eating me from the inside out. The mere thought of food is nauseating. I go to my room with every intention of going to sleep early, only sleep won't claim me. Every noise and bump in the house has me on edge. My conversation with Kai, waiting to hear from Oaklynn, being unsure about my mom and Mila, all of it is crushing my chest with pressure. I wish there was a way to know what the future holds. I wish I could be one of those people who didn't surrender to anxiety. I would give anything to be one of those people who shrug things off and keep going. Instead, I overthink, and when I overthink, I create a bigger problem out of a smaller problem and then I create an even larger one for those problems to live in. It's messed up how my brain works against my body and emotions like that.

Frustrated, I slide out of bed and walk over to the dresser to get my iPod. Right as my hand closes over my lifeline, a loud bang sounds from downstairs, and I'm instantly frozen in place. Cold sweat breaks out on my skin. I struggle to listen over the sound of my own breathing and heartbeat. Footsteps climb the stairs and enter the bathroom.

"Shit," I hear Ciaran's voice, followed by a clatter of bottles and boxes falling onto the counter. I finally let out my breath and throw my sweatshirt over my head, before opening my door to see what he's doing.

The bathroom light is on, a package of band aids and gauze sits on the floor. Ciaran leans against the sink, a strip of cloth in his mouth, holding it while he uses one hand to wind the material tightly around his knuckles. Red droplets of blood stain the fabric.

"Do you need help?" I ask, hating the timid way my voice sounds.

Ciaran's head snaps to mine, his eyes are unfocused for a minute, almost like he's confused at how I'm standing there.

"I'm fine," he bites out.

Heat rushes up my neck and I take a step back out the door, ready to flee to my room. Anytime I think I can take a step forward with Ciaran, he sends me ten steps back.

"Fuck," he mutters. "I didn't mean it that way. I'm just almost done."

"Okay," I say, before preparing to leave again.

"Actually, can you open that bottle for me?" He nods to the Tylenol on the floor.

I bend to pick it up and unscrew the top for him. "How many?"

"Well, it hurts like a bitch, so three?" He laughs.

The sound sends rings of warmth through me. A genuine smile cracks his perfect lips, and I'm stunned for a moment.

"Are you okay? Did you hit your head or something?" I question, moving closer, in case he's going to pass out. What if he has a concussion?

"No." He smirks. "This is the worst of it." He nods to his knuckles.

"Hmm." I pour three tablets into my palm and hold them out to him. He scoops them from my hand, his fingers dragging lightly across the sensitive skin. "Okay, well, night," I say and turn to leave.

"I'm sorry." Those are two words from his mouth I never thought I'd hear. My body instantly tenses, waiting for another attack. I whip around and almost collide right into his bare chest.

Small bruises decorate the whole left side of his abdomen, their color marring his golden skin. My eyes drag over the loose black joggers, sitting on his hips, showing off and highlighting the perfect V, before moving up above the waistband to his cut, six-pack that tenses under my watch. It's honestly not fair that such a jerk can be wrapped in such a beautiful package.

My mouth is dry by the time I can actually meet his gaze again. He's watching me watch him. A blush forms on my cheeks again. I really checked him out this time. "Saylor," he swallows, his eyes moving up my bare legs to the edge of my sweatshirt that ends mid-thigh.

"You're apologizing to me? For real?" I ask, hating to be hopeful.

Ciaran's long fingers touch the edge of my jaw, before sliding strands of hair behind my ear. "I guess I am." The words leave his mouth, and his eyes never leave mine. A current moves between us. Flames dance over every inch of skin that is in contact with Ciaran. Even my hair can feel his touch. He cradles my face between both his hands. My body sways into him. I place my hands at his sides, holding gently, so I don't fall.

"Don't say it unless you mean it," I choke on the words, not wanting to kill the moment we're in. Maybe we need a healthy dose of reality, though.

Ciaran's stare moves over my face. Learning it. Memorizing it. Pink creeps its way up to my hairline from being under his scrutiny. "I do," he clears his throat. "I'm sorry I hurt you."

My brain skips over the part where he doesn't actually apologize for what he said, only that it hurt me, and stashes it away for another time. Ciaran will probably always view me and my family as the enemy. My dad wronged Silas' family in some way, enough for all three of them to hate my family. I can only hope Ciaran sees me separate from my dad, one day, and not as part of the mistakes he made.

Tears leak over the rims of my eyes. Ciaran tilts my head back, before lowering his head to mine. A soft kiss lands on the corner of my jaw, before his tongue darts out, catching the fresh round of tears that are spilling over, and licks them up. Heat and wetness cling to my skin from his mouth, making my stomach clench and heat flood my core. Ciaran pulls back, dropping one hand to my waist, and pulls my frame up against his. His other hand palms my face and tilts my head. He kisses me so hard, my lips bruise. It's an angry, all-consuming kiss that steals my breath and forces me to hold on tight. My fingernails scrape his skin in their quest to keep my body upright. My bottom lip is pulled between his teeth and sucked on until it's red and shiny when he finally lets it go. The pad of his thumb traces over the bite mark from his teeth, a predatory gleam in his eyes.

"Just like a raspberry," he mutters, before squeezing my jaw in his hand and kissing me again. My hands fly to his biceps, enjoying the way the muscles flex under my hold. He groans into my mouth, and I swallow the noise. Our tongues meet and clash in battle. He tastes like mint and sugar from an energy drink. I don't feel his hatred or dislike, only the tightening of his arm around my back, forcing me onto my tiptoes to give him deeper access to my mouth.

A pained expression crosses his face, when he pulls away panting. I like that I make him breathless. His lips are glossy and even puffier than before. "Matt's truck just pulled up." His voice is hoarse. My brain processes his words slowly as he lowers me to my feet.

"Oh God." I jump back from him.

"Shh!" His finger comes to his lips, a smile dancing in his eyes. Ciaran pulls me behind him, keeping watch over the banister, covering me until he reaches my door.

"Go," he whispers and nods to my door. I crack it open and slip inside. Ciaran reaches out to pull it closed. I race to my bed and hop in quietly, right as the front door opens, and

Matt stomps his boots off. That was close. My fingers trail over my now sensitive lips. Ciaran kissed me. He touched me, and I let it happen. I liked kissing him and being in his arms. I sigh and turn in my bed. My emotions are all over the place, scattered around with my thoughts, but one thing I know for sure, I want it to happen again.

# #Thirteen

*Saylor*

C iaran has become an addiction. One kiss wasn't enough for him or me. He's been a frequent presence in my room every night for the past week. By morning, he's gone, and we go back to being at odds with each other. I keep my distance, and he goes back to ignoring me. If Oaklynn knew, she'd tell me I'm his dirty little secret. I'm glad, for once, that my best friend isn't around. There is no way I could tell her that I don't mind. Ciaran is a force, and he is feared as much as he's respected. He's complicated. He's well-known, and I don't want that much attention on me. By some miracle, no one has figured out yet that we live together, much less that he sneaks into my room every night and whispers dirty things in my ear until I moan his name. In a way, he's my little secret, too, and I love that. A part of me loves that he's different in the dark than he is in the light of day.

"Tell me something about you," I ask, while dragging my fingers through his hair.

"Are we sharing feelings now?" He cocks his eyebrow, and for the first time since he walked through my door, his voice hardens a little. I roll my eyes.

"Kai says you're enlisting in the Army after graduation." He stills while I'm talking.

"You and Kai best friends now?" His eyes flash to mine. Possessiveness and irritation radiate off him as goosebumps rain over my skin.

"Work gets slow sometimes, so we make small talk." I keep my tone light, feeling like I'm suddenly treading on thin ice. Ciaran's eyes swing around my room and silence hangs in the air, acting as a barrier between us.

He clears his throat. "I want to run Rogue for Matt someday." His shoulders lift. His face tenses, and he looks uncomfortable. "Part of that plan is needing military training. One of Matt's friends is a recruiter, so he hooks us up with where we need to go and what we need to do."

"What's your favorite color and your favorite thing to eat?" I rattle off basic questions, hoping he'll be more willing to answer.

"What are you doing?" he counters, a hint of frustration lacing his tone.

"I'm just curious," I lift my shoulders, "I don't really know anything about you."

"I didn't realize we were the sharing kind of friends?" His voice is mocking, and now, I'm getting upset. I sit up, and he rolls to his side. His face is guarded.

"Are we friends, Ciaran?" I lay out the real issue, not caring anymore.

His ice blue eyes are watching me intently, his jaw hardens to stone. His body unfolds and lifts off my bed. My heart thumps painfully in my chest, but I don't stop him. He stands and swipes his shirt off my floor, before throwing it over his head. Without a word, he takes two steps to my door before stopping, his back still facing me. My stomach twists and drops.

"Green." His head turns halfway to meet my gaze. "And, can you stop eating all those fresh raspberries Matt buys? Some of us like them, too."

Without waiting for a reply, he stalks out of my room and closes the door behind him. I slide down farther into my covers stunned, elated and confused. Ciaran gave me a piece of himself then took his physical presence away. I don't know if I won the war or lost the battle. He didn't deny that we're friends but he also didn't confirm it. How he feels about me is still in a limbo without a name. I don't need him to label his feelings. I just want to not have the rug pulled out from under me one day, if he all of a sudden decides to freeze me out again and goes back to ignoring me. Ciaran is loyal to his friends. My chest aches to be on that level.

I wake up the next morning with a sense of dread in my bones. It's still dark, the sky barely carrying a hint of light, which is not unusual for this time of year. My room is abnormally cold. The kind that makes you ache and want to layer up, before sliding under a mountain of covers. Turning onto my side, I pick my phone up to silence the alarm going off when it dings in my hand.

> Winter: Ugh! I can't believe we have to go to school today.
> It snowed almost a foot overnight.
> Ariel: Great. Just what we need. More snow. :-(
> Winter: My car is almost buried. My dad is bringing me in before work. Can you get a ride?
> Ariel: Yeah, I'll figure something out.

"Ugh!" I fall back on my bed. That sticky ball of dread rolls back around in my stomach because I have to ask Ciaran for a ride. Since that first day, I have not ridden with him again. I usually get a ride with Winter. Matt has given me access to his vehicle, but I usually decline when going to school. Would it be easier? Yes. Do I want people to recognize Matt's vehicles and wonder why I'm driving it? No. Thankfully, Winter has told me numerous times I'm on her way in, and she doesn't mind giving me a ride.

After giving myself some breathing time, I push myself out of bed. I scramble into my favorite pair of black jeans and a chunky rose gold sweater, before throwing my hair back in a high ponytail. I grab my backpack off the desk and saunter into the hallway. When my stocking feet hit the stairs, I realize the house is quieter than usual. The coffee machine is not running either, which almost heightens a state of panic in my chest.

"Matt's out of town." Ciaran's voice jumps at me from the shadows, and my heart rate increases.

"You scared me," I mumble, placing my hand over my heart. My brain grapples with my mind's fight or flight instincts. "What are you doing here?" He usually is up and out of the house before I get up; yet, somehow, he barely makes it to school before the bell.

He shrugs. "It snowed a lot. We have to take the sleds in."

I blink. "Say what?"

Ciaran rolls his eyes. Rolls. His. Eyes. "Come on, Princess, your chariot awaits," he lays the sarcasm on thick while handing me an extra-large pair of black snow pants and the snow jacket Winter had told me I needed to get before the snow fell.

I take the items from his hands, and he takes my backpack while I put them on. As expected, the snow pants swallow me whole. Ciaran laughs. "Shit. I thought for sure those would fit."

"You're like a foot taller than me," I explain, my hand swinging wildly between us.

"They're mine from the seventh grade." He laughs again.

With my cheeks flaming, I push my arms into my coat and quickly zip it up to my chin. I feel like a bulky, uncoordinated disaster. Ciaran is trying to hide a grin. I raise my eyebrow at him, not above delivering a swift punch to his abdomen right now. Not that it would matter much. I've learned from a lot of heavy touching that Ciaran's whole torso is solid muscle. I pull my lip between my teeth, wishing we didn't have to go to school at all and could start over in my bedroom. Last night was cut way too short by my stupid mouth.

"Let's go." Ciaran cuts into my daydream by handing me an all-black helmet. Sighing, I follow him out the door. Sitting on top of the snow in the driveway is a white and black snowmobile with the engine running.

"Is this even legal? Taking a sled to school?" I ask, raising my voice that is now muffled by the helmet.

His eyes slice to mine sharply like he thinks I'm joking. The smirk on his face confirms it probably isn't, but we're doing it anyway. I narrow my eyes, even though he can't see, and follow him to my new waiting ride. He hops on first and scoots forward. Hesitantly, my hands touch his shoulders to boost myself on.

"Hang on," he hollers back at me. That's all the warning I get before we lurch forward. My arms jump out and hold tightly to his middle while we glide across the snowy road, before dipping into a ditch. My stomach drops like I'm on a rollercoaster. I want to laugh and scream at the same time. Snow flies past us, and soon, we're tailed by two other sleds. I don't have to guess who they are. The way they're driving, jumping over drifts, whipping their back ends, it gives them away.

My heart drops when we get about half a block away, and Ciaran lets our sled slow down. I slam my eyes closed in denial. There is so much snow; he wouldn't really make me get off and walk, right? He lets Silas and Kai pull past us, before turning into the parking lot. I have to take a couple of deep breaths to keep calm. My emotions jump all over the place. Instinctively, my arms clutch around Ciaran tighter, as if he could shield me from all the looks we're about to get.

Even with the side of my head pressed to his back, I can still make out the lines and rows of other sleds in the lot. Red ones, black ones, green ones and even a loud bright orange one. A few trucks and SUVs are there as well. Ciaran swings us around, before backing into a spot next to Kai who already has his helmet off and is shaking snow from his hair.

"Decided to give the evil spawn a ride in today?" The darkly sarcastic comment comes from Silas. My cheeks instantly heat. Part of me wants to lash out, while another just wants to beg for forgiveness for whatever business or money his family probably lost because of my dad.

Ciaran lifts his eyebrow but doesn't comment. My chest automatically deflates. Guess we're going back to being enemies today. Kai ignores everything going on, only eyeing the few stragglers still heading into the building. He's arranged his longer hair into small top-knot. Normally, that look wouldn't do much for me, but on Kai, it looks sinful. My thoughts automatically flash to Oaklynn. She would practically be panting if she saw him.

"Get inside," Ciaran's voice interrupts my thoughts. He lifts his chin to the building, waiting for me to start walking. They're all watching me, varying looks on their face: rage, indifference, and wait, hunger? My stomach lurches, and that's all it takes to get my feet moving as fast as I can through the inches of snow. The farther away I walk, the louder their voices begin to get until there is only silence. A quick glance over my shoulder lets me know they're following; they're just keeping their distance. This should make me happy; yet, a tiny fraction of my heart cracks. I frown at the emotion and walk faster, until I'm practically running to get into the building. This gets me even more curious looks.

We only made it three hours in before the principal calls it an early release day. The snow has continued to fall outside, and suddenly, everyone is worried about how buses and students will get home. I stand from my desk, a frown creasing my forehead, while I slip down the hall to my locker.

"Who shit in your Fruit Loops?" Winter asks, suddenly appearing next to me.

"I don't think that's something people actually say," I reply, even though my brain isn't really comprehending how things are working right now. How am I going to get home? Do I assume Ciaran will take me?

"It should be," she answers, while shrugging her shoulder.

"Hey," I glance at her. "How are you getting home?"

"We're not going home, silly." She chuckles at my confusion. "It's a snow day," she says, like it's something new I should know about.

"Exactly, we were excused to go home," I remind her.

"I forget you're so city sometimes." She smirks. "Snow days here basically just set us up for a day of fun. A bunch of people are taking sleds up to the Ridge."

"What's the Ridge?" I ask, trying to keep up with her lingo. I'm positive she's never mentioned it before.

"A small resort on a lake about an hour and a half from here. A couple kids' parents have property up there," she answers and starts handing me the snow pants and jacket from my locker. "I'm going to go get mine. Wait for me, yeah?" I nod, but she's already taking off down the hallway.

I quickly shove my materials in my locker and pull the snow pants and jacket on. Since we had no homework assigned today and I'm current on my project in history, I decide to leave my backpack here. I pocket my cell phone and iPod, though. The minute I shut my door, I collide against two stone hard chests covered in thick winter jackets. My head snaps up in surprise, while my eyes collide first with pale blue eyes then dart to Kai's brown ones.

"What are you doing?" I murmur, my head whipping around to see if anyone is paying attention to us.

He smirks. "We're heading to the Ridge."

"I know. Winter told me about it," I let him know, still confused by his presence here in the first place.

Kai laughs, and Ciaran's eyes narrow. "No, you're leaving with us to the Ridge."

"Your escort is here to pick you up, Gossip Girl." Kai leans in to tell me, before being shoved back by Ciaran, which only earns another round of laughter from Kai.

"I promised I'd go with Winter," I tell him, worrying my lip with my teeth. His eyes dart to my mouth, before snapping up to mine.

"It's covered," he answers, before reaching out to take my arm.

"I'll go handle, Snow," Kai thumps him on the back, before heading in the direction of Winter's locker. I frown.

Ciaran leads me out of the building to where we parked earlier today. For the first time, I notice Silas is not sulking in the background. "Where's your other half?"

"He had some stuff to take care of," Ciaran states, while handing me the same helmet I wore this morning. He doesn't offer anything else, and I don't pry further. It's easier to breathe around Ciaran when Silas isn't there. I know they're best friends, and I would never come between them. It's not a secret, though, that Silas hates me and my family.

By the time I'm situated on the back of the seat, Kai and Winter are finally making it over to us. Kai's face looks tense while Winter talks animatedly beside him. I chuckle to myself. Ciaran waits for Kai to be ready before we leave. Once he gets a thumbs up, we're fly out of the parking lot. I almost lose my balance, falling backward, before slamming forward into Ciaran's back. My arms instantly wrap all the way around his waist this time, gripping for dear life. Our sled sways side to side while it gains the momentum needed to keep us soaring over the snow. Instead of heading in the direction of the house, Ciaran coasts through town to the main highway. Once there, he jumps into a ditch, heading north.

Almost two hours later, my legs are shaking from being locked to the sled. The muscles in my arms burn from their frigid hold around Ciaran. I'm seriously surprised he can even breathe still, and all I want to do is lay down and sleep. When we bank through a clearing of trees, it suddenly becomes apparent why everyone decides to make this trek on days like this.

A massive wooden cabin, surrounded by pine trees, comes into view. Behind the house is an opening that leads down to a huge lake. A few snowmobiles are racing across it, while a few people are out playing boot hockey. With the snow continuing to fall in giant fluffy flakes, the scene looks like it belongs in a snow globe or on a calendar. I'm in awe as Ciaran lifts the helmet from my head and shoves a black stocking cap on me instead.

"Thanks." I touch the edge of the material. I'm assuming it's one of his since I didn't have my own. He shrugs, before tugging on the sleeve of my jacket to follow him.

To my surprise, Kai and Winter arrived before us. She comes bouncing through the snow to get to me. "Finally!"

"How long have you been here?" I ask, not even remembering when they could have passed us.

"We took the back roads." She laughs. "Probably about fifteen minutes ago." Her nose scrunches up.

"The heck. Why didn't we take the back roads?" I turn to Ciaran accusingly.

His eyes turn to the sky before looking back at me. "Like I could drive the back roads when you're stiffer than a corpse on the back of my sled."

"I've never ridden on one before!" I exclaim, defending myself. "What the hell am I supposed to do?"

"Not make it so the guy can't drive in any direction but straight," Kai chimes in. I whip around to face him. His usual playful smirk tugs at his lips.

"You could have said something." I look back at Ciaran whose eyes are looking off in the distance.

"It's over now." He shrugs.

We make our way, mostly in silence, down to the edge of the lake.

"Is it thick enough?" Ciaran turns to Kai.

"It's damn near perfect. Get the ice castle out here in a week, and we'll be golden," Kai answers, while rubbing his gloved hands together.

"Ice fishing," Winter leans down to answer my unspoken question.

I smile. "You're scary when you do that."

"You ever been, Gossip Girl?" Kai asks me. I shake my head no. The most winter leisure my family did was booking a vacation to somewhere tropical.

"You'll have to go with us then," Kai answers, at the same time Ciaran shoots him a look. It isn't hard to miss the message passing between them. I most likely am not invited because Silas will have a problem with it. Instead of answering or even giving my opinion, I walk over to where Winter has walked off to chat with Jamie and Ella.

I have a lot of fun over the next few hours we spend out here. We take breaks inside the cabin, every now and then, to stay warm. I learn that the cabin belongs to Aiden, the senior, whose house we also partied at the other weekend, while he was gone. According to Winter, his family is super rich, and they also have a home in Florida. They do not work for Matt's company, though, so he is oblivious to the hidden families and children around him.

The whole time we're here, Ciaran doesn't approach me or talk to me much. He stopped me one time on my way into the cabin to ask if I was warm enough. Once I reassured him I was, he left me alone again. When the sky is starting to turn darker, everyone starts to leave. Ciaran and Kai purposefully wait until most people leave, before they quickly usher Winter and myself to their sleds.

"You braving it this time?" Kai jokes with Ciaran.

"Just tell me what I'm supposed to do!" I pipe in, raising my voice.

"Chill." Ciaran chuckles with Kai. "You're just too tense. You need to move with the sled. When I turn, you have to lean into it. We're going to hit some banks but, again, just ride the movement."

"Yes, just ride it with your body." Kai winks at me, grinning. I flip him off with my gloved finger.

Ciaran and I get on, and he fires it up. Kai and Winter take off before he turns to face me. "As much as I like having your arms wrapped around me, you have to let me move. Just keep them at my side. I promise you won't fall off."

His tone becomes softer and concerned, as if he can read my thoughts and fears. Unable to form words from the emotion lodged in my throat, I nod. Even though we haven't talked much today, we also haven't fought or exchanged hurtful words. I want to hope we're turning a new leaf and our time together is beginning to mean something. That instead of nemeses, maybe we can turn into...frenemies. But every time I let my guard down around him, he ends up changing his mind about letting me in, leaving me with nothing except his cold shoulder.

We make it back into town a lot faster by taking the back roads. I tried my best to follow the direction Ciaran had given me. I must have done better, since he didn't stop us to find the main road. By the time he pulls into the garage, the sky is dark, and the snow has finally stopped. A thin blanket covers the driveway, and I wonder who was here to clear it. The house is dark, and Matt's vehicle isn't anywhere.

"Matt's not home," I state.

"He won't be back until tomorrow night sometime," Ciaran shares with me. It's on the tip of my tongue to ask where Matt is, until I realize I'll be home alone in the house tonight with Ciaran.

My cheeks heat, and even in the darkness, I have to turn my head away, so he can't see. "I'm going to go inside," I call back, before dashing up the front steps. I peel off my soaked winter gear and lay it out over the banister to dry. Taking the stairs two at a time, I duck into my room and change into sweats and a long sleeve t-shirt. My heart is racing, thinking about being alone with Ciaran. Even though he's been in here, he leaves before Matt comes home. After that night in the bathroom, he's been extra cautious of not being on top of me when our guardian gets here. I'm not sure how Matt would react if he found out. The rules about dating are pretty strict. I don't think Matt would make me leave after he promised to help my mom, but he also probably isn't going to kick his nephew out.

My breath blows out, while my hands tangle in my hair. Pacing, I strain to listen for Ciaran moving around the house.

"What are you doing?" His voice startles me, practically sending me in the air.

"Why do you have to sneak around like that?" I snap back. I didn't hear him at all over the sound of my blood pumping in my ears.

He shrugs. "I wasn't sneaking." He peels his shirt off over his head, and I'm, once again, met with his perfect torso. My eyes rake over him, heat building low in my stomach, as my core clenches in anticipation.

"Like what you see?" His lips pull into that perfect side smile. I want to kiss that corner and drag my tongue across his bottom lip. Without shame, I nod. I do like what I see. The way his eyes blaze to life from my answer wipes away any doubts I had earlier.

In two strides, he reaches for me, hoisting my body up against his half-naked one. With our height difference, I have to wrap my legs around his waist. Judging from the low growl in his throat, he likes my decision. He's instantly hard, and I can feel him cradled against me.

"Ci," I gasp his name against his lips, right as they descend on mine. He drops me to the bed, his body following after mine. It's on my tongue to ask him again about where we stand.

"I don't know," he answers, finally addressing our conversation from last night, before pulling back, so our eyes lock. Heat, confusion, and want pass between us in the invisible current that pulls us together and pushes us apart. "I don't know what we're doing or what it means. I can't give you that right now."

I love that I make him talk. It's an intoxicating feeling to know he wants me as much as I want him, even though he isn't supposed to even like me. "I don't need that right now. I just don't want to be a joke to you and your friends later."

He shakes his head, his lips dropping to place open mouthed kisses along my jaw and down the sides of my throat. He zeros in on the pulse point at the base of my neck and sucks. My body jolts, slamming my core right into him. "You aren't a joke or a secret. I need to be the one to tell him, though."

I pull back, forcing him to make eye contact. His blue orbs shine with lust but also honesty and truth. I may not understand fully, but if that's what he needs, I'm fine with it. "I understand," I tell him. "Ci?"

"Hmm," he answers.

"I'm not ready for anyone else to know anyways. I don't," I look away, trying to organize my thoughts, "I don't want the school to know we live together."

He stares at me puzzled, before his features soften. He almost looks relieved for a second before his jaw clenches. "Why not?"

"You guys drive enough attention and gossip the way it is. I'm supposed to be staying under the radar, remember?" I throw his own words back at him. I don't miss the way his gaze slants like he wants to argue. "We have things to work through, and while we're figuring this out, can we just take those things in stride?"

"I think you're the only girl who would probably ever want to keep this a secret." His shoulders shake under my hands, and I realize he's trying not to laugh.

"What can I say," I shrug, "I'm weird."

"I like it," he tells me, running his fingers through the strands of my hair.

The mood from earlier has simmered, and I realize how tired my body actually is. Ciaran falls to my side and wraps his arm around my waist. My leg slides between his, and my free hand relaxes over his chest. In a scary way, our bodies fit together perfectly. My curves fill in the harder planes of his. I bite my lip and keep these thoughts to myself. I wonder again, for the hundredth time, if I can survive this Midwest Boy and keep my heart in one piece.

# #Fourteen

*Ciaran*

Saylor is officially in my head. I can't breathe or think straight, and it's becoming an issue. Even though I visit her every night, I hate being away from her during the day. Not even the guilt I should feel when my best friend is around is enough to stop the storm inside me. She's addicting and maddening. She doesn't want me to claim her publicly, wants to be my friend and still allows me to shove my tongue down her throat on a nightly basis, while she grinds her pussy against me, and I have to stop myself from reverting back to my fourteen-year-old hormonal ways.

The tension when I'm around the guys, though, has become too much. Without me having to say it, I know they know something has shifted in my dynamics with the demon princess. My own monster likes her too much. He's pussy whipped, without even actually having a taste. I settle every night just for her lips and her body against mine. I sound like some sappy lead in a romcom, and I hate it, but I like her more. She's mine. My enemy wrapped in a small package of fuck you attitude and purple hair.

I bend over the engine of the car we're working on, my eyes briefly catching Kai's. His eyes widen, and he nods at me mouthing *Just do it already*. I drop my gaze back to the engine, concentrating on the right words to say. I'm about to break many years' worth of pacts that were made over PB&J sandwiches, the first joint we snuck together, and the first night we got wasted when we were thirteen.

"She's in my head." The words fall out of my mouth, and I instantly want to take them back. The delivery was not so smooth. It definitely sounded better in my head. I clear my throat when Si pulls back, turning to face me. He rubs his hands in the oil rag. Kai's arms cross over his chest, and he's watching intently. "Saylor, I mean." Fuck my words suck today. Not like he wasn't going to know who I meant.

I watch a myriad of emotions flash over his face: anger, betrayal, and acceptance, before he shuts it down. His jaw locks, and his eyes zone out. It's a look I've seen many times. Usually when anything touches on his past, Si will shut down. He nods while his feet step back.

"You're okay with this, too, Liu?" He addresses Kai, while his steely blank eyes never leave mine.

Kai's arms drop. "You both need to settle this and put it to bed. She's *not* her mom *or* her dad."

Silas nods his head aggressively, backing farther away from us, as if our presence is painful and too much. "I see how it is."

"Si—"

"Nah," he shakes his head, "You'll learn, Jakobe, you'll learn." He stalks out of the garage. A few moments later, the sound of his truck peeling out of the lot can be heard.

"That went well," Kai says sarcastically.

"Shut up," I tell him, before going back to the project in front of me. Now that Silas left, it's going to take all night to finish setting this ride up, and Matt asked for it to be ready by tomorrow.

"Are you serious, though?" he asks, his head tilting like he's trying to decode one of his stupid transcripts.

I don't answer, just flick my eyes to his then back to the engine. I'm at a loss for words, just like the first night she asked me about my feelings. When she asked for my favorite color and food. Mundane things, yet, I had to remind myself she doesn't know me. I may have an endless file on her, but to her, I'm a stranger. I'm a mystery, but, damn, that girl is wasting no time unraveling me. I've let her in more than anyone else in the past ten years. Next to Kai and Silas, she now knows me the third best.

I doubt even Matt knows that I love fruits, let alone my favorite color or that I'd rather watch a comedy over a horror film. Matt is my uncle, and I love him, but we aren't close. I do the work he asks of me, and in return, he leaves me alone and ignores when I'm not home at a decent time on a school night.

"Well, we're not about to go out and get matching tattoos or anything. I'm not planning any big Valentine's date." I give him that tiny bit of information. They may now know she's on my mind, but they don't need to know the extent to which she's wrapping herself around me.

Kai's lost in his thoughts when I look back up at him. The worry line that creases his forehead is there. His one major tell that he's deeply disturbed by something.

"What?" I ask. Something is clicking too fast in that genius brain of his.

"Fuck," he mutters, bringing his hands up to cup his neck.

"Dude." I stand back, my hands twisting around the wrench.

"She's supposed to tell you," Kai winces. I freeze, waiting for him to continue.

"Well, she didn't, so maybe you should," I bite the words out. For a brief moment, I'm almost wondering if Silas' point has already been made.

"It would be better if you heard it," he clips out, running a hand through his hair. He nods his head toward the office. I follow behind, my heart rate accelerating. I can feel the adrenaline pumping in my veins. Whatever it is, I know I'm not going to like it.

We walk in, and he brings a computer screen to life. A few clicks later and a box opens. "One minute," he mutters, his eyes moving from one screen to another.

I'm about to ask what the hell he means when Saylor's voice cuts through the audio.

"O?" Her voice sounds sad and so filled with hope that I pause.

"Oh my God, Say!" Another girl's voice answers.

My gaze flashes to Kai. "Take it down," I order. Anger radiates over my frame. My stomach tightens with realization.

"Just wait," Kai pleads. I'm about to tell him off when I hear the sob on her line.

"I miss you," she chokes out. Her friend, on the other line, is crying, too.

"I thought you were dead. Your house," her voice trails off.

"I didn't know if anyone knew," Saylor answers. "It wasn't on the news."

"They're keeping it hush hush," Oaklynn answers.

"Who?" Saylor asks, her voice so small. I lean forward to listen and even Kai stops breathing.

"I don't know. The investigators, I think. Maybe Nash's parents. My mom tried really hard to get it to that level, but it kept getting covered up. I thought you were dead, Say. We were going to offer a reward for information, but they wouldn't let us," she explains hurriedly. Saylor's intake of breath is sharp and audible.

"Doesn't matter, I'm just glad you got the phone," she replies. I can hear the difference in her voice, the happiness.

"You scared the living shit out of me. I've been waiting for weeks to open it, scared that pictures of your dead body would be on there or some shit like that," Oaklynn rambles.

"That's pretty gruesome," Saylor replies. I can tell, without seeing her, that she's smiling.

"So, is this #MNGirl account you?" Oaklynn asks her. I raise my brow at Kai, questioning, but he waves me off.

"Yeah," Saylor answers. "I just wanted to let you know I was alive."

"Thank fuck, Say." Her friend sounds like she's going to cry again. "I miss you, bitch."

Saylor laughs. "I miss you, too. Look, I don't have much time. My friend can only keep this line secure for short amounts of time. I'm alive, though. I'll keep posting to that account as often as I can. Until I have to close it."

"Are you coming back?" Oaklynn asks, and I freeze.

"I don't think so. It's not safe." Saylor's voice is barely a whisper when she says it.

"Say," her friend sobs a little, "Same thing next time?"

"Same thing," Saylor answers.

"Love you, wild," Oaklynn tells her.

"Love you, crazy," Saylor answers, before the line goes dead.

Kai's fingers start clicking across his keyboard. Things are decrypting and dissolving on the screen. I'm at a loss for words.

"Kai." I want to lay into him, only the anger I had been holding onto was fleeting.

"She set it all up. I told her I'd give her a clean line, so, at least, it's as safe as possible. She was really upset over her friend not knowing about her. I caved. She was supposed to tell you and Matt, though," he answers, at least trying to look guilty.

"It was safe, though?" I ask again. They're conversation, the hurt in her voice followed by pure joy is slowly killing something inside me.

"Yeah," Kai replies, going back to clicking his screen.

"What's this #MNGirl thing?" I ask.

Kai chuckles. "Oh, I'll save that for your girlfriend to answer."

"She's not my girlfriend," I shoot back. I hate labels. I barely understand my own feelings, right now, and Saylor is in the same boat. We agreed not to label or define what we're doing until we've had some time to figure it out. I like that about her, too.

"Yeah, yeah," Kai answers, "we better get back out there."

I nod and follow him out of the office to the garage. I check around the room, making sure we really are alone. No one else is scheduled tonight. Years of training, though, has heightened my sensitivity. After what I just saw and heard, the last thing I need is someone here, knowing about it, too. The less people, the better.

"No one else knows about that, right?" I ask, not liking the way his face tightens. "Just you, Ariel, and me?"

"And Reed." Kai winces when he says the name. My hands ball into fists. Of all people, it would be Reed. Kai did say she told him she figured it out herself, and while I do believe she is smart, there is no way she'd have known how to pull that off.

"Fucking great," I breathe out, before hurling the wrench against the back door.

"Talk to her," Kai admonishes, sprinting over to pick it up.

I give him a scathing look, while he holds his hands up in surrender. There were many things I had been imagining doing to Saylor when I got home tonight. Talking to her about her little escapades was not one of them.

The rest of the evening passes slowly. Silas never returns. Kai and I work in silence. I'm pissed, and he knows it. At least he stays quiet. The drive home sets me on edge. I go back and forth between being pissed off at Saylor, wanting to shake her, to feeling bad for the girl who lost everything after witnessing her mom's assault. Black and white is how we operate within Rogue. It's what I've been trained to do, the lens I've been forced to look through. Since Saylor's arrival, everything has become shades of grey. She's everything my mind has been taught not to do.

The lights are still on when I pull into the driveway. I send a small prayer to the big guy upstairs that Matt won't get back until tomorrow before he leaves again. He's been taking more trips out of town than usual. Not that I'm complaining. It just gives me more alone time with Saylor.

I find her alone in her room, laying on her stomach, with a textbook sprawled out in front of her. She looks up and does a double take. Her chocolate eyes widen. Whatever she saw on my face has her scrambling to her knees. In only a t-shirt and leggings she looks beautiful and a small part of the anger I'm holding onto slips away.

"Hey." Her voice is timid. Guilt laces her words, and I cock my head to the side, wondering if she feels that way because she did it or if it's because she doesn't feel bad about it.

I look away from her, needing the time to sort my thoughts. Even after hours of contemplating what I was going to say, I have no words. I made a fatal mistake letting my emotions put me in this position. I'm already in too deep. She may not know it, but this is tearing me up inside.

I slide my phone from my pocket and open the account I found on Instagram that she created with Reed's help. It's so embedded that I can see how Kai was able to conclude she didn't do it on her own.

"Is this you?" I ask, holding up her latest picture, where she's pointing to the time on her watch. The exact same time she asked Kai to open a secure line for her today. Her face pales. To her credit, though, she doesn't back down. Her spine straightens and that small pointed chin lifts.

"Yes," she answers, her voice hoarse but strong. I almost wish she had lied to me, so, at least, I could stay mad at her.

"What were the rules, Princess?" I ask, unzipping my sweater and hanging it over her chair. Her throat bobs with emotion. Her eyes shine, but she holds her tears in check.

"Don't stand out, stay under the radar and--"

"And don't make stupid decisions. Think smarter. Under no circumstances contact anyone from your previous life," I practically growl at her. She has no idea the danger she potentially put, not just herself, but the others in.

"What were you going to do if the people looking for your family were watching Oaklynn and *her* family?" I can tell my question startles her. Her skin takes on a greenish tinge. The thought makes her sick, and I can tell by the way her brain spins that she didn't think that part over.

"I did everything I could to make the package not look suspicious. It's been weeks, and nothing's happened. I thought," her voice breaks. My chest squeezes involuntarily. "I thought it would be fine."

I scoff. "You had no way of knowing that, Saylor. You not only could have compromised yourself and our whole operation, you could put her entire family in danger. Don't you think there's a reason why your disappearance hasn't been reported? It's being covered up. Who are the people they are going to watch the closest?"

"Friends and family," she mumbles, and the tears finally flow free. She's getting it. And I still feel like an asshole having to tear her down like this.

"You can't do it again. Post to your little account or whatever, but no more calls." I shake my head. "Kai's good, but it's still risky."

Her head falls in defeat. I've won this round; yet, it still feels like I lost. She shuts down in front of me, closing herself off in agony. The hairs on my neck start to rise in reaction. I don't want her to shut me out. I realize it makes me a hypocrite because I'm so hell-bent on sharing as little about myself and my emotions as possible. Still, the minute she starts to build a wall around her, my mind spirals for a way to break it down, to demolish and destroy it.

I stalk over to her and grab her face between my hands; she gasps before my lips crash onto hers. She resists, at first, making the victory that much sweeter when her lips finally surrender, letting me in. I kiss the shit out of her, wanting to bruise her mouth, mark her, anything to keep her from trying to shut me out. I envelop her, crowd her space, and force her body into mine. So far, we've been keeping things over the clothes, while we figure this shit out between us. Tonight, I'm not so sure I can keep my monster from devouring his demon princess.

I force her off her knees until she's lying underneath me; a soft whimper escapes her mouth, as she also realizes things are about to cross a line we definitely can't come back from. Stolen kisses and sharing favorites in the dark is elementary compared to where my thoughts are heading.

Her eyes open to see me watching her. The rich brown color is almost swallowed up when her pupils dilate. From chocolate to oil. They say when a person sees something they like or is attracted to that this will happen. I can't take my eyes off of her. My breathing shallows out, and I have to mentally talk myself down from rushing too fast. I want her in a way I've never felt for another person.

Reclining back on my knees, my fingers graze her sides, pulling the thin fabric of her t-shirt up and over her head. The motion causes her tits to bounce free. I close my eyes to keep my dick in check. Rowdy fucker has a mind of his own when it comes to Saylor. Sliding off her bed and to my feet, I reach back and pull my own shirt over my head, never looking away from her. Her cheeks turn pink, the blush chasing down her chest, creating little splotches everywhere.

"If we do this, things are going to change," I try to rein everything in on the chance she isn't ready. Her eyes glance over my bare skin, dragging up my torso, before holding my gaze. Flames dance in the depths of her eyes, momentarily stealing my breath. Her teeth sink into her bottom lip.

"I know." The words slip from her mouth quietly. My eye brow rises.

"You look nervous." I lean toward her and place kisses along her neck and collarbone.

"I'm not nervous," she answers quickly, her voice becoming husky, "it's not my first time but,"

"But, what?" I pull back, forcing her eyes to mine. The air shifts around us, emotions coiled in my stomach tighten in knots.

"This *is* going to change things. We probably shouldn't, but I want you." Her words are my undoing.

"I want you, too," I reply, before leaning over her again and silencing her with another kiss to her lips.

I easily hook my index finger into her leggings and pull them down in one fell swoop. My head slants, taking in the fact that she isn't wearing anything underneath.

"The princess likes going commando," I chuckle softly.

"Bite me, Jakobe," she huffs, from her prone position on the bed. Her eyes are roaming all over me, taking everything in, and I know she's not actually mad. It's a façade, just like when I pretend to hate her.

"I plan to, Baby." The words sound gruff coming from my mouth that I barely recognize it. If it's possible, her cheeks turn redder as her chest falls and lifts rapidly. The tip of her tongue darts out to wet her bottom lip. Purple locks of hair now fall loose around her face while she holds my gaze. "You're so beautiful, Say."

Without taking my eyes off hers, I sink to my knees at the side of her bed. My hands land on her hips and drag her forward. She lets out a burst of air that quickly turns to a moan, the minute my lips graze against the sensitive skin on the inside of her thigh. I repeat the same pattern, biting, sucking, kissing on both sides, until she can't lay still anymore, and she's wet, so fucking wet. I slide my fingers between her folds, enjoying the way her hips buck into my hand, eager for more. Her head falls back, and her eyes close, when I start fucking her with my index and middle fingers, swirling her clit with my thumb. Her legs tense, before falling over my shoulders on their own, like they were made to be there, just like my shoulders were sculpted to hold them perfectly in place.

"That's my little demon," I whisper against her flesh, before replacing my hand with my tongue. Of course, Saylor tastes better than I could have imagined. I have to close my mind off from the way she grinds against me, seeking out the orgasm she knows I'm going to give her.

*Don't come. Don't come. Don't come.*

The wind kicks branches against the outside of the house, reminding me how frigid it is out there. In here, though, things are burning up like an inferno.

"Ci, I'm going to..." She bites on her bottom lip, at the same time I suck her hard little clit into my mouth, and she comes so hard, she yells my name and draws blood from the lip held hostage between her teeth.

I pop up the second her hips stop seeking my face and grab the condom from my wallet on the floor. I roll it on and line up the tip with her entrance, before leaning over her and wrapping those lilac strands around my fist. Her head snaps to me, her eyes unfocused and her lips definitely bruised. My mouth crashes over hers, my tongue sliding against hers, forcing her to taste how delicious she is.

Her hands come up to grip my shoulders, and I shift my hips until my cock slides all the way inside her in one go, burying myself to the hilt. She groans in pleasure and not pain. Crazy thoughts fill my mind while I pump my hips in and out of her. Things like I'll be the last one she ever has, I'll ruin her for anyone else, and that she's made for me. All these feelings swirl inside my chest until they threaten to rip me apart from the inside. I fight to regain my control and remind myself who exactly I'm fucking right now, I don't want to scare her, but my monster is too far gone. He loves how she feels and the grip she has around my dick, so hard and so tight, that my balls tense up sooner than I want.

I have to pull back to watch her face. Our eyes clash, the molten chocolate of hers burns me alive. Even as I try to hold part of myself at a distance, she is still fighting to bring us closer together with a fire under her touch. Scorching my skin and branding what's left of my soul. She's melting the hardened pieces I keep locked away. I only last a few more minutes before I come, the hardest I've ever in my life, following after her and emptying into the condom.

Decorum probably states I should roll off her to let her breathe, but I can't force myself to pull away from her contact. Our stomachs are slick and slide against each other easily. I wonder, for only a second, what she's going to think once she learns the truth about Rogue and the twisted history connected to her mom. I should tell her now; instead, I force her head up to mine and give her another hard kiss. Her hands wind around my neck again, holding me to her. It's the final nail in my coffin. There is no escaping from me now, Princess.

# #Fifteen

*Saylor*

After that first night with Ciaran, we've done a one-eighty flip. I can't keep my hands off him when he's around, and he's the same with me. Even at school, where we've agreed is a no-go zone, he finds small ways to touch me. His fingers graze mine in the hallway, he accidentally grinds against my butt in the lunch line, small things that send a livewire connection right to my core. His eyes never leave me. He finds me the minute I walk into the same space he's in, and I find him, too. With my lashes lowered, I practically stalk him during the lunch period. While we agreed not to cling to each other at school or be open about this budding *friendship* between us, my heart jumps around in my chest when he keeps other girls at a distance now.

Over this past week, Matt has been home more often again, which has made him sneaking into my room more of a challenge. When we happen to be home in the evenings together, it feels like we're on borrowed time. Work has suddenly picked up momentum, which feels like a bad omen. I check any chance I get on my mom and sister's dot on the board in Matt's basement. Every time, the light is shining bright.

It's finally the weekend again, and Ciaran tells me I'm going with him and the guys ice fishing up at the Ridge. Kai is excited about it and sends me texts all week, trying to goad me into a competition for the biggest catch. Loser has to down three straight shots of tequila. He's grown on me, and I think he's accepting of my position in Ciaran's life. It's Silas who still has a problem. While he doesn't call me out in public or sneer at me from across the room anymore, he isn't exactly friendly either. If anything, he goes out of his way to continue ignoring me. At first, it hurt my feelings, but now, I'm only worried he's hurting Ciaran. I never want Ci to feel he's in the position to choose between us. A, because I know he won't choose me and B, I would never recover from the loss. He's become as essential to be as air and that scares the shit out of me. It's a secret I plan to take to the grave.

When I wake up Saturday morning, the sun is shining for once. The reflection of the snow is almost blinding, and I need my square frame sunglasses just to avoid a headache. Jumping out of bed, I quickly throw on the clothes Ciaran said I'd need and grab the bag I had packed before bed. After brushing my teeth and securing my hair in its usual top-knot, I make my way down to the kitchen. The room smells delicious. My eyes widen in surprise to see Matt at the stove. I wasn't aware he was home again.

"Take a seat, Gossip Girl," Kai calls from the direction of the table, which is when I notice that all three boys are sitting and waiting. Their eyes all follow me as I sit in one of the empty chairs. Ciaran's eyes narrow on me because I took the one next to Kai and not him. Kai loves it and smirks. Matt serves up plates of food and sits with us. They talk about the shop, orders and extractions. I can tell they're tiptoeing around how much information to share with me. On some level, I'm bothered by this, and yet, also grateful. I'm not ready to completely immerse myself into their world when I plan on checking out at some point.

After breakfast, I help Matt clear the dishes, while the guys pack up all the bags and supplies and hook the trailer to Ciaran's truck.

"Have fun," Matt says, skeptically, when I head for the door.

"Why? What's wrong?" I question, feeling uneasy with the look on his face.

His shoulders lift and an easy grin pulls his lips apart. "Your mom wasn't one for ice fishing," his eyes fade to the past, "I wonder if you'll be the same."

I roll my eyes. My mom hated anything that had to do with the outdoors and nature. Sometimes, I'm surprised she lived this life and wonder if that's part of the reason she decided to leave it behind. She was way more comfortable in our living room working on a crossword all weekend than camping, fishing, or even renting a boat on the Fourth of July at the Hamptons. Just remembering her brings a smile to my lips. Even with her quirks, I love her.

"I miss her," I tell Matt, knowing he'll understand.

"They're doing well," he assures me, and it works. I'm building somewhat of a life here, while away from my family. Knowing they're in a good spot eases the guilt that I'm happy, too, even when they're gone.

"Let's go, Ariel!" Silas yells inside, sounding irritated. I frown, not missing the way he continues to use my fake name, even when it's just us.

"He'll get over it," Matt pipes up.

"Yeah," I nod. "Right." I grab my jacket, hat and gloves, before sliding my feet into some snow boots.

The drive up to the Ridge goes better than planned. It probably helped that I chose to sit in the back with Kai and didn't talk much the whole way up, unless I was forced to. Ciaran drives the long way around until we pull into a parking lot where a sign reads boat launch. My hand moves toward the handle to get out.

"What are you doing?" Kai questions, watching me.

"Getting out so we haul all this stuff," I answer. All three of them howl with laughter, until I'm ready to smack them.

"That's cute, Gossip Girl," Kai gasps between laughs. I'm about to open my mouth and let them have it when I realize we're driving over the ice to the middle of the lake.

"What the actual fuck!" I roll my window down and stick my head outside, confirming what I see.

Silas snickers from his seat upfront. "How did you think we'd get out on the ice?"

"Walk!" I practically yell, my eyes swinging over all of them, "Like normal people. What if this big ass truck falls through? We're all going to die."

"Relax." Ciaran's icy blue gaze connects with mine in his rearview mirror. "The ice is hella thick. My truck isn't going to break through it."

"Yeah, relax," I mumble under my breath, my eyes squeeze shut, and I force my mind not to think about it. *One, Two, Three, Four....*

"I think we broke her," Kai jokes next to me.

I ignore them and the way they try to bait me, keeping my eyes closed. Maybe if I don't see it then it's not really happening. After what seems like forever, the truck comes to a stop. Their doors pop open, and they hop out. My body is frozen in fear.

"Are you going to stay in here?" Silas asks, suddenly next to my window. "If you're inside the vehicle, and it falls through the ice, you're going to have a helluva time getting out."

My eyes snap open with new panic, and I spring from the truck. Silas laughs again. "Glad to be your entertainment," I remark snidely. He walks away, shaking his head.

They roll the ice house off the trailer and work on securing it in place. I stand outside, regarding it like another death trap.

"You need to chill." Ciaran's mouth is right next to my ear, his breath warm against the cold shell. Tingles spread down my arms from the sensation.

"Are you going to move your truck?" I ask, all kinds of worst-case scenarios are playing in my head.

Ciaran glances at me and back to the truck, putting together where my thoughts have gone. "Having my truck next to us isn't going to cause the ice to break."

"You don't know that," I tell him, shaking my head.

His jaw clicks, before he reaches into his pocket and takes out his keys. He stomps angrily to the truck and hops in.

"Are you serious?" Silas asks from beside him.

"Would you rather she continues to shout and be hysterical out here? She's scaring all the fish away," Ciaran answers. I stick my tongue out.

His idea of far away and mine are clearly not the same. I swear he only moved it a few feet from the ice house. Enough distance for the band around my heart to cease, yet not far enough away to allow my body to relax. After a lot of convincing, Ciaran finally gets me inside the ice house. It's larger than I imagined. The middle of the room has two holes dug and scooped out. Silas and Kai are both sitting in fold out chairs with their poles in one hand and a beer in their other. There is a small countertop area and a set of bunk beds on both ends. Despite the chill outside, the space is actually warm.

Ciaran takes an empty chair and uses his free hand to pull me down onto his lap. I tense when Kai and Silas watch us. This is the most public display of attention he's given me, and it's in front of his best friends. My cheeks tinge pink. Ciaran doesn't comment, he only rubs circles over my back, trying to ease the muscles. Eventually, they go back to talking amongst themselves. Kai pulls his phone from his pocket and turns on some music. My ears instantly pick up on Brantley Gilbert's "Man of Steel."

"Good song," I murmur to myself. Kai hears me, though.

"You like country?" he asks. Genuine curiosity laces his tone, making me feel more comfortable.

I shrug. "I like a little of everything."

"Same." Kai smiles. "Some of his stuff is the best to rip chords to." He strums his fingers on an air guitar, and I laugh. "Speaking of, that one blonde chick, the one with Rhodes. She's after me again to play for their stupid talent show act."

"Didn't she do that last year, too, after you told her 'no' a hundred times?" Silas asks.

"Yes! I had to publicly turn her down to get it through her head I wasn't doing it." Kai shakes his head, scoffing at the memory.

The hours tick by with them mostly making small talk. I learn from their interactions that Kai is the peacekeeper. Silas is genuinely more hot-headed, and he's also the first one to throw down a bet or a good joke. Ciaran rarely engages. He prefers to sit back and let them talk, only offering his voice when requested or he has something important to say. He emits dominance and control, even in his close group of friends, the guys he trusts with his life. A new appreciation for their bond starts to form. I instantly miss Oaklynn again but shut that thought down as soon as it arises. I haven't set up another call, just like I promised, and I have no plans to go back on my word. Ciaran could have ruined me that night. I gave him the key to the kingdom to have me sent away. Besides chewing me out when he found out, he hasn't mentioned it again.

"Aiden just got here." Kai leans across to show Silas his phone. Silas' eyes glance at the screen.

"Let's go." They stand up and reel in their hooks.

"Where are we going?" I ask, turning to face Ciaran.

"They're leaving." He nods to the guys. Silas averts his eyes while Kai gives me a shit eating grin.

"No offense!" He puts his hands up. "But I'm not about to share a hut with the two of you tonight. All the sexual tension in here is making me horny."

Silas reaches out and slaps Kai upside the head. "Move."

Kai laughs and follows him out the door, calling over his shoulder, "Have a fun night, kids. Remember, no love without a glove!"

"Jesus," Ciaran groans, while I laugh.

"They didn't have to leave," I tell him, feeling unsure of myself. "We could go to the party, too, if you want," I offer.

He turns me in his lap until my chest is resting against his and my legs dangle on either side of the chair, straddling his lap. His hands rest on my hips, before reaching up to push my coat off my shoulders. I watch him, watching me, loving the red flush that appears high on his cheekbones, and his eyes glaze with desire. He's so beautiful, my chest squeezes before beating wildly in my chest. Ciaran reaches up and pulls the hat from my head, running his fingers down the long strands of my hair.

Tentatively, I reach my fingers out to his jaw, gripping it in my palm, before sliding my fingers across the sharp angles. His jaw is so powerful, it could cut glass.

"Why do you like ice fishing?" I ask, keeping my voice light.

He shrugs. "It's quiet. We get to chill away from everyone and let things go." I nod, taking his words to heart. Thinking about the pressure these boys are under, the positions they've been thrust into, it has to take a toll on them.

"Why do you want to take over Rogue? It always sounds like the place is tearing you in half, but you still want it for yourself someday. Why not leave?" I question, my fingers continuing their dance over his cheeks, his nose, his perfectly thick and shaped eyebrows and down over his lips.

"For them. The families, kids...they need us. When your own government can't keep you safe; sometimes, you have to go rogue." His eyes lock on mine, his fingers twisting in the material of my sweatshirt. Before I can blink, he whips it off over my head, until I'm sitting in my jeans, boots and bra. The chill creeps over my exposed skin, tingling my skin with goosebumps and hardening my nipples.

Ciaran's lips touch my neck and collarbone, sprinkling light kisses up and down. I squirm in his lap, which only makes him groan.

"What was your favorite meal your mom made when you were a kid?" I ask, breathless, my thoughts starting to scatter.

"Mac and cheese," he answers quickly.

I laugh. "For real?"

"My mom can't cook for shit." He shrugs. "Love the woman to death, but if it wasn't for my grandma, we would have starved. Plus, my mom worked nights at the hospital when I was young, and it was rare we ate together."

"What about now?" I question further.

Ciaran laughs. "She still can't cook. I think she tried to learn once, and it didn't go well. Matt banned her from the kitchen. She's gone a lot, but when she is home, we try to take her out to eat or we grill. I guess I really love steaks."

"Mmm," I answer, my head tilting back to give his lips better access while thinking over the information he shared.

"What did your cooks make?" He asks, quirking an eyebrow at me.

I roll my eyes, before pushing him back into a seated position. "You know I was only really rich for the past few years, right? I didn't grow up that way. My mom always cooked our dinners. She makes a wicked lasagna."

We eye each other. His hands rest against the bare skin on my back. "I forgot," he admits. My shoulders lift before I lean in to press a light kiss against his lips. I'd rather not fight with Ciaran. Soon, his lips move with mine, and his tongue dips into my mouth, running along my own. We tangle and fight against each other. My arms wind around his neck, and my legs squeeze against him. It literally looks like I'm trying to burrow his body into mine.

Ciaran stands, his hands flexing around my butt, holding me in place against him. My legs lock around his waist while he carries me over to the bottom bed. My back hits the rail as I'm propped against it. His hoodie comes off, followed by his t-shirt. My fingers greedily scrape and pull against the skin he's just bared to me. He grunts, before his hand dips between us, and opens me wider. My legs drop suddenly, and the jeans I'm wearing hit the floor with his. He sighs in frustration, before coming back to my boy shorts and yanking them down, too. I'm picked up again, this time, my center rubs along the ridges of his washboard abs, leaving my wetness against his skin.

"Fuck," he breathes out against my mouth, finally pulling away. We're both breathing hard, taking each other in, and I can't get enough. I want to be closer. Over him, under him, next to him, it doesn't matter.

Ciaran turns to sit on the edge of the bed, situating my legs, so I'm straddling him again. He hands me a foil packet, and I waste no time opening the condom and rolling it down his erection, before lining us up and sliding down his length in one go. He fills me to the brim, stretching and creating a delicious ache in my abdomen. I start to grind against him, alternating kisses between lifting and lowering myself back down onto him. Beads of sweat trickle down my back from trying to stay in control, to make the connection last as long as possible. His blue orbs are wild beneath hooded eyes. His lips swollen from the kisses and pulls my mouth has taken from them.

We move in rhythm, kissing, touching, and biting. The air turns thick with the smell of sex. All I can feel, see, smell and touch is Ciaran. The first wave of my orgasm chases into another, buckling my body forward, when it crashes.

"Fuck, Saylor, *Fuck*!" His hips jolt up against me, bouncing my breasts against his chest, as he chases his own release, grinding against me as he empties into the condom.

My head drops to his shoulder, exhaustion taking over. For the first time today, my body is completely relaxed. Ciaran rolls me onto the bed and pulls the covers up around me. I watch as he walks, naked, to the trash and wraps the condom in a paper towel, before shoving it out of sight. He comes back to me and slides under the covers. The bunks are barely a twin size. His long body curls around mine, blocking the chilled air. I bury my head under his chin. It doesn't take long before his breathing lulls me into unconsciousness.

### ###

The next morning, Ciaran wakes us up early enough for one more round of desperate, on the verge of meaningful, intense sex. We're close to crossing that boundary when 'just sex' becomes making love. At least for me anyway. Every time we touch, a new wave of lust burns through me. I'm terrified that, at this rate, I'll never be able to let him go someday. After, we scramble to get dressed and air out the room before the guys return. Kai was kind enough to send a warning text a half hour ago.

When they do get back, Kai grins widely and waggles his eyebrows at me. "Shut up." I push him away, which only earns more laughter. Silas looks pissed at the world and disappointed, like he lost a high stakes bet. I try not to examine how that makes me feel. We waste no time getting back to Savage Lakes and unpacking. Matt isn't home, but he did leave a note, telling the guys to get to the garage when they get back. I end the night alone, in my room, with leftover pizza and an English paper. Between last night and this morning, Ciaran wore me out, and I can't even keep my eyes open to wait up for him.

The next morning, I wake up alone, Ciaran's usual scent gone from my pillow. My lips pull down in a frown. He must not have come home last night. I quickly shower and get ready for school. One look around the kitchen confirms that neither of the guys came back last night. I try not to think too hard about the fact I spent all night completely alone in the house. My hand slams to my chest when a horn honks outside. I peek out the window to find Winter parked in front of my house. I quickly grab my bag and lock up.

We catch up on our weekends during the drive. Winter's jaw drops when she finds out I spent the weekend with the guys. "All three of them?" she asks again.

"Stop saying it like that." I roll my eyes, laughing at what she's insinuating.

"I'm sorry, it's just never happened that one girl, any girl or a group of girls, for that matter, has ever spent time alone with them," she explains. For some reason, her words warm my heart. I can't say that Kai and Silas were happy to be around me, but they didn't flat out ignore me or be rude to me either.

Pulling into the parking lot, I notice that none of their vehicles are here yet. My fingers itch to send a text to Ciaran, asking him if everything is okay. I push it down, frowning, thinking it would be something a real girlfriend would do. We still haven't made any decisions on what we're doing, but Ciaran has been adamant he doesn't want to have the boyfriend, girlfriend label. I tuck my phone back in my pocket and ignore the uncertainty coursing through my mind. I replay the events from the weekend over in my memory. Nothing was out of the ordinary. The car ride home was just as uneventful as the ride up. There was no sign I did anything that could have pissed Ciaran off for him to ignore me.

After the first three hours and lunch, I've still not seen any of the guys. I finally cave and send a generic *you alive?* text to Ciaran. It is delivered and opened, but he doesn't respond. As soon as lunch is over, I'm up out of my seat and sprinting to my locker. The irrational idea to skip the rest of the day and head to Rogue's Car Repairs infiltrates my mind. I'm about to grab my jacket when a chest pushes against my arm. My head snaps in his direction, only to find Bentley standing there instead of who I wanted it to be.

"Can I help you?" I ask, wondering why he's at my locker and invading my space. My feet shuffle to the side, trying to put some distance between us.

His lips crack into a blinding smile. "Haven't talked to you in a while, Waters. You weren't at the party this weekend either. Come to think of it, neither was your boy, Jakobe." His fingers drum against his lips.

I fight to keep my face neutral, pulling that mask of indifference back on. It's been so long since I've worn it, I almost forgot how it feels to pretend not to care. "What a coincidence." I shrug, acting like his words humor me more than anything.

Bentley's eyes narrow. My reaction is not at all what he wanted. His hand lands on my forearm, yanking me to him. I'm about to scream, when a fist flies to the side of his head. Bentley rears back, letting me go, cupping his face. Blood pours out the side of his mouth. Ciaran stands in front of me, Kai and Silas off to the side, ready to jump in if needed. By now, there is a crowd gathering. I force myself to stand still and not reach out for Ciaran.

"How many more times do I have to tell you not to touch what's mine, Rhodes?" Ciaran taunts, before slamming his leg up into Bentley's face. The impact causes him to fall backward on the ground, Ciaran towering above him. "You fucking touch her one more time, I'll break both your arms. We'll see how far you get in your college football career then. Stay the fuck away from her."

Bentley shuffles to his feet, his eyes wild, and teeth bloody. "Yours, huh?" He spits at the ground. My breath hitches when it clicks for me, too. Ciaran just claimed me in front of a large chunk of the student body. Our relationship is against the rules. Bentley shoulders his way past the crowd, leaving everyone behind.

I keep my eyes on the floor, my heart beating out of rhythm. Ciaran looks ready to step in my direction, before Silas curses and leaves out the side door. Kai jogs after him, followed by Ciaran. Without thinking, I chase after them, too. I follow them into the parking lot where Silas and Ciaran look like they're about to go head to head. Kai stands between them, a hand on each of their chests.

"Please stop!" I beg, tears gathering in my eyes. I don't want to destroy them. I can't hurt Ciaran this way.

"Go back inside," Ciaran yells in my direction. I ignore him and keep stepping forward.

"You should listen to your family wrecking girlfriend, Ci," Silas growls back. The sting of his words feel like a slap to the face.

"Shut your mouth, Si," Ciaran barks back. For the first time, he looks unhinged. Guilt spreads through my veins like wildfire. I won't be my dad. I won't destroy lives.

"I'm sorry, Silas," I yell, pulling all of their attention to me and off each other. "Whatever my family did to yours, I'm sorry. I had no way of stopping it. You guys can't let this happen to each other, though. What do I need to do to fix it?"

"You want to fix it." Silas takes a few steps toward me, and Kai scrambles to keep him from reaching me. I shrink back from the look of pure hate and rage dancing in his eyes. "Leave. That's how you fix it. Everything you touch, everything your family touches is ruined."

I struggle to breathe. Ciaran's head hangs down, defeated. Like he believes what Silas just said. Like he thinks the same things about me. Kai and Ciaran don't argue with him or defend me.

I shake my head. "I can't right now, Silas, even if I wanted to. I can't go---."

He pulls out of Kai's hold and stomps over to his truck, cutting me off. A sob escapes my throat, my face in agony with embarrassment. I sprint back into the school and away from the boy who just broke another piece of my heart with his quiet defense for his friend. It no longer matters that he claimed me just minutes before. He may want me, but he'll never choose me over Silas. I won't destroy their friendship. And the truth is, eventually, we'll go our separate ways anyhow. He's graduating soon. I have no idea when my expiration date is in Minnesota, but at some point, I'll be leaving, too.

I grab my jacket and bag out of my locker and dip out the door again. My heart pounds so loudly in my chest, it aches after being stomped all over. Blood rushes in my ears, blocking out all noise, except for my erratic breathing. I'm desperate to get away. My eyes burn with unshed tears when I finally make it to the fence and hop over. My feet jog over the ice and snow until I reach the main road. Once I know where I am, it's easier to walk. I pull my iPod from my pocket and press the headphones in place. I listen to Natalie Taylor's "Surrender" on repeat, until I reach my destination. Once I get to the clearing by the lake, I slip my watch off and change the time. I take my phone out and snap a pic of my watch surrounded by my hair and post it to #MNGirl. Within minutes, the post is liked. My chest heaves. I fall to my knees and sit back on the edge of my jacket to keep from getting completely wet and hug my legs to my chest.

Time slips by, and before I know it, my phone vibrates in my pocket. I swipe up to accept the call.

"S?" Her voice filters through the phone. I sob in reply. We sit while I cry. She keeps talking, telling me stories and letting me get it all out.

"I'm sorry," I croak and wince at the sound.

"It's okay," Oaklynn responds, "Is there anything I can do?"

"No," I give a watery chuckle, "I just needed my best friend."

"I'm always here for you, Babe," she responds. Her phone bumps and rubs against fabric. I hear her voice muffled, and she sounds like she's walking. "Sorry, I had to change rooms. Ollie is home on break, so, of course, he's always around."

"How is Ollie?" I ask. Her twin brother attends a prestigious school in England. He's rarely home, but when he is, Oaklynn loves spending time with him. They're close, and I know the distance hurts her.

"Same old, same old." She laughs lightly. "He, uh, he's actually been spending a lot of time with Nash."

"Nash?" I ask, noticing that his name doesn't affect me anymore like it used to, only months ago.

"Yeah," she explains, "You know they were friends before Ollie left. He's been here almost every day since Ollie's been back."

"Well, that's nice for them at least," I reply.

"Nash has been weird since you disappeared," Oaklynn rushes out. "At first, he was mopey. He was fighting everyone who had something negative to say about you or your family. Now, he's here all the time, and I swear him and Ollie have brought you up to my parents a handful of times now. My mom even was contemplating going back to the authorities." Her voice gets lower during the last few parts, like she's trying to keep quiet, so no one can hear her.

"Well, that's nice of your parents and Ollie to be concerned," I tell her. My feelings about Nash swirl in my chest. I wait for the usual tension to appear. If you had asked me six months ago, I would have sworn he could be the love of my life. Now, I realize how stupid that was. I replay that last night over again and how he ghosted me by not showing up.

"Nash probably just feels guilty he didn't show up and then I was gone. It's all honestly over with now. I know we weren't meant to be together," I explain, the best way I can. Even while she talks about my ex-boyfriend, all I can think about is startling blue eyes and messy blond hair.

"Oh, yeah." Oaklynn giggles. "Is there a certain guy who has your attention there?"

"No," I answer too quickly, and Oaklynn practically cackles with glee.

"I just...I have no connection with Nash. I wanted to be accepted," I tell her.

"What's his name?" she asks, seeing through my bullshit, like always.

"Oak," My voice cracks with laughter.

"Is he listening?" She fires off more questions.

"God, I hope not," I laugh, not even anticipating that could be a thing.

"You really like him, huh?" Her voice is judgment free and understanding. This is what I needed. This is why I risked everything to hear her voice. Tears clog my throat again.

"I only see him, O," I break into the phone.

"Our timer is going to go off," she replies.

"I know. I'm sorry, Oak. I know this could be dangerous. I shouldn't have called," I apologize, feeling like the worst friend ever.

"Don't you dare." Her voice turns hard. "I'm not losing you for good. We promised to live in a big house someday and drink lemonade on the porch, wearing big ugly sun hats."

I laugh, remembering that pinky promise after our first time dipping into her mom's Smirnoff Ice coolers. "I promise," I tell her.

"Good," she replies. The phone starts beeping. "Love you, wild."

"Love you, crazy," I reply, before the line shuts off.

I ugly cry the entire walk back to town. It started snowing again, the huge flakes catching in my hair and swirling it around. Each time it pelts my face, the flakes melt against my hot tears. I haul my ass into Rogue's, prepared to grovel with Matt to let me stay and work. Instead, Ciaran meets me in the parking lot. My spine straightens, prepared to go to battle again. Nothing surprises me more than when his hands bury in my hair, and his mouth slams on mine. His warm lips grind against my cold ones. He kisses me hard and angry, like he wants to swallow me whole. My arms circle around his neck.

"I only see you, too," he breathes against my lips. A blush creeps up my neck to my cheeks. Those fuckers were listening. Before I can say anything, he picks me up, my feet dangling, and carries me over to his truck that is parked far enough in the back, away from anyone who may see us. He throws my body into the passenger seat and follows me in. He hits the lock, before going for my mouth again.

"Cameras?" I gasp against his lips, luckily half my brain is still working. This is twice in one day that I've seen Ciaran reckless, and I'm not sure how to handle it. He usually operates on instinct and the orders he's given.

"Kai will fix it," he assures me in-between kisses.

His hands are an unstoppable force, yanking my jacket down and ripping apart the buttons on my flannel shirt. I'm just as greedy for him, tugging his shirt and fumbling to push his joggers down. Shoes hit the floorboards in our efforts, my bra lands somewhere on the dashboard, before I'm laid back across the seats. Ciaran's body covers the top of mine, and I'm thankful for the snow covering the windshield and windows. Even though they're tinted, giving the auto shop a peep show is not on my list of things I want to do.

I barely breathe, before Ciaran slams into me, pinning me to the seat, with one hand twisted in my hair. The burn on my scalp, the dominating way he holds my body, makes me wetter for him. My back arches off the seat, his teeth pull and suck at my nipple, while his free hand squeezes and pinches the other. The sensations are too strong and too much; it pushes me right over the edge into an orgasm that steals my breath, silencing my scream and blacking out my vision momentarily. Ciaran doesn't give me a chance to recover, before his hips pick up speed, each thrust deep and penetrating. His teeth clamp down on my shoulder, and I cry out, moaning his name. When he empties inside me, a flush makes its way all over my skin.

Ciaran swoops down, dropping kisses anywhere the red patches show up. I feel him tense suddenly, my eyes follow his gaze to where we're joined.

"Shit," he mutters and looks back to me, eyes wide.

I know what he just noticed and I bite my lip. "I have the implant."

Ciaran's eyes soften again and the tension leaves his shoulders. "I've never forgotten before."

"Me either," I reassure him, while dragging my nails down his back. He groans before falling back to me. I don't know how long we stay locked together, and I don't care. I tuck my face into his neck and breathe him in. He smells like sweat, mint and his body wash. He also smells faintly like my body wash. Like mine. He's mine...for now.

# #Sixteen

*Ciaran*

I 've always wondered what one of those alarms would sound like when it goes off on that board in the basement. In the last five years I've lived with Matt, I've never experienced it. In my eighteen years, it's not been mentioned more than a handful of times that the alarm went off. I figure it out around four in the morning on a Tuesday in March. My heart jumps in my throat. Matt flies into the house, slamming doors. I jump out of bed and almost collide with Saylor in the hallway. Her eyes are big and anxious. I slam my hoodie over my head and take her hand, leading her to the basement. Matt is pulling out maps and has a cell phone to his ear, before setting it down and putting it on speaker. I grab the radio off the shelf and skip over dials.

"Channel 12," Matt instructs, pulling up his monitors. I flip to the one he wants right when Kai, Silas and Jason get into the room. Jason's eyes flick to Saylor. I grip her arm and pull her behind me, away from all of their eyes.

"Where are you now, Andy?" Matt asks.

Saylor's head snaps up, her eyes rimming red, she frantically looks to the board. Sure enough, the button on her mom and sister is blinking.

"We're just shy of the Missouri border. I couldn't stop any sooner at one of the other safe houses. I'm not sure if they're following or not. I didn't want to chance it," Andy's voice floats in the air.

"What the hell happened?" Jason demands, arms crossed, glaring at the phone.

"I have no idea," Andy answers. "I came home, and the place was trashed. I got out, picked up Kell from the flower shop, and we hightailed it to the school to get Mila. A dark van pulled away from the curb when they saw me. I started driving right away."

"Have you changed vehicles?" Matt asks, looking at his map and circling locations.

"This is the first time," Andy replies.

"How long can you drive this one for?" he asks.

"Until empty and it's a full tank...probably to the border, but it could be shy of that."

"Just drive as far as you can." Matt looks at his watch. "I'll meet you there to extract you. Don't stop for anything else if you don't have to."

"Is my mom okay?" Saylor asks, unable to hold back.

There's a slight pause before Andy answers. "They're okay, a little shaken, but okay."

Saylor's body sinks into mine. My arm wraps around her head, pulling her closer and shielding her from prying eyes. I don't miss the way Matt's gaze flicks over us or the disapproving look on his face. I keep my features straight and deadly.

Andy disconnects from the phone after giving us an ETA. Matt radios into the shop to get a rig put together with extra storage. He's bringing guns, which means he thinks things are more serious than Andy has let on.

"I'm coming with you," Jason speaks up. Silas glares at the ground, his shoulders tensing.

Matt nods, his eyes flickering over Silas, before coming back to me. "Kai, I need you on the monitors. I need open lights from Missouri to the border. I need eyes on that highway. Any car that passes the same three lights as Andy, you call it in."

"On it," Kai answers.

"Si, Ci and Saylor, I want you to get your asses to the garage. Set the house into lockdown until I get back." Matt continues rattling off instructions.

"Okay," Si and I answer at the same time. Matt and Jason race up the stairs.

"Let's leave in ten," I tell them, before ushering Saylor back upstairs. I pull her into my room.

"What's happening, Ci?' Her voice sounds small and vulnerable. She's hurting and confused. The calm before the storm.

"Matt wants us to take refuge at the garage. There's a chance the house isn't safe right now, and we need to move you," I explain to her. "Matt and Jason are going to meet Andy and your mom and Mila."

I pull one of my sweatshirts out of the closet and slip it over her head. The end hits her mid-thigh. I pull out a pair of my joggers and help her dress. She cinches the ties tightly around her waist to the point they start to look bulky. The sight makes me grin, while also squeezing my gut painfully. I like seeing my clothes on her. I like when she needs me.

"Let's go." I grab her hand and lead her out of my room and down the stairs. Kai and Silas are waiting by the door. Kai's backpack, with the necessary files, hangs off his shoulder. Silas pulls a 9mm from inside a holster that's covered by his jacket, checks the chamber before slamming it in, and flipping the safety before handing it to me. He takes another gun from the other side, goes through the same process and hands it to Kai, before pulling his own weapon out from his back waistband.

"Ready?" He cocks his eyebrow at us, his tone low. Kai and I nod. He opens the door, breaking left, while Kai goes right. They circle the perimeter, before whistling the all clear.

"Hold onto my shirt and keep your head down," I tell Saylor. Kai whips my truck into the driveway, and Silas opens the door. With one arm around her, my other still holding my gun, I half run and half drag Saylor out of the house and into my truck. The minute the door slams, we take off toward the garage.

We arrive right as Matt and Jason are leaving. Saylor notices the bulletproof vests, and her eyes widen again. "It's going to be okay," I tell her, bringing her forehead to my lips. We quickly get inside and make it to the office. Kai locks everything down and flips on the perimeter cameras around here and the house.

"Go lay down." I nod toward the couch in the office and hand her my jacket. She takes it and walks over. She sits and curls her legs up, hugging them to her.

"Well, this is fucked up," Kai announces, while setting up his monitors how Matt wanted. Silas grabs the radio and switches to twelve. He sits in a chair, not saying anything. I know having Kelly come here is going to really fuck with his head. Having his dad going after her probably didn't help. Old wounds are re-opening all-around me. My gaze swings between my friend and the girl who holds my heart with a vice grip in her hand. This is fucked up.

"What do you need me to do?" I ask Kai, but he shakes his head.

"Let a man work, Ci," he admonishes and goes back to clicking his keyboard. I walk over to the couch and pull Saylor onto my lap. She comes willingly and wraps her arms around my chest, burying her tear stained face in my neck. The wetness tickles and creates shivers over my skin. I continue holding her, though. She can soak my whole shirt for all I care.

Saylor sleeps, off and on, over the next twelve hours. Kai reports no incidents to Matt and Jason. Andy makes it to the border and all three of them are picked up. Across the room, Silas tenses. We've been monitoring the outside feed here and at the house. Any cars that drive by we've run through our system and each one has checked out.

"Do you think this was an inside leak?" He finally voices the worst thing imaginable. It's also the only thing that makes sense.

"I hope not," I answer, even though we both know that it was. There is no way anyone should have found them unless the information was given freely.

"They could come here next," he voices my fears again. My eyes swing to his.

"I know," I tell him, my arm instinctively pulling Saylor closer to me. I won't lose her.

"We're ten minutes out," Matt's voice breaks over the radio in Silas' hand.

"Code-four," he answers, standing up and flipping the switch for the automatic doors.

Saylor is alerted by the commotion and gets to her feet. She paces by the door. Her anxiety is written all over her face. Ten minutes later, the door opens, and the rig pulls in. Silas closes it behind them. Kai comes out, looking exhausted, his hair sticking up in all different directions from his hand running through it.

The door to the office unlocks, and we head down the stairs.

"Mom!" Saylor runs to her mom and sister, both of whom are running toward her. They meet in the middle, hugging, crying, and laughing. Silas comes to a halt next to me, his gaze intense on Jason who watches the huddle of women with a smile on his face. It's the happiest I've ever seen Jason, and I can only imagine what that does to Silas. He storms out of the garage, Kai on his heels. I'm conflicted for the first time. My first instinct is to follow Silas and Kai, like I always do. But my heart deflates thinking of leaving Saylor right now. My eyes roam over her, taking in everything that's happening. She's crying happy tears and surrounded by her family. My gaze drops to the ground, guilt eating my insides. I'm Silas' family. When Jason gave up, Kai and I stepped up to the plate. I follow after my friends, my brothers, and leave the girl who holds my heart.

# #Seventeen

*Saylor*

W e didn't leave the house over the next few days. There was constant chatter between all the safe homes and families. Everyone is taking extra precautions and reporting in. Someone is always around, checking the perimeter, watching monitors or scouring the news feed. We are constantly monitored. I almost feel like I have to ask to be excused to go to the bathroom.

I want things to go back to normal. I'm ready for this quarantine phase to be over with. Matt wants to keep my mom and Mila here for at least another week or more, until they have definitive answers. I want them to stay here permanently. Mila fills me in on her life in Arizona. She was going to school and planned to play softball this spring. She made friends and was feeling normal again. After the incident in New York, she and mom were seeing a therapist to talk through the trauma. She tells me mom was working at a flower shop and even started making friends with the booster club parents. I'm happy for them, even while being sad that they were doing okay without me.

Mila is sleeping with me, which ends any chance of seeing Ciaran alone. He distanced himself the minute my mom and sister arrived. I figure it has something to do with Silas, who constantly wears an angry scowl and is ready to pick a fight with his dad over every little thing. I want to yell at him to stop being so petty. Jason is not upset to have my family around. If anyone, he should be the one upset, since my family screwed him over. He acts professional, which is something the guys are clearly lacking. Even Kai has lost some of his friendliness. I chalk it up to everyone's emotions running on high alert with the safe house being discovered. A small inkling in my mind, though, is whispering that there is something bigger going on, only my heart refuses to see it.

"How are you holding up, Love?" My mom asks, curling up next to me on the couch. I shrug, and my gaze darts back to Ciaran involuntarily. Her eyes follow mine and a knowing smile pulls her lips apart. "He's cute," she whispers behind her hand and laughs.

"Stop." I laugh along with her, a blush painting my cheeks. "I think he's mad about something," I confide in her.

Her forehead scrunches, and she frowns. "I think Ciaran has a big responsibility to fill, and he just has a lot on his plate right now. You don't see it, but he's stealing glances at you, just like you are of him."

"Really?" My head lifts and so does my smile. She nods and smiles.

"Are you dating?" she asks, while rubbing my arm. I nod my head yes then no.

"I'm not really sure," I tell her, lifting my shoulder in a shrug. I tell her our story, and her eyes cloud over. A darkness I've never seen before from my mom shakes through her.

"Silas is Jason's son?" she asks. I nod my head yes.

"Are you okay?" I ask, my hand slipping into hers.

She grips me tightly. "I'm fine. Just surprised, I guess."

I nod, even though her statement doesn't really make sense. We're both lost in thought when Silas and Jason start yelling back and forth from the kitchen. My mom stands and walks over to them. I get up to follow her.

"Ever since she came here, you want to be super dad. Fuck you, Jason. You've never done shit for me!" Silas' face is red.

"You have no idea what you're talking about, Boy." Jason shakes his head. He's tense, his shoulders vibrating.

"I know that when mom left, you didn't bat an eye. You used a bottle to get over it. Now Kelly's back in town, and you want to know what I want for dinner and if I finished my homework... fuck you," Silas hisses, his voice falling into a growl.

"Jason, you need to tell your son the truth." My mom suddenly jumps into the conversation. All eyes swing to her. Silas lights up again with fury and hate.

"Whatever you've told him, Jase, it's messing with his head. You need to tell him everything." Matt adds his opinion, and suddenly, everyone doesn't know where to look anymore. I try to get Ciaran's attention, but he purposefully keeps his eyes averted.

Jason takes a deep breath in, his eyes watering when they land back on Silas. "I was in love with Kelly all through high school. Over spring break, our senior year, I got drunk at a party and cheated on her. I told her about it, and we were going to try and work through it, until your mom came to me saying she was pregnant. I wanted to still be part of your life and co-parent. Your mom gave me an ultimatum that if I didn't marry her, she was going to get an abortion or put you up for adoption, without me knowing. So I married her."

Silas is shaking from head to toe, his hands clench and unclench. My eyes dart to Ciaran who's watching his friend. Kai's gaze swings back and forth between Jason and his friend, unsure who he's supposed to feel more sorry for. Silas' mom left and at the same time Jason was trying to protect Silas from being used as a pawn by his mom. It's a messed up situation.

"When your mom left, she was pregnant," Jason keeps going. This time, Matt reaches out a hand and lays it on Jason's shoulder. "I tried to get her to come back. I thought maybe this baby would bring us close again. She always held Kelly over my head, and I couldn't make myself love her when she was so manipulative. I feared every day I was going to come home, and something would happen to you. She tried to run away with you once, faked that you were kidnapped. Matt and I spent four days looking for you, before she showed back up at home. I have no idea what happened to the baby she was carrying, Si. I feel guilty over it every day. I know I drink, and I know I used to yell at you. You just held her to such a high standard that I didn't want to ruin that for you, but it also wasn't fair to me."

Silas stomps out of the house, the front door flying against the wall. Ciaran and Kai start to go after him. "You two stay." My mom glowers at them. I feel her maternal, mama bear about to kick in and heaven help us all. "Jason, you go after that boy. You made the choices you did and maybe your marriage wasn't perfect, but you got one hell of a kid out of it. He needs you right now. Get going. Be his goddamn dad." Jason flinches, but when he looks at my mom, the adoration he still has for her is clear as day on his face.

"We need to talk later," he says, holding her gaze hostage.

"Fine." She nods. "But first, go be a dad. Now I have to take my daughters upstairs and explain to them what you two knuckleheads have been keeping under wraps here." Her gaze lands on Ciaran and Kai, the latter at least has the decency to look guilty.

The whole time I've been here comes flying back to me in clips and pictures from my memory. The minute I arrived here, I was met with hostility. Silas, Ciaran, and Kai flat out said they didn't want me here and that I basically deserved to die and not be saved by Matt because of what my family did. I was bullied, ignored, diminished and broken, little by little, ever since I got here.

"You hated me because Silas thought my mom ruined his parents' relationship?" My eyes focus only on Ciaran. He lifts his gaze to mine, and everything I see on his face only confirms the truth. He was making me pay for sins he and Silas thought my parents committed, almost twenty years ago. Before I was even born.

I turn and flee up the stairs as fast as my legs will move. My cheeks sting and they're flushed so red that I fear all the blood will rush to my head. I'm embarrassed, confused and heartbroken. I thought apologizing would help Silas get over his parents losing money because my father was a criminal. I had no idea he wanted my head because he blamed my mom for his parents' marriage failing and his mom leaving him. Not once, in all the nights he spent with me, did Ciaran even attempt to tell me the truth. He never would have let go of that contempt for me, while still thinking my family was to blame for his friend's pain. I can vividly remember Matt telling them over and over that they didn't know what they were talking about. They never bothered to find out, though. The *perfect* Midwest Boys believed they were never wrong about anything, even without knowing all the facts.

My bed dips, and Mila scoots next to me, resting her head against my shoulder. A few seconds later, my mom lays on my other side, running her fingers through my hair. "I met Jason when we had the same teacher in second grade. Matt was also in my class that year. The three of us instantly bonded. We were inseparable. They never treated me as less than equal, even if I was a girl. When we reached middle school, my feelings for Jason started to change. I noticed him more. My heart skipped faster when he was nearby. I was so scared of losing one of my best friends, I didn't say anything. Our first day of freshman year in high school, this older boy came up to me and wanted my number. Jason told him to eat dirt and that I was his. He kissed me for the first time, and we were together after that."

"I thought Dad was your high school sweetheart?" I ask, feeling like my whole life has been a lie.

"Your dad came to live with my family during my junior year of high school. We took him in for Rogue." My mom's voice trails off. Mila and I turn to look at her, confused.

"Dad was hidden?" Mila asks, pushing herself into a sitting position.

"He was." Mom nods. "He was being ordered to take over his family business, and until then, he had been okay with that. Then one day, he saw what they were doing to make money. Trafficking young girls. Some of them were younger than you, Mi. So he told the authorities, and they instantly contacted Matt's dad, who was head of Rogue at the time. Your dad's biological family was dangerous back then: a large criminal family with strong ties to the mafia. They had their own people inside the government, law enforcement, everywhere. No one could be trusted, so he was given a spot in Rogue. He lived in my house; we grew close and became friends. Jason was jealous and going through a tough time at his own home. He started drinking more at parties and not really caring if he spent time with me or Matt. Then he cheated. When Jason told me he was going to marry Stacy, I fell apart. I was depressed and hurt. I didn't lose the man I loved to another woman but to a baby. How do you stay angry at an innocent baby? Your dad wanted to go to New York for college, and I decided to go with him. Along the way, we developed deeper feelings for each other, and before I knew it, I was pregnant with you, Say. And the rest is history." Her shoulders lift, and she offers us a small smile.

My head continues spinning with all the new information and things from my past that make sense now but didn't before. "Matt said that dad accepted money from his old family, is that why he bailed and disappeared?"

My mom's hand pauses in my hair, before she continues stroking. I knew the topic would be painful for her. "We believe so, yes. Your dad's family is very wealthy. Despite the crime, your dad is accustomed to that lifestyle. Having to be here, where everyone wore Wranglers and boots or Converse, rather than designer brand, was something he couldn't handle. We had to work in college to save money in order to have things. He wanted everything to just come to him, without having to put in the work for it."

"Did you love him?" Mila's young voice asks.

"I did. I wanted a family, and he gave me you two. I will always love him for that," she responds, but I hear the deeper meaning in her words. She loved my dad, but she wasn't in love with him, not like with Jason. If they had stayed together, Jason could have been my dad. It's a weird feeling and thought to have, considering all Silas has ever done is belittle his own father and tear him down.

Mila and I both take the night to process the revelations my mom made today. Matt drops dinner off for us in my room, and we spend the evening retelling old stories and painting each other's fingers and toes. My heart is full for the first time since we said goodbye outside that motel, six months ago. I don't miss the texts Ciaran sends. I choose to ignore him. For now, I just want to put him in a box and shove it deep into the closet, where I'm keeping all my other skeletons that I know I'll have to deal with someday.

### ###

We get another full week together, before Matt announces that they have a new location. Matt, Jason and my mom have been working diligently to figure out who is behind the attack, so we can live normally. They have a plan in place that they think shouldn't take more than a few more months. Mom and Mila are leaving tomorrow. They wanted to be here for the talent show tonight, though. Ciaran, Kai and Silas are always around, and I go out my way to ignore them. Part of me isn't ready to open the box and the other part of me just feels plain vindictive. They deserve a taste of their own medicine. It doesn't escape my notice that Matt is treating them harsher as well, and I wonder if he's doing that for my benefit. I have a feeling my mom, Matt and Jason have all shared what's been going on here for the past few months. My cheeks color, just thinking about it.

"I'm happy you'll be here for the talent show," I tell Mila, while she curls my hair, before I leave for school. Now that Matt has lifted the quarantine, since we aren't in immediate danger, I've been insisting I go back daily. The show is tonight, and I've been a ball of nerves all week.

"Which song are you singing?" Mila asks.

I smile and shrug. "You know me, Mi, probably won't decide till the day of. It's got to hit me just right, ya know? I like when songs speak to my soul."

"You're so weird." She rolls her eyes at me, and we laugh. I missed my sister. I'm happy to see she's been well and that she looks healthy. She no longer has the haunted look in her eyes that she did our last day in that motel room. She's thirteen going on seventeen and beautiful.

Another text pops up on my phone, and I swipe it away with the others. I've been ignoring him. I don't know what to say to him anymore. I start to hum while Mila continues adding curls around my head, when the perfect song clicks. "I need a guitar," I whisper to myself, before picking up my phone and shooting a text to Kai.

Ariel: Since you owe me for being a douche, can you play guitar?
Kai: I will play anything you tell me.

His answer is quick, and I smirk. I quickly shoot back my song choice and a guitar version I found online, along with instructions that I want to sing a slower version. Kai texts back immediately that he will have it learned.

A few hours later, I wait in the wings of the school auditorium for the performances before me to be over. Everyone is in the crowd. My family, my new friends, the whole school and even Silas. I rub my hands down my destroyed jeans. I chose a country vibe for tonight, pairing the jeans with my white button up top and a black leather jacket. It's comfortable, and for once, I feel like myself. I pace back and forth, lost in my own thoughts, when a hand snatches my wrist and starts pulling me out the back doors.

"What the hell, Ciaran?" I yank my arm, but it's no use. His grip is steely. "You keep ignoring me," he accuses, yanking me around and shoving my back to the brick wall of the building.

"I don't want to talk to you," I tell him and try to step around him, only to have him crowd my space further.

"You could give me a chance to explain." He grips my chin between his fingers. Tears rise to the surface of my eyes, and I will myself not to cry.

"Nothing you say can change what you guys put me through." My voice comes out gravelly and low. His face turns harder, that jaw of his locking up. "You made me miserable for months. I was ignored and bullied; you tore me down as a person. Ridiculed me for wanting to be me, like I was this horrible person. I took everything you gave me to heart, really thinking it was because of my dad and what he did. I lost things that night, too, but I didn't think I could feel that pain because your friend lost more. You hate me, but you don't know me. You're blaming me for events I had no control over. My world is destroyed, but you're breaking my heart."

Tears fall freely from my eyes and cascade down my cheeks. Ciaran dips his head down with a growl and licks them away. My body betrays me and leans against him. The truth is I want him to take my pain away. I want to move on, but I don't know how to do that.

"Don't," I whisper, my hands fisting in the fabric of his jacket.

"I can't walk away from you, Say. I know things are fucked between us right now, but I'll talk to you until I'm blue in the face if that's what you want. Just don't ask me to stay away from you. I don't hate you," he tells me fiercely, before his lips attack mine. His body grinds into my chest, shoving me back and farther up the wall. His hands roam and tug at the different articles of clothing, trying his hardest to get to as much of my skin as possible. I feel his fingers at the button of my jeans before they give way and are pushed down by his hand. His fingers shove between my legs and push my panties to the side. His thumb swirls around my clit, and everything clenches. Ciaran drops to his knees and tugs one of my legs out of my jeans, before throwing my leg over his shoulder and opening me wider for him. His mouth dives in, licking between my legs, until my fingers are twisted in his hair, and I grind shamelessly against his face, riding the pleasure he's hell-bent on giving me. His teeth graze around the sensitive nub and that's all it takes for the wave of my orgasm to crest and crash through me. It's powerful. The physical experience of it robs the air from my lungs, and my legs threaten to give out.

Ciaran doesn't rise until my hips stop moving against him. He helps me put my booted foot back into my jeans and shimmies them back over my legs. He comes back to my mouth and bruises my lips with another kiss, running his lips all along my mouth and thrusting his tongue, so I'm forced to taste myself on him. It's a dirty kiss that I can't get enough of.

He pulls back when we're both breathing hard. "I need to go back in," I tell him. In my post orgasmic moment, all the reasons I'm still mad at him come rushing back.

"When can we actually talk? I need to talk to you, Say. I can't take the distance anymore." His forehead rests against mine, his hands resting on the wall on both sides of my head. I'm caged in, surrounded by Ciaran, enveloped by his warmth.

"I want to spend time with my mom and Mila before they leave," I tell him.

"Okay, so after?" He pushes again.

"Yes," I concede, my heart throbbing painfully.

"Go sing, Baby." He kisses me again, before disappearing around the corner.

I take a few deep breaths, trying to calm my racing heart. My face is flushed, and my hair is sticking to the wall I'm leaning against. Running my hands over the strands, I rush back inside, right as Kai takes out his guitar. "There you are, I couldn't find you, but we're next."

"Okay." I nod. The butterflies from earlier are gone and replaced with the knowledge that Ciaran is going to be out there. I honestly didn't expect him to come. My song choice suddenly feels too personal.

"We're up," Kai calls to me. Cheers erupt from the crowd when he steps on the stage, echoed by whistles and chants once I join him. Right away, I find my mom and Mila in the crowd. They're standing and waving their arms in the air, cheering me on. My stomach settles instantly. I feel Ciaran's fiery gaze and the sharp tingle between my legs flares to life again. I don't search him out, though.

Taking a seat on the stool next to Kai, I scoot the microphone closer. The audience dies down. Kai looks at me, and I nod for him to start. I put my heart and soul into singing Elise Lieberth's version of "Holding Out For A Hero," holding nothing back. Kai's eyebrows rise, and he grins when I hit all the notes with perfect precision. I love singing, and I've been blessed with the ability to carry a note. I don't flaunt it. I appreciate music, and all the gifts it has to offer.

When the last note from Kai's guitar strum dies out, the auditorium erupts in cheers. Kai takes my hand and pulls us down into a bow. I flash a smile, and we walk off the stage. Once we're in the back, Kai lifts me off my feet and twirls me in a circle.

"Holy fuck, Gossip Girl!" He laughs. "I had no idea you could hit notes like that."

I shrug. "It's not something I do often."

"You should." He smirks. "I honestly had no idea how this whole thing was going to go. I was thinking, even if you sucked, at least I played and then we'd be one step closer to burying the hatchet."

I laugh. "I'll consider us even for now," I tell him. We don't stay too long at the school, anxious to get back to Matt's house. My mom and Mila only stayed long enough to see me then left right after. Matt reminds us I'm supposed to be parentless, and it would be weird if I, all of a sudden, had a mom show up. We make it work just for the night, and I've never felt more grateful.

I spend one more night sharing my bed with Mila, snuggling like old times. They both are leaving again tomorrow. My chest feels heavy with emotion. Our reunion was too quick. Knowing it could be months before I see them again, doesn't bring me comfort. I want more than anything to go back to normal. My mom plays with our hair until we fall asleep. She hasn't been staying in the room with us, and I don't even want to think about what that could mean. The realization that everything is going to change is starting to sneak past my defenses.

"Wake up, sleepyheads," she calls to us, planting a kiss on my cheek.

"What time is it?" I roll over asking. My shades are already drawn aside, and the sun is shining. For the middle of March, the weather has been warmer, and some of the snow is already melting.

"Nine," my mom calls cheerfully, and Mila groans next to me. I laugh.

"I want to talk to you both about something quick," she says. We both sit up, watching her closely. Her eyes sparkle, and her skin is glowing.

"Ew." I laugh. "Are you with Jason?"

"Saylor!" She jokingly hits my shoulder. Mila and I fall into each other laughing. My mom's face blooms red. She looks younger, the years of strain are finally disappearing.

"I mean," she pauses and looks down, biting her lip, "We may try dating again when all this is over."

"That's great, Mom," Mila answers right away, taking her hand in mine.

"Yeah, Mom," I tell her. "You deserve to be happy."

She sighs in relief. "I was worried how you would take it. Things are just crazy right now. The heart can be demanding, though. True love doesn't fade."

I nod and have to look away. Her words hit truer than she knows.

"Okay, hurry and get ready. We're having breakfast before our ride gets here," she calls over her shoulder, before leaving my room.

"Are you really okay with that?" Mila asks, her little brow is raised quizzically.

"I don't really want to start having family dinners with Silas," I tell her honestly. "I also want her to be happy again, though."

"Me too." Mila nods thoughtfully.

I help her get ready and make sure all her stuff is packed before we head downstairs. Everyone is already at the table when we get there. We eat and laugh. My mom and Jason are sickeningly affectionate. I catch Silas watching them at times, too. I want to know where he stands on all this. Mom shared with me that he and Jason had a really tough and honest conversation and that they are going to work on their relationship. He doesn't appear to be shooting daggers at her head, so I guess, for now, he's okay with it.

After breakfast, we clean up, and everyone starts a round of goodbyes. My stomach twists painfully, having to do this again. I just got them back, and it feels like I'm losing them all over again. My eyes take in my mom's face, memorizing it. I can't explain where it comes from, but I, suddenly, want to just stare at her like it's the last time. When Mila wraps her arms around me, I grip her tightly and breathe her in. "I love you," I tell her, that same sense of fear crawls over my skin.

She pulls back and pokes my cheek with her index finger. "It's not forever," she repeats the same thing I told her last time in the motel bathroom. Tears sting my eyes at the memory.

I'm swept into my mom's embrace next. I mold myself to her, soaking in her strength and love. My arms tighten reflexively. It's on my tongue to beg her to stay and not leave. I don't want to be without her. "I love you so much, Saylor," she whispers into my ear. "You are the greatest gift I never knew I wanted. I dreamt about you my whole life."

"Mom," I choke, while she rocks me slightly. I don't want to breakdown and cry in front of our audience. I grip her tighter, scared, a sense of foreboding trickling in my veins.

"It will all be okay, Love," she tells me, pulling back. "We'll be back together soon." I'm sure she assumes I'm just sad to see her leave again and maybe that is what's wrong with me. I'm desperate to have my family together again.

I nod, too scared to speak, in case the dam of tears breaks. I watch as they slide into the car with another Rogue member. I don't move while they drive down the street or even once they're out of sight. I don't know how long I stand on the porch, before I feel a presence next to me.

"Hey." Silas clears his throat and shoots me a side look.

I'm instantly on alert and hyperaware. "What do you want?"

He sighs. "I'm sorry. I was an ass, and you didn't deserve it."

My gaze flicks to his face, looking for signs of a set up or the usual moody expression he wears. He just looks tired, though. "You talked with your dad?"

He turns his gaze back to the street. "Yeah. Looks like we might be siblings someday." He attempts a joke and actually chuckles at the freaked out look on my face.

We stand in silence for a few more moments, before he speaks again, "You should forgive Ci. He was being a loyal friend. We both should have worked harder to understand what was going on. That was on me."

"You didn't make Ciaran do the things he did or say what he said," I scoff.

"I think you know more than anyone else how important your closest friendships are, and you'd do anything for them, right... #MNGirl?" he asks.

I turn to give him a piece of my mind, but he's already at the door. A shit-eating grin on his face. "Later, Sis," he calls, and I flip him off in response.

I hate that, of all people, Silas is the one to make the biggest point. I would do anything for Oaklynn and her for me. Those are the kind of friends you keep and you hold onto. It's why I haven't been able to give up the #MNGirl account.

I sense him before he touches me. His chest brushes against my back. My eyes slam shut. My traitorous heart beats to life when he's near. It's unfair in an almost beautifully tragic way. Enemies to lovers usually is.

"Talk?"

# #Eighteen

*Ciaran*

I keep my eyes on Saylor across the room. She still insists on eating lunch away from me, just to piss me off. She says it's to not draw attention, but I call bullshit. Everyone already knows she's mine anyway. Saylor is still scared. I've tried multiple times to talk to her about everything. Anytime I think we make progress, we make a turn, and then keep going in circles. So we sit apart at lunch.

"You need to tone it down a bit, Dude," Kai jokes next to me. These jackasses have already been cleared for their crimes, and I'm still in isolation.

"Yeah," Silas agrees, "quit eye-fucking my sister."

I flip them both off. They laugh and joke at my expense, and I don't care. I keep Saylor in my line of vision. She cut her hair recently. The strands hit her shoulders now. She's not wearing her usual get up of sweats and hoodies or leggings and oversized shirts. Something she also blames me for. She's back to skirts and tight fitted jeans and even tighter shirts. She looks perfect no matter what she wears. For fuck's sake she'd make a pillow case look sexy. I've stared down, and even threatened, at least five guys today who were brave enough to look at her for more than two seconds. I've never been one for labels, but, for Saylor, I'm ready to make the concession. She's mine, whether she wants to admit it or not.

When lunch is over, we get up to dump our trays. I take one step into the hallway when the announcement comes.

"ATTENTION ALL STUDENTS. PLEASE REPORT TO YOUR NEAREST LOCKED DOOR ROOM. THIS IS NOT A DRILL."

"What the hell?" Kai starts walking faster down the hall. People start clearing out and rushing into classrooms. It's unorganized chaos.

"Grab your target," I fire off orders, following the protocol Rogue set in motion years ago. My eyes scan the sea of bodies for purple. I see Winter dragging her down the hall toward me.

"I got it," I tell her, taking Saylor's arm, while Winter dashes off to a room.

"What's going on?" Saylor's eyes are round, and she looks terrified.

"We're going into a lockdown. Follow me, so we can figure out what's going on," I instruct, leading us to the designated empty classroom, pulling her in with me. Kai and Reed are already here, and Silas and Bentley sneak in right before the door closes.

"I fuckin knew it." Rhodes laughs when he sees Saylor. Idiot just made the connection she's being hidden like him. Reed's eyes roll.

"Is there a school shooting or something?' Saylor asks more questions. I can tell this is really getting to her.

"I just sent Matt an alarm message. Kai's pulling up the news." I wrap an arm around her shoulders and pull her into my chest. She automatically wraps herself around me. I hide my grin in her hair.

"This isn't good," Kai finally announces.

"What?" I ask, moving closer to his phone.

"It's a live news broadcast. All the schools in the country went into a lockdown for a threatened shooting. Like every single school in the country," he reads off the information.

My phone vibrates. "Matt, you see the news?"

"You need to get to the shop. Something isn't right," he bites out. "Do you have all your targets?"

"Yeah, we got em'," I answer. "Do we have a clear path?"

"As far as I can see, the parking lot is empty, move now, Ciaran," Matt orders, before hanging up the phone.

I nod to Kai and Silas. "Let's go."

I pull Saylor into my body, shielding her with my back. We sneak across the empty hallways and out the side door in the gym. The exit leads right to the student parking lot.

"Clear," Silas calls out. We jog single file to my truck. I fling my door open and have Saylor climb across to the passenger seat.

"Buckle up," I order. I gun the gas and we speed out of the parking lot. Kai follows between Silas and I, while we roll down to Rogue's. Matt has the doors open, and we pull all the way through.

"What's happening?" I ask Matt's retreating form, as he jogs back up to the office. We follow close behind, bringing our targets with us. Once we're in the office, Matt locks it down. Jason, Randy and Kai's dad are already here.

"We got a distress call a few hours ago from one of the safe houses. Then nothing. We attempted contact a couple times now. About thirty minutes before the schools went into lockdown, we got another call. There was a lot of gunfire. I sent the nearest extraction team to the area to check it out." Matt's pale and his hands are shaking.

"Which house?" I ask, even while a pit of dread stirs in my stomach. I can see it written all over his face. My eyes swing to Jason who's cradling his head in his hands, taking deep breaths.

"Matt?" Saylor's voice cracks. I can see her body sway, and I instinctively step closer to her, ready to grab her if she falls.

"It's your mom and Mila," Matt confirms, his eyes glistening.

"They could be all right, though," Saylor states, trying to sound hopeful.

"Say," Matt starts to say, but she cuts him off.

"You don't know for sure yet." She backs out of my hold, her arms wrapping around her middle. Her face is so pale, her skin almost looks translucent.

"We'll know soon." Matt lowers his head, spinning the radio between his hands.

"So the school thing was just, what?" Bentley asks. "A ruse to take attention off the safe house?"

Matt nods. "That's what we're thinking."

My eyes scan the room. This is fucked up. Saylor's breath hitches, and I take a step in her direction, before she holds her hand up stopping me.

"I can't right now." She shakes her head.

"Okay, Baby," I tell her, stepping back to give her room. "Just breathe."

The radio in Matt's hand flickers with static. "Rogue command two, come in."

"This is Rogue," Matt answers.

"This is extraction team WY1223. We're on the property." The voice sounds strained. Everything in me can feel that whatever happens next is going to change everything.

An ominous feeling surrounds the room. "Go ahead," Matt says the words, his eyes closing.

"Multiple rounds of ammunition were used on the exterior of the home. We extracted two DOA's from the building. One is a Caucasian female, the other a Caucasian male. We're airlifting another Caucasian minor by air for life support," the voice responds.

"No!" Saylor cries, the sound echoing in my soul. The anguish she feels is written all over her face. Jason lands on his knees, reaching for her. She falls into him, and he rocks her, while sobs rip through her body, over and over again.

"You need to see this Rogue." The voice over the radio flips back in. Kai hits a button on the screen and the feed from the extraction team comes into view.

"Fuck," Kai breathes. My eyes roam over the image. Anger swirls in my veins until I see red. Bullet holes decorate the walls. Blood splatter in various parts of the house are a stark contrast against the white walls. The camera zooms in on the written message on the wall.

"What's that say?" Matt asks, trying to look at it sideways.

"It's Latin," I reply.

Eye for an eye," Reed translates.

I can't think. The image is more gruesome and real now that I have a personal connection to the lives lost. My eyes swing to the girl in my best friend's dad's arms. I walk over to them and fall to my knees in front of her, pulling her body into mine. She comes willingly. Her tears leak onto the skin around my neck and all over the collar of my shirt. I hold her to me like I could absorb her under my skin and keep her safe forever. The emotions and realization hit me like a truck. I love her. I don't know if I'll get her past this, but I won't give up until she gets justice. I won't quit until she's safe.

## The End...for now

# #More from A.M. Brooks

**Coming Soon...**
<u>Midwest Boys Series</u>
My#MNGirl- Book 2
#SummerGirl- Book 3
#NYGirl- Book 4

Warrior- The Salvation Soceity

Scar (Trent's Story

**Available Now....**
<u>The Hearts Series Duet</u>
Hearts and Bruises
Hearts and Flowers

Where Demons Hide

# #Connect with A.M. Brooks

Website: www.ambrooksbooks.com

Facebook: www.facebook.com/ambrooksbooks/

Twitter: @brooksauthor

Instagram: ambrooksbooks

Pinterest: www.pinterest.com/ambrooksbooks/

Printed in Great Britain
by Amazon